MAD COW

MAD COW

A Novel

ALEXIS KIENLEN

N_1 O_2 N_1

CANADA

Library and Archives Canada Cataloguing in Publication

Title: Mad cow : a novel / Alexis Kienlen.

Names: Kienlen, Alexis, author.

Identifiers: Canadiana 20200168606 | ISBN 9781988098982 (softcover)

Classification: LCC PS8621.I53 M33 2020 | DDC C813/.6—dc23

Printed and bound in Canada on 100% recycled paper.

Now Or Never Publishing
901, 163 Street
Surrey, British Columbia
Canada V4A 9T8

nonpublishing.com
Fighting Words.

We gratefully acknowledge the support of the Canada Council for the Arts
and the British Columbia Arts Council for our publishing program.

For the ranchers

CHAPTER I

Allyson sat by the flagpole, waiting for her father. Her friend Amber sat beside her. They watched as Amber's brother's truck drove up, blasting loud, angry rock music that filled the entire street in front of the school. The bright yellow truck had a decal with the words "Rig Piggy" scrawled in huge letters across the back window. A shiny, clean quad sat in the truck bed. Amber sighed and picked up her flute case.

"I wish he wouldn't be so obnoxious," she said. "I'll call you later."

Amber's brother leaned out the window, holding a smoke in one hand. He was friends with Allyson's brother Colton, and Allyson knew they partied together frequently. Amber's brother was named Murray, but everyone called him Booger. It was a nickname he'd picked up in high school. Even if people did call him by his given name, he told them to call him Booger. One time, Allyson asked Amber about the origins of the nickname. Amber raised her eyebrows. "Trust me, you don't want to know."

Booger was back from the rigs. He still came home to crash once in a while and hang out with his buddies. Allyson had been inside his truck with Amber, but she usually ignored him when she saw him driving around town. He was known for driving up and down Main Street, and then sitting in the 7-Eleven parking lot where he drank Slurpees and smoked, watched traffic and waited for other people to come talk to him. Allyson knew he smoked weed with Colton. She suspected Booger might be into E too, or even something stronger. Rig piggies like Booger had more money than God and they wanted to share their wealth with their friends.

Booger waved at Allyson once Amber was in the truck.

"Still hanging out with that chink?" he yelled.

Allyson didn't bother to answer. She gave him the finger as the truck sped away. Allyson hoped her dad would be on time today. Last time he picked her up, she'd had to wait for over half an hour. She stared out into the street, resting one arm over her trumpet case. She missed the days of the previous year, when she and Chloe had been in band together. But Chloe said she didn't need the extra credits she would get from being in after-school band, so she'd decided not to take it. Chloe used that time to go into town and hang out at the coffee shops with her friend Jamie. Thank god Amber was still in band. Allyson always felt she should have more friends than she did, because she'd lived near the town her whole life. But she had spent a lot of time hanging out with her cousin until recently. And she just didn't want to hang out with other people. Why were people supposed to have so many friends? She would rather stay in her room, draw, listen to music and read. So what if she ended up spending a lot of time alone?

Her dad's tired red pickup trundled down the street through the dust. It was so dry this year, a carryover from the drought last year. He pulled the truck up to the curb in front of the flagpole and honked. Allyson stood up, picked up her trumpet case and walked toward him.

"Thanks for coming to get me," she said as she did up her seatbelt. "Dad, you should buckle up," she said, looking over at him. "Seriously."

Her father nodded but didn't say anything. He fumbled around him, found the seatbelt and pulled it across his body.

Her father looked more tired than usual. Even his face looked slack, as if his cheeks wanted to slide off his face and onto the ground. He was in his mid-forties, and that was impossibly old to her. Would she ever be that old? Would she look like him, with cheeks that were permanently wind stained? Not if she couldn't help it. She didn't want the same kind of life he had.

Her father's belly had grown rounder in recent years and her mom gave him a hard time about it.

"You need to watch what you eat," her mother would say to him. "No more snacks out in the truck. No more chips in front of the TV."

"I work hard," her dad said when he sat down at night, falling into his La-Z-Boy to watch the news or the Oilers. "Sometimes I just want a beer and chips. Is that too much to ask?"

"It's going to your belly," her mother said. "And that's not healthy."

Shania Twain was on the radio, singing about feeling like a woman. Allyson thought about turning it off, but didn't. They only got two stations in town. Allyson looked out the window at her school. Only three more years. Then she could finally get out of here.

Her dad tapped his hands on the steering wheel. Allyson's mom said it was a good thing her dad had a job that allowed him to be physical, because he wouldn't have been able to sit at a desk all day. He needed to move.

"Your dad never would have survived in the city," she said. "He needs to be out on the farm."

Allyson looked out the window at the town. It was the same old. Her mother said the entire town needed a new coat of paint. Her dad turned the pickup away from the school and drove towards the main drag. But instead of turning towards the road that would take them to the highway, he continued up the street.

"Aren't we going home?" Allyson asked.

"Nope," her dad said. "We're going to Joe's. I need to talk to the guys. Something big happened today."

Allyson looked at him, not wanting to ask.

"Everything's fine," her dad said. "Everything's okay. I just need to catch up on the local gossip."

Allyson would have preferred to go home, eat her supper and watch TV, but she didn't mind hanging out at Joe's. She might be able to talk to Jeff, who was in a few classes with her at school. His dad, Joe Chin, ran the restaurant.

Her dad drove up the street and circled the block, looking for a parking spot.

"Dad," Allyson said, letting her voice go into a slight whine. "Why can't you just park and walk a few blocks?"

Her dad kept on driving around the block, until a truck pulled out from a spot just in front of the Dewdrop Inn.

"See," her dad said, smiling. "We can park like the rock stars we are if we just wait."

Allyson opened the door and jumped out. "I'm going to leave my trumpet in the car, so maybe you should lock it."

"Why don't you just bring it in?" her dad said.

"Just lock the door," she said. "It's not going to kill you."

She locked her own door, and then listened to make sure her dad locked his side.

Allyson walked into Joe's first, her dad following behind.

Inside, Joe's smelled like cigarette smoke and the oily scent of grease from French fries and the buffet table. Two tables full of people waved or nodded at Gord and Allyson as they walked by. Allyson wondered what it would be like to live in a city, where you didn't know half of the people around you. Her dad always liked to say you couldn't fart in town without half of the town hearing about it.

Gord caught up with Allyson and then walked ahead of her, waving at two guys who were already seated. Doug Miller was wearing a Co-op cap and drinking a coffee, while old Ray Sharp sat beside him.

"Are Craig and Al coming?" Doug asked as Allyson and Gord approached the table.

Gord shook his head. "Nah. I think Dad went to Hills' and Craig is driving some cattle to the border. He had a long haul ahead of him. He's not back yet."

"Nice to see you," Ray Sharp said as Allyson sat down next to him. Her father sat on the other side of her. Ray squeezed her arm and gave her a big smile. Ray's wife has passed a while ago, but he was still in cattle. All of the neighbours helped him out when he needed it. The farm wives doted on him, bringing him pies and fresh baking. His sons, their wives and his grandkids came back all the time for visits. Allyson liked Ray, his aura of genuine kindness, and his big smile, filled with teeth that gleamed so white that they were probably fake.

Allyson looked around for Jeff, but didn't see him. Before she could blink, Joe came to their table with an armful of menus.

"Nice to see you all," he said. "Don't you ever work?

Doug crossed his arms over his large belly and laughed. Allyson found it hard not to stare at his gut. She wondered how Doug could move about, balancing his huge belly on his skinny legs. She hoped her father wouldn't end up like that.

"We don't want you to go broke," Doug said. "Need to be able to feed your kids."

Joe laughed and gestured around the table. "Coffees for everyone?"

Allyson shook her head. "I'll have a Coke."

Gord put his menu down on the table. "I don't know why you brought us these menus, Joe. We all know these menus like we know our wives' cooking. Unless you got something new?"

Joe shook his head. "No, still same."

He had a Chinese accent. The Chins had immigrated from China, but they had been in the community for many years and were well-known. Their two children were both born in town.

"I don't even have to look at this," Doug said, placing the menu back on the table. "I'll have fries and a double burger."

Allyson ordered a small cup of wonton soup and tuned out while Ray and her father ordered. The TV in the back corner was showing an episode of *Jeopardy!* The Chins always had close captioning on, so you could focus on the TV if you didn't feel like talking to the other people at your table.

"Shame about the border," Ray Sharp said. "I'm just glad that I downsized last year after the drought. I'm not feeding many cows."

"I heard it earlier today. And it's just going to be trouble. I've got a lot of cows ready to go," Doug said.

"We're just going to get slammed again," Gord said. "I'm trying not to get worked up about it, but this could be a major hit in the pocket book."

"What can we really do about it?" Doug asked. "Those government guys need to figure it out. All I know is I'm going to be watching the news. Hopefully they'll get it resolved before I need to ship my cows. If not, I'm going to have to get down on my knees and pray."

"If they don't take any of our beef, this could affect the whole country," Ray said. "The whole thing makes me mad. The beef is safe. It's just the one cow so far. But this could kill the industry."

Allyson was used to farming conversations, about how there wasn't enough rain, or it was too cold or too hot or prices were down. The cows were too skinny or the bull was shooting blanks, or the equipment was broken and parts hadn't come into town yet. Nothing was more boring than news, unless it was news about farming. But today had a different feel to it. The men were resigned and subdued. Her dad kept on fidgeting with the salt shaker, and Ray, who smiled constantly, looked serious and hadn't even offered her gum, or asked her about school, or if she had a boyfriend. Doug propped his head up with his hand, as if it was too heavy for him to hold up. As Allyson watched, he patted the breast pocket in his plaid shirt, putting his hand on a square package.

"I'm going out for a smoke," he said, standing up.

"Thought you gave that up," Gord said.

"Most of the time, yeah," Doug said. "But today is a smoking day. I'm going outside for some fresh air." Allyson watched as he stood up and walked out of the restaurant. Nobody said anything when he left. Normally, the men would have been laughing and joking, telling stories about what some of the other farmers they knew had been up to. But today, they sat in a reserved silence.

"I wonder if we can get Joe to change the channel," Gord said. "It's got to be on the news."

Jeff showed up with the coffees and Coke and Allyson caught his eye.

"I'll be in the back booth in a few minutes," he said as he put her drink in front of her. "If you want to wait for me, I can hang with you for a little bit."

Allyson took her Coke and stood up. "Dad, I'm going to go sit in the back."

Gord nodded, but he was staring at some far-off spot over her head.

"May 20, 2003," Ray Sharp said, taking a sip of coffee and shaking his head. "We're not going to forget it."

"I'm just hoping this doesn't end up like the UK," her dad said.

Allyson walked away while her dad continued to talk. When she looked back at him, he was slouched over the table, waving his hands about the way he always did when he was emotional about something. The way he hunched over made him look old. She didn't want to keep on thinking about that.

She sat down at the table in the back nearest the kitchen and kept on watching *Jeopardy!* Jeff's homework was piled on the table. All the regulars knew this table belonged to the Chin kids and no one ever took it. She recognized his copy of *The Stone Angel* that they'd been studying in English class, along with his math textbook and a couple of his notebooks. Jeff had told her it was too quiet at home and he found hard to study there.

One of Jeff's large sketchpads lay on the table. Allyson looked at the whirling loops of his doodles on the front cover. Jeff liked to draw anime characters and he was good at it. He was the one who had introduced her to anime. One time, she'd gone over to his house to watch *Akira*. No one else had been home and the Chin house was small and quiet. It was too neat, as if they were expecting company. The house was only a few blocks from the restaurant.

Allyson looked at the pictures of Chinese people on the walls. The pictures were black and white, and the people in them stilted and formal. Allyson liked hanging out with Jeff, but she'd been uncomfortable while they were alone in his house. Immediately after they'd finished watching the movie, she called her mom to come get her.

After a few minutes, Jeff's mom, Winnie, came and put a bowl of soup in front of her.

"Thanks," Allyson said. The warm, salty taste of the broth was comforting and she realized how hungry she was. She picked up a wonton with her china spoon and examined it. Colton always said wontons looked like calf testicles. After he said that, the image haunted her but that didn't mean she was going to stop eating wontons. She was a farm kid, after all.

Allyson studied the restaurant, taking in the plastic table top in front of her and the green of the carpet. She liked the wallpaper in the restaurant, its iridescent peacocks edged with flecks of gold. Her mother said it was garish, but Allyson thought places in China must have wallpaper like this.

Jeff walked by and waved. "Just have to serve a few more tables," he said. "I'll try and take a break soon."

Allyson nodded and kept on eating her soup.

The bell over the front door chimed, and her cousin Chloe entered the restaurant, followed by Jamie. Allyson wondered if she should wave at them. She stared down at her soup. Chloe was laughing about something. Her dad saw Chloe and raised his hand in acknowledgement.

"Hi, Uncle Gord," Chloe said. Jamie nodded at him and walked over to the corner, choosing a table with two chairs near the window. Allyson waved at Chloe, trying to catch her cousin's eye. Chloe ignored her and went to join Jamie.

For a second, Allyson wondered if her cousin hadn't seen her. Why wouldn't Chloe say hi? She watched as Winnie went to their table to give them menus. She looked back down at her soup, which she had nearly finished, before turning her eyes up to the television again. Should she go over and talk to them?

She looked over to see if they had noticed her. They were talking and laughing, oblivious to everyone else in the restaurant. They were too far away for her to hear what they were saying. She looked around for Jeff.

"I'll be there soon," Jeff said, as he passed through the door, holding a tray with four Cokes and a plate of fries on it. "We're a bit short-staffed today. One of the waitresses called in sick." He stopped for a minute at her table before walking towards Chloe and Jamie, delivering Cokes and fries to the table of seniors beside them.

Allyson wished she'd brought her school bag in from the car. She picked up Jeff's copy of *The Stone Angel* even though she had already read it twice and was sick of it. Anything would be better than sitting here, pretending she wasn't alone while her cousin and her friend sat at one table and her dad sat at another. She hoped Jeff would join her soon. He put Cokes down at Chloe's table. What would happen if she pulled up a chair and joined them?

She got up and walked toward their table, abandoning her empty bowl.

"Hey," she said, as she pulled up a chair and sat down beside her cousin and her friend. "What are you guys up to?"

Jamie fiddled with her straw. Chloe sighed. "Not much," she said.

Jamie said, "Want to go over to Ben's later? I think Josh is going to be there too."

"I need to spend more time with Josh," Chloe said. "We've been chatting on MSN, but I don't think he knows that I like him yet. Although we were talking about the movies, and he said that sometimes he likes to drive to Lloydminster to go to the movies there. He actually typed, 'Maybe it would be fun to drive to the city to see a movie.' I couldn't believe it. It was almost like he was asking me out on a date."

"He's totally into you," Jamie said. "Ben thinks so too. I've been asking him to find out for you, but he's not sure how to ask. He doesn't want to ask in front of the other guys."

"Why don't you just ask him if he likes you?" Allyson asked. "Or why don't you just ask him out?"

Chloe looked down at her hands on the table. Her cousin's nails were a bright lilac colour. This was new. Her cousin didn't like to draw attention to her hands. She had bitten her nails for years, and even used to bite at the cuticles around the nail bed.

The silence was uncomfortable. Why was it taking so long for her cousin to answer her? Jamie and Chloe looked at each other, and in their glance, Allyson could tell they wanted her to leave.

"You don't do that," Jamie said, taking a long sip of Coke. "How can you ever expect a guy to like you if you ask him out first? I had to flirt with Ben for weeks before he finally clued in. And then I had to wait for him to make the first move. That's just how you get a boyfriend. If you ask him first, he's going to think you're desperate or something."

She leaned in closer and whispered, "Or you can be like Lily, if you want."

Lily Stevens, who was currently dating Colton, had a repu- tation of being forward. Lots of guys had dated Lily, and most of them had probably slept with her too. There were rumours that Lily had come from the rez, that she had been in jail. No one knew the real story. The girls in the high school couldn't under- stand why guys all loved Lily so much.

"She's not anything pretty or special," Chloe said to Allyson when they'd been hanging out on the farm last summer, sitting on the fence, staring out into the yard. "Honestly, her round face reminds me of the sun."

"Yeah, I don't know," Allyson answered.

Allyson and Chloe used to hang out all the time. Things were easier when they were younger. She thought back to when she was thirteen, and Chloe was the age that she was now. Back when she was twelve, she remembered wishing she was fourteen because that's when the boys in town would get cute. Now that she was fourteen, she thought the boys around her might be bet- ter looking when she was twenty.

"You're daydreaming again," Chloe said to her, snapping her out of her memories and back to the present. "You're a space cadet," she said. "Makes it hard to talk to you."

Allyson was confused. Why was her cousin being so mean to her?

"Well, if we don't go into the city with the boys this week- end, we should do it some other time," Jamie said. "Maybe you or I could drive into Edmonton for a day or a weekend. Go to West Ed and do some shopping. Maybe even go to the water park. Stay with my sister. It would be a blast, and she'd love to have us."

"I'd love it," Chloe said.

"Hey, did you see *Buffy* this week?" Jamie asked. "Wasn't it amazing?"

Buffy was one of Allyson's favourite shows. "I know," she said. "I can't believe what they're doing with Willow."

"I taped it," Chloe said. "I haven't had time to watch it yet. My parents are making me help out on the farm all the time. Plus, I have to write that English essay."

"Oh yeah, the one for Mrs. Henshaw," Jamie said. "She's a hard marker."

They continued talking about their English essays. They weren't going to acknowledge her. She wanted to grab her cousin by the shoulders and shake her.

"I'll see you back at the farm," Allyson mumbled, pushing out her chair. She slunk back to Jeff's table, hoping no one else was watching her. She sat down and stared at the front of Jeff's sketch pad, willing herself not to cry. She took a deep breath, and realized her shoulders were up by her ears. Relax, she said to herself. Calm down. Don't let them know they pissed you off.

She opened Jeff's sketch pad and flipped through it. There were drawings of anime girls and a portrait of his sister. As she flipped further, she saw realistic drawings of naked female torsos. He had drawn breasts of all sizes and shapes. She giggled before flipping to another page. Then she saw a picture of herself. Her head was bent over a book, her long dark hair gathered around her face. It really looked like her.

"What are you doing?" Jeff said. "That's private."

He grabbed the sketchbook away from her.

"If it's so private, you shouldn't have left it here on the table," Allyson said. She could feel her cheeks turning red, the way they always did when she got flustered.

Jeff held the sketchbook close to his chest and went back through the door into the kitchen.

Allyson waited a few minutes for him to come back. He walked by, carrying a tray full of Cokes and beers, but didn't even bother to look at her. Allyson took a pen off the table, and wrote, "I'm sorry. Hope to talk to you later," on a napkin. Then she went back to her dad's table.

Her dad's friend, an auctioneer named Tony, sat in the seat she'd abandoned. Allyson stood by the table. The men were talking in murmurs.

"This could screw the industry," Tony said. "We could be completely ruined."

Her dad shook his head. "I can't even talk about this anymore," he said. "The whole thing is just too much."

"Dad, can we go?" Allyson asked. "I have lot of homework and I'm not getting anything done here."

She shifted her weight from foot to foot.

Her dad stood up. "Talk to you guys later," he said. "Maybe we'll have time for a coffee tomorrow."

"Keep your chin up, Gord," Ray Sharp said. This was his standard goodbye. "You too girl."

"Go ask Chloe if she needs a ride home," Gord said.

"She doesn't," Allyson said. "She's with her friend."

"Ask her anyway," Gord said. "It's the right thing to do.

He started towards the door. Allyson followed, but he gave her a look and she walked over to Chloe's table.

"Do you need a ride back to the farm?" she asked, speaking more to the floor than to her cousin.

"Jamie will give me a ride," Chloe said. "Thanks." She didn't even bother to look at her cousin as she spoke.

Allyson ran out to the truck. The hum of the truck's engine was comforting. She pulled on the door, opened it and climbed onto the dirty, dusty truck seat. Allyson swept a few strands of hay off the seat and wondered why she hadn't noticed them before. She rested her arm on the hard shell of her trumpet case and the curve of her backpack. Her dad backed the truck up and started towards home.

"So much bad news," he said, sighing.

He turned on the radio and a country singer wailed about how much it hurt to lose love. Allyson sympathized with his sadness, even if the sound of his voice annoyed her. She turned away from her dad and faced the window, looking out toward the expanse of prairie, and familiar farmhouses. It was still so dry. At least the coffee shop talk had been about something different, rather than about the lack of moisture from last year. They drove by the Stamps' place, and Allyson strained her eyes, looking for the shapes of the bison in the yard.

They drove past one of their own pastures and her father slowed the truck down the way he always did. Her mother said her father was a born cattleman. He could read cows the same way some people could read other people. He could look at a herd of cows and immediately tell which ones were sick and needed to be isolated from the herd. She didn't even know how many times she'd watched him pull a calf. He was so good at it that you could almost feel the cow's relief.

"Watch the cows' ears and eyes," he always said. "They can tell you all you need to know."

Her father had taught her how to be gentle with cattle, and how to walk in a way that would force the cattle to move, so you didn't need to yell at them. Her mother, Donna, didn't like cattle. She had been hurt by a cow when Allyson's oldest brother Clay was just a baby. The cow charged her, knocked the wind out of her, and sent her tumbling to the ground. She'd hurt her wrist. Donna had been trying to look at the cow's calf and hadn't noticed the cow getting protective. No one else had been around when she'd been hit. She crawled to the corner of the pen, shivering and yelling until Gord and Grandma Abby came to help her. After that, Donna rarely went around the animals.

"Gramma and Aunty Linda tried to help her get over her fear," Gord always said when he told the story. "They would hold her hand before she went into the pens, try to make her go in with the calves and ask her to come into the pens with them. But she was just too scared. She tried for a long time, but she couldn't just get over her encounter with that one cow."

The sun wouldn't set for a few hours, but the sky was already the paler blue of evening, the colour it turned before slipping into purple and pink. The red cows clumped together in the field. Some of them looked at the truck, curious, their big brown eyes wide. Calves followed close behind. The calves had a look of innocence, a cuteness about them that made them look like toys, especially as they struggled to keep up to their mothers with their babyish, jumping gaits. Gord inspected the animals and sized them up. He turned off the radio, rolled down the window and leaned out of the truck, starting at one lone cow standing near a willow.

"Allyson, your eyes are better than mine. Can you see what she's looking at?"

Allyson shook her head.

As they watched, the cow circled a lump in the field. The rest of the herd meandered, moving back towards the pasture that led to the home quarter. They knew the routine and sensed Gord might be there to move them.

Gord opened the door of the truck. "I'm going to have a look," he said, hopping down from the cab. Allyson fiddled with the radio the minute after he closed the door, searching for the rock station. She watched as her dad opened the barbed-wire gate, closed it behind him and strode off across the pasture. The lone cow watched him, shifting away from him as he approached.

The cow circled and started to moo insistently. The other cattle watched, but stayed their distance. Gord bent down and examined the lump in the field. He knelt down and picked it up. When he rose again, she could see it was a dead calf, one that had just been born last month. All four of its legs sagged over Gord's arms as he walked towards the fence. The cow followed behind Gord, bawling as he walked to the gate. The limbs and head of the calf bobbed and flopped with each of Gord's steps. As her father got closer, Allyson saw the calf's mouth was open, its eyes big and scared. Dried blood coated the calf's limbs and head. She shifted over to her dad's side of the truck, and leaned out the window to take in the scene. Though she couldn't hear him, she knew her dad was making calm, shushing noises. He talked to them as if they could understand what he was saying, speaking in a low, calm voice. Her older brother Clay called it, "the voice Dad uses when he talks to his girls."

Her dad didn't have to say the words; she got out of the truck and scrambled across the ditch. The wind blew strands of her long brown hair into her face as she opened the barbed-wire gate. Her dad cradled the calf's dead body and walked through the small opening in the fence.

"Shh," he said to the cow, who followed close behind him. "They got your baby." The cow let out angrier bawls as Gord carried the dead calf to the truck. He leaned over the side of the truck and let go of the calf's body. Allyson turned so she didn't have to watch it fall into the truck.

"Damn coyotes," Gord said, sighing. The front and sleeves of his dusty, dirty jean jacket were spotted with dark red patches of blood.

"I always knew those beasts could take down a calf," he said. "Guess I'll have to tell your uncle that we need to go hunting. We'll get that sucker."

Gord ran his wet hands down his pants, leaving rust-coloured streaks on his jeans. He swung up into the truck and started it. The cow stood by the fence and watched as they drove away. Allyson and Gord sat in silence until they got back home.

At the farm, Allyson leaned over the side of the truck bed to get a better look at the calf's body and the hole in its side where the coyote had attacked the animal. The calf's entrails spilled out, the white sticks of its small ribs visible. The calf was so small. Its delicate red eyelashes surrounded scared-looking eyes. The animal's tongue stuck out of its open mouth, as if it had been caught mid-scream.

"Why did you bring the body back?" she asked.

Gord walked over and stood beside her. "Needed to remove the source of food," he said. "Don't want it in the pasture. I'll throw it in the bush later."

Allyson smelled the dark iron stench of the animal's blood. She looked away, willing herself not to gag. Rascal, their border collie, came to greet her and she reached a hand down, burying it in his long, dark fur. The dog sat down beside her and looked up with his eager, dark brown eyes. As Allyson stood beside her father, she felt tears welling up. She slumped against the back of the truck, pressing her spine against the cold metal. Her tears weren't for the calf, though the sight of its mutilated body was disturbing. She thought about Jeff's notebook, and Chloe's dismissal of her. She leaned down and put her hands over her face. The evening air had a chill to it, and she could feel a breeze on her bare arms.

Her dad hummed a mournful lament. She wasn't able to identify the song. Allyson straightened up and faced him.

"Why are you crying?" he asked. "It's one calf."

Allyson didn't answer. Instead, she leaned over to pick up her backpack and trumpet case and started towards the house. The screen door banged shut behind her. She slipped off her shoes and climbed the stairs, headed for the sanctuary of her bedroom.

CHAPTER 2

The accident happened two weeks after the border closed. It was a Saturday night and Gramma Abby and Grandpa Al had gone into Lloydminster for dinner and a movie.

"We can't stay out too late," Al said to Donna, who was out in the yard in a lawn chair, enjoying some of the late afternoon sun. "Someone's got to get up early. I'll have this girl back in time," he said, putting his arm around his wife.

"Have fun on your date," Donna said. She thought it was great her in-laws went on dates and still looked at each other with love. They were in their sixties, and completely smitten with each other. Gord said sometimes he'd go looking for Al in the yard and catch his parents sharing a kiss, Al the red-haired, red-bearded mountain bending over to kiss Abby, who was barely five feet tall. Abby and Al were prone to driving around the back country, taking back roads and staying away from the farm for hours.

"I think they park like teenagers," Linda said once when she and Donna were having coffee.

"Better them than the actual teenagers around here," Donna said, and she and her sister-in-law laughed.

Donna watched as Al and Abby drove Al's old truck out of the farmyard. Al's window was open and he hung his elbow out. Abby always teased him for driving like that, said you could see how much he had driven by how red his arm was. She said it made him look even more like a hillbilly, even more than his red hair, or his weathered face and the crow's feet around his eyes. Abby had grown up on a farm just outside the city, but hadn't worked cattle until she married Al. Donna had never met anyone tougher than her mother-in-law. The woman was barely one hundred pounds soaking wet, but she would get up in the night to pull calves, drive the truck to bring bales into the pasture and wrestle sick calves into the bathtub if needed. Abby was the matriarch of the ranch, the one everyone deferred to. But she was so sweet about everything nobody minded taking direction from her.

The truck rolled down the long driveway, through the gate and down the road. The horses Temple, Crow and Cassidy stood in their pen looking out at the yard, swishing their tails to keep the flies off. The sun shone and there were no clouds. They hadn't had a lot of rain yet this spring, and everything was dusty. Allyson's allergies were acting up and she kept sneezing and rubbed her eyes all the time.

"I wasn't meant to live on a farm," she said earlier that morning after sneezing three times in a row.

"Well, this is where you live until you're old enough to move out," Donna snapped. "I'm sick and tired of your whining. Just think, it could be worse. It could still be winter."

Donna moved to a deck chair on the porch behind the house. She lit a citronella ring and allowed the smoke to waft over the deck. Rascal and Maggie had come in from the yard and lay near her feet. It was still light out, but the sun was fading, even though it was warm for the beginning of June. She shivered a little and pulled up the blanket that rested over her legs. It was one of Abby's quilts. She was always knitting or quilting or doing something crafty when she wasn't farming. She and Al had an inability to rest.

"Idle hands are the devil's workshop," Abby liked to say. She wasn't an overly religious woman, but she believed in God, went to confession and attended church every week. Gord, Donna and their kids had never gone because Donna never wanted to, but Gord's brother Craig and his wife Linda kept the faith. Abby and Al never said anything about it, but Donna knew they wished her kids had been confirmed. She'd baptized them because she knew Abby wanted it, but they'd never gone further than that.

She heard footsteps running across the yard, the slam of the front door. Craig inside the house, his voice loud. She couldn't make out what he was saying, but she heard Gord's voice answer him. The screen door to the deck opened and Allyson ran out. The next thing Donna knew, her girl was in her arms, sobbing.

"What?" Donna asked, putting her arms around her daughter. Allyson was fourteen, too old to ask for hugs on a regular basis. She'd seen her daughter cry recently—she was a teenager, after all—but she hadn't seen waterworks like this for a while. Her daughter sobbed, nose running, her face blotchy and red.

"What's wrong?" Donna asked. "Honey, what happened?"

This was no ordinary teenage problem. Her daughter had been unhappy a while ago, something about issues with Chloe, but Allyson was crying too hard for this to be something as simple as a fight with her cousin.

Donna heard footsteps and looked over her daughter's shoulder to her husband's face. Something terrible had happened because he couldn't look her in the eye. He stared out at the space over her head, out into the yard. When Gord spoke, his voice was calm and terrible.

"There's been an accident," he said. His words were without emotion, as if he was telling her he was planning to become the treasurer of the Elks' club.

"What?" Donna asked, letting go of her daughter. Allyson moved away, leaving Donna alone in the chair. Donna sat up straight. "Is it Linda? Where's Chloe? Is Colton okay?"

When you lived on a farm and someone said there had been an accident, you never knew what you were dealing with. The last time there had been an accident, Gord cut himself badly with a bandsaw and was rushed into town to get stitches. The sight of Gord with blood streaming from his hand down the front of his t-shirt and onto his jeans haunted Donna for weeks.

"Mom and Dad. Someone hit their truck out on the highway."

"Oh my God," Donna said. "Jesus. No."

"It's bad," he said. "We don't know if they're alive. Craig and Linda are going to the hospital in the city. I'm going there too."

"What happened?"

"We don't know. Rita called Craig. The ambulance just brought them in. She said it's bad."

"I can go too," Donna said, standing up.

"You better stay here," Gord said. He looked at Allyson who stood in between them, taking in their words. "The kids."

Donna nodded. Her eyes itched and she could feel tears starting, but she willed herself not to cry. Abby's voice popped into her head, telling her crying would do no good and she should focus on getting things done.

"Are you okay to drive?" Donna asked.

"I know where the hospital is," he said. "I'll be fine."

Even though Gord did most of the driving on the highways and in town, he hated driving in cities. Said all the stopping, starting, twisting and turning was enough to make a man throw himself under a truck.

Gord walked down the deck stairs and around the side of the house. Donna followed him. She heard a truck start up and sprinted across the yard. She ran to Linda's side of the vehicle and leaned in. Linda always bragged about how she wasn't a crier, but she was dabbing at her eyes with a Kleenex. She shifted towards the window, grabbed Donna's arm and held it tight. "I'm already praying," she said.

Donna wished she were a believer—that she could ask God to save two of the people who mattered most to her.

"Call me when you know something," she said.

Linda nodded. "Give my girl a big squeeze if she gets home first," she said.

Then Gord's hand was in Donna's, and she walked away from the truck towards their vehicle. Craig and Linda drove off. Donna's legs were heavy and wobbly. How could this be happening? Were Al and Abby dead? Everything was far away and distant, as if she was looking at the world through the wrong end of a telescope. She couldn't finish a thought. Gord's arms circled her and she inhaled the familiar smell of Old Spice and his warm body.

"Breathe," he said, and she realized she had been taking shallow sips of air, heading towards an anxiety attack.

She closed her eyes and tried to suck in as much air as she could. She couldn't have a panic attack now. Gord gave her a kiss on the top of her head, got into the truck, started it up and rolled down the window.

"Drive careful," she said. "Call me when you have news."

He drove out of the yard. Donna watched the back of her husband's head, a silhouette she'd seen thousands of times. The worn-down red truck kicked up gravel and dust and turned down the driveway. The horses stood in their pen, calm, staring off into space, oblivious to what had just transpired. Worries began to trickle into Donna's thoughts. What if someone hit Gord's truck while he was driving? What if Linda and Craig hit a deer on the road? Where were Colton and Chloe?

She was shaking, and wrapped her arms around herself. Her teeth chattered and her chest was tight and sore like she'd been punched in the sternum. She walked around to a tree and braced herself against it, feeling the bark against her hands, inhaling the scent of emerging leaves. She looked across the yard towards Al and Abby's big white house and Craig and Linda's smaller brown house, leaned into the tree, and let its sturdiness prop her up.

"Mom," she heard, and Allyson was there, hugging her, pinning Donna's arms to her sides.

"Breathe," Allyson said, and Donna closed her eyes, concentrating on the sound of her daughter's own jagged breathing, the quick beating of her daughter's heart against her own chest. Rascal had joined them and his cold, wet nose brushed the back of her hand. She reached out and buried her hand in his warm fur. She felt a tickle on her forearm and turned her head to see a wasp land on her arm. She moved her arms, and her daughter let go of her. The wasp flew off. Rascal licked her hand. Donna tried to concentrate on these things, rather than the cloud of worries in her head. A therapist had told her years ago to concentrate on the things around her, the physical details she could see, feel and smell, and use them to ground her.

"Let's go inside," Allyson said and Donna leaned on her daughter. As they walked toward the house, Donna had a flash of what she would be like as an old woman, scared and confused, relying on her daughter for guidance. That wasn't the way it should be right now. She was the parent, the one who should be strong. She heard Abby's voice telling her to pull herself together.

"I don't know what we should do," Donna said, once they were inside. "We should probably sit in the front room to watch for Chloe. And go get the phone."

Allyson walked out of the living room and returned with the white phone in her hand. Donna took it from her and checked to make sure the ringer volume was turned up high. The phone was covered with fingerprints.

"Stay by the window," she said to her daughter, before walking to the kitchen to grab a dishcloth to wipe down the phone. She brought the cloth back to the front room. Might as well do some dusting while they were waiting. Allyson kneeled on the couch, staring over the back of it, out into the yard.

"Chloe is probably with Jamie," she said. "Should I try to find the number?"

"I don't think we should call," Donna said. "It's probably best not to tie up the phone."

Donna wondered where Colton was. Probably driving around town or sitting in a bar somewhere. Maybe he was out in the bush, making a fire and drinking beer. Should she try to find him? It probably made more sense just to wait and see when he turned up. He had been talking about getting a cell phone, and now she wished he had one.

The phone rang while she was holding it in her hand, and she jumped.

"Hello, any news?"

"What?" The voice on the other end of the phone was low and groggy. "Is Colton there?" The caller exhaled, as if he was letting smoke out of his lungs.

"No," Donna said. "He's not. Do you know where he is?" The minute after she asked, she realized how stupid the question was.

"If I knew, I wouldn't be calling," the caller said, emitting a low laugh.

"Is this Booger?" she asked.

"Yeah."

"If he turns up, tell him to come right home. There's been an accident." Donna hung up without saying goodbye.

Allyson was still sitting on the couch, looking out the window.

"I wish we had a TV in here or something," she said. "I need something to distract me. I don't want to think what I'm thinking."

She had stopped crying. Donna studied her daughter's face. Allyson's eyes were blotchy. She had only started puberty last year, and it still surprised Donna to see adult features on her baby girl's face. When she looked at Allyson's face, she could see a glimpse of what Allyson would look like when she was in her thirties. But she could still see the remnant of the child toddling around the yard as well. Right now, her daughter looked young and vulnerable, and Donna remembered Allyson when she was small, the feeling of holding her entire body, the way her hair smelled like Johnson's baby shampoo. Her daughter's eyes were too big for her face.

"Put on some music. It'll be okay if we play something quiet," Donna said. "I'll keep watch while you go get some CDs." She stood and looked out the window. The sky was starting to darken. Even though it was after nine, she could still see the yard as clear as day.

Allyson returned with a stack of CDs and put one in the player. Piano music and mournful vocals filled the room. Allyson turned the volume down low and moved back to the couch. She'd brought her sketchbook and started doodling, stopping once in a while to look out at the yard. Donna dusted the top of the mantel and the china cabinet. There was no dust on anything, but the physical movement of cleaning was calming. If she concentrated, she could pretend it was an ordinary day. She was doing something, accomplishing something. She wished she could run the vacuum cleaner, but she didn't want to make noise. What if they didn't hear the phone? She was still holding it, scared to put it down.

She didn't want to start thinking about what had happened, if Abby and Al were still alive. Years ago, her therapist had told her she should always try to imagine the best scenario, rather than the worst. She closed her eyes and pictured Abby and Al. In her mind, Al was out in the yard, looking at the cattle, surveying everything in the place he called "his little piece of heaven." Abby was in the kitchen, quilting or outside working in her big vegetable garden, her small hands clad in her favourite purple gardening gloves. They were going to be okay, she thought. But even as she said those words to herself, she didn't believe it. There had been so many horrific accidents on that highway. And Rita had said it was bad. She opened her eyes, and tried to make herself focus on her surroundings. She walked over to the old rocking chair and fluffed the pillows on it, and tried to make herself concentrate on the music. Someone with a sad voice was singing about "Yellow".

"What is this music?" Donna asked her daughter. "This is way too sad. Put something else on."

Without complaining, Allyson got up from the couch and changed the CD. Soon Jim Morrison's voice filled the room.

"When did you start liking The Doors?" Donna asked.

"I saw that movie on TV late one night," Allyson said. "The one with Val Kilmer."

Donna put the phone next to her daughter's head, checking again to make sure the ringer volume was high. She walked over to the mantel to dust pictures. She picked them all up: baby photos of Clay, who had been a huge Doors fan when he lived in the house. Photos of her and Gord and Clay, all smiling. How young they had been. Just babies themselves. There were baby photos of Colton, who hadn't bothered to crawl, but ran as soon as he was able to pull himself upright. School photos of all three of her kids with gap-toothed grins, and then Clay's smile, full of shiny silver braces that cost a fortune. Photos of her girl, of Chloe, of Craig and Linda, and Pam, her own sister. She stopped dusting before she got to the photos of Abby and Al's fortieth wedding anniversary. She didn't want to pick up those photos right now. Instead, she moved back to the couch and sat down beside her daughter.

"Want me to make tea?" Allyson asked.

Donna nodded. "I'll sit here and watch."

She hummed along to the CD, glad to be listening to something so familiar. Sang along with Jim as he sang about being untrue and a liar. Her singing was off key, but it made her feel better, helped take her mind off things. Donna looked at the clock on the mantel. Why hadn't anyone called? It took about an hour to drive to the city. She hadn't kept track of what time everyone had left. It was a little after ten now, finally starting to get dark.

The kettle bubbled in the kitchen, and she could hear the sound of her daughter opening drawers and cupboards. Allyson returned with two steaming mugs. Donna took the Co-op mug, inhaled the calming smell of peppermint, and blew on it before taking a sip. Allyson sat down next to the window and looked out.

"I wish they would call," she said.

Donna saw the dust before she saw the orange Celica barrel up the driveway and park beside Craig and Linda's house.

"That kid is driving too fast again," Donna muttered. She turned to her daughter. "You need to go out and talk to her. Tell her what happened."

Allyson didn't move. "Maybe you should go." She took a sip of tea and grimaced.

"Don't be silly," Donna said. "Go get your cousin. One of us needs to wait inside."

Allyson put her mug down on the coffee table. Donna thought about asking her daughter to use a coaster, but now was not the time for lectures on proper furniture maintenance.

Chloe stepped outside the car and walked toward her house. Rascal and Maggie ran over to greet her, and she leaned over to pet them. Their wagging tails made Donna feel a bit better. At least two of the kids were home safe.

Allyson sighed and pulled herself off the couch. Her movements were slow and reluctant, as if her limbs were weighed down. Donna wondered if the two of them had had another fight. When they were little, they had been like sisters, but they were spending less time together lately.

"Hurry up," Donna said. "I'll feel better when Chloe is in here too."

Allyson shuffled towards the door. Donna watched out the window as her daughter walked across the yard. God, that girl was getting tall.

Her daughter caught up to Chloe. Chloe turned and looked at her, and Donna shivered. She'd seen that look before, but not on Chloe's face. A look of disdain and annoyance, a look she remembered on the face of a girl who bullied her in high school. Donna watched as the girls talked. Chloe stood a few steps away from her cousin, but then she took several steps forward, crumpled towards her cousin and embraced her. Donna couldn't see either girl's face. As she watched, they broke their embrace and ran toward the house. At the same moment, the phone rang. She fumbled around for it, before finding it on the back of the couch, near Allyson's sketch pad.

"Gord, is that you? Any news?"

"Dad's dead," he said.

"Oh God," she said. "Abby?"

"Still alive. But she's not doing well."

She wanted to cry, but tears wouldn't come. She was a crier, but here she was, unable to cry. There was a rush of heat, as if she was developing a fever. Then she was freezing, and she went to the couch and wrapped a blanket around her, teeth chattering. Al couldn't be dead. This wasn't supposed to happen. He was too young. He was supposed to grow to be an old man, a man in his eighties or nineties, hobbling around his land with a cane, practically deaf, keeping watch over all he had created.

She heard Gord's sobs and it was the worst sound she'd ever heard, long low moans like an animal in pain. She didn't know what to say, so she just let him cry. They had been married for over twenty-five years and she had never once heard or seen him cry. He'd slipped and fallen, cut himself and needed stitches on one of his knees. He'd been kicked by cows and had more black eyes and skinned knuckles than she could count. She'd watched him bury his favourite farm dog and warm his toes in the tub after he'd given himself frostbite staying out in the yard to help a cow calve in minus forty-degree weather. They'd survived so many emergencies together, some of them caused by farming and some of them caused by life and the stress people encounter when they have three children and live out in the middle of nowhere. But Gord never cried in front of her.

She wasn't sure what to say, so she just listened, waiting for him to speak. His sobs were so horrible that she forced herself to stare at the window, out at the yard, which was now almost dark. The girls were nowhere to be seen. As she listened to Gord cry on the phone, she heard Jim Morrison sing about riders on the storm. The juxtaposition of the two sounds was surreal and she knew she would never be able to listen to this album again. Still holding the phone to her ear, she ran to the bathroom, the acid in her stomach rising and burning.

"Just wait a second," she said and she held the phone away from her head with one hand, and pulled her hair back with the other as she heaved, retched and threw up in the toilet. When she finished, she flushed and sank down next to the toilet, holding her head up with one hand, inhaling deep, shuddering breaths.

"I'm okay," she said into the phone. "I'm okay. Don't worry about me. Just talk when you're ready."

"Donna," she heard on the line. "It's Craig." His voice was calm.

"Tell me everything," she said. Her teeth chattered against each other.

"Aunty Donna?" Chloe's voice came from the other room. "Are you okay?"

"In the bathroom," Donna called. The door to the bathroom was still open.

"The girls are here," she said to Craig.

Allyson and Chloe entered the bathroom, their bodies filling the tiny room as the three women squeezed into the space. Chloe hugged her aunt. Donna smelled vanilla, the scent Chloe always wore.

"Chloe's here," she said to Craig.

"Let me talk to her," Craig said.

Donna handed the phone to her niece, who took it and moved down the hallway. Allyson backed out of the room and stood just outside the doorway, watching Donna turn on the faucet. The cool water felt good on her hands and she splashed her face, letting the freshness wash away the sickness. She turned off the tap, dried her hands on the fluffy purple towel and looked at her daughter.

"They're dead," Allyson said. "That's the only thing that could make you throw up like that."

"Your grandpa's dead," Donna said, before wiping her face on the towel. Allyson started to cry. Donna put her arms around her, hugged her close, felt the fast beat of her daughter's heart against her chest.

"Gramma?" Allyson asked, pushing her hair back from her face.

"She's alive. That's all I know."

Chloe came back up the hallway and handed the phone to Donna. "Dad wants to talk to you," she said.

Donna walked away from the girls and down the hallway. Chloe was still wearing her jean jacket. The sleeves of the jacket were dirty and grass stained. She leaned against the wall. The cool sturdiness of the wall was solid against her back.

"Tell me everything," she said.

Craig's voice was strained and he spoke faster than he normally did. Craig usually talked in a slow drawl that made him sound like he was from Texas rather than Alberta.

"They were coming back from the city and were turning onto the highway. A car drove through the turnoff on Highway 21, blew the stop sign and t-boned the truck on Dad's side. Truck rolled into the ditch. Some people behind them saw the whole thing and called it in on their cell phones. They were both alive when they arrived at the hospital, but Dad's injuries were really bad, and he didn't make it."

Craig took a long shuddering breath. "Mom's in rough shape. She broke one of her arms and she's still out of it. Doctors say she's going to make it, but she'll have extensive injuries."

There was a long silence on the other end of the line as Donna waited for him to go on.

"His body was banged up. The crash did a number on him. Must have gone flying through the window. He was all cut up and bruised, bones broken everywhere. Those yahoos must have been gunning it."

Donna felt like throwing up again.

"Linda is taking care of the arrangements," Craig said. He lowered his voice. "Gord's a mess. He started wailing as soon as he saw Dad. Just sat near his bed, held Dad's hands in his and bawled. It was so terrible, like something out of those tearjerker movies. Might be best for Gord to go home, but I don't want to leave, and I don't want him to drive himself back. He wouldn't be able to concentrate on the road right now."

Donna knew Gord would never forgive himself if he wasn't there to help out. If he missed out on making some critical decisions, he would never let himself forget it. Gord prided himself on being tough, and things would be better if she did whatever was needed to help him get through this. Gord's favourite sayings were "Cowboy up" or "Git 'er done." She'd never hear the end of it if he ran away from this one.

"He'll pull himself together," Donna said. "Do you want us to come down?"

She waited for Craig to answer.

"I don't think we need you right now. I think you should stay with the kids. I know they're all old enough, but I don't want Chloe to be alone."

"What if we all drove down?" Donna asked. "We could all be there."

"The three of us can handle it," Craig said. "Linda and I can do most of it even if Gord needs to take a time out. I don't want you guys on the road. It's dark, everyone's emotional and there are lots of deer out tonight. We saw a whole whack of them on our way up here. I was a little distracted, worried that I might hit one. I don't think Chloe and Allyson need to be here. I don't want them to see Dad's body. I'd just feel better if everyone stayed put. If we need to, we'll grab a motel room in the city and sleep. You can come out in the morning, when everyone has rested. Maybe we'll know more about Mom by then."

"Okay," Donna said. She wasn't going to argue with him. This wasn't the time to rush in and try to be a hero. Craig and Linda were there and they would deal with things. She was good at taking orders. She'd been doing that since she moved to the farm. "Is Gord around?"

"I just saw him walk down the hallway. I think he was going to get a coffee or a water or something. You know how he is."

"Well, tell him to call me if he needs to," she said. Her mind raced. What were the next steps to take? She started to talk through things out loud.

"I'll try to get hold of Clay. Wait up for Colton. Call me back and tell me if there's more news. Let me know if there's anything I can do. Just say the word. I'll get in the car the second you ask."

"You don't need to start calling people right now," Craig said. "It can wait until morning. We don't have any news about Mom and Dad's gone."

"Where's Linda?"

"I think she was talking to the nurses, signing some forms. We'll call Sutter's funeral home in the morning. Make all the arrangements."

She heard the catch in his throat. "I can't even think about this stuff right now. Linda's handling it all. She's such a trooper. Don't know where Gord and me would be without her."

Donna didn't know the right thing to say and so she stayed silent, trying to digest everything Craig was telling her.

"Just tell me whatever you need me to do," she said. "Call me if you need anything. Ask Gord or Linda to call. I'll do whatever needs to be done."

"We know that," he said. "We'll keep you posted. We might come home. Just take care of the kids. I need to go."

"Okay," she said, trying to think of the right thing to say, the perfect thing that would make this terribleness just a little bit better. "I love you. Tell Gord and Linda I send my love."

"We'll keep praying," he said. "I gotta go."

Donna let him hang up first, then clicked the button to hang up the phone. She checked the phone's battery levels and carried it into the kitchen, where Chloe and Allyson sat at the round wooden table, a large box of Kleenex between them.

"Chloe told me everything," Allyson said. "I know Grandpa's dead."

Her daughter's face was even paler than normal. Donna looked at Chloe. Her niece's mascara had run off, and blackish-grey marks streaked down her face.

"It's the most terrible thing that could happen," Donna said, sitting down at the table with them.

"Gramma is going to make it," Chloe said. "We need to concentrate on that. Mom and Dad told me they were praying for her. That's what Gramma would want."

Allyson and Donna said nothing. Donna hadn't been brought up in the church, and had never taught her children to pray. Gord wasn't a believer and he was more than happy to stop going to church when they'd married. Every Sunday, when Chloe, Linda, Craig, Al and Abby made the drive into town to go to the Blessed Sacrament Church, Donna, Gord and the kids stayed home and watched old movies, cartoons or westerns on TV. Sometimes they made pancakes and stayed in their pyjamas until noon.

Donna stood up and hugged Allyson. As soon as she felt the warm sturdiness of her daughter, she knew she didn't have the luxury of crying any more that night. Allyson started crying as soon as her mother hugged her. Donna squeezed her, made shh sounds and stroked her daughter's long, brown hair. Her daughter may be turning into a woman, but Donna could still feel the bony points of the shoulder blades on her daughter's back. She was the adult here; she would need to take charge. She had two kids to take care of, and she couldn't just go to bed, pull the covers over her head and start bawling, even though that's what she wanted to do. She looked at the clock, wondering if it was too late to call her sister. Pam's voice would be a comfort. But she couldn't lean on Pam right now. Abby's voice came into Donna's head, reminding her that she needed to take care of things. She let her daughter go and hugged Chloe for a few minutes, before grabbing a Kleenex from the box on the table. The box was

covered in a crocheted cozy that was a gift from Linda. Donna
hated it, and had taken it only to appease her sister-in-law. She
bit her tongue every time Linda went to Country Treasures in
town and came home with a new ornament shaped like a farm
animal, or a sign embossed with a pat saying like "Live, love,
laugh" or "Home is where your heart lives."

Donna stood up and went to the cupboard for a glass, leaving
the phone on the table. She glanced at it, daring it to ring. "Do
either of you want some water?" she asked.

Chloe nodded and Allyson shook her head. Donna filled
three glasses of water anyway, and brought them to the table one
at a time. Chloe picked up a tall glass with a Coke label on it and
took a long drink. Donna watched the movement of her throat.
When Chloe put the glass back on the table, Donna spoke.

"I think you should stay here tonight," she said. "Unless you
really want to be in your own bed. You can stay in Allyson's
room if you want."

Chloe looked at her fingers, which were still gripping the
water glass.

"I think I'd sleep better in a bed than on an air mattress," she
said. "Can I stay in Clay's room?"

Donna nodded. "The bed is made up."

Chloe stood up. "I'll go get my stuff and come right back."

She walked out of the room. The screen door slammed a few
minutes later. Allyson sat at the table, staring at the Kleenex box.

"Honey, are you okay?" Donna asked.

Allyson turned to her and gave her a baleful look. Donna was
familiar with that face. She remembered the first time she had
seen it, shortly after Allyson turned thirteen.

"My Grandpa just died and my Gramma might die," she said
and stood up. "How am I supposed to feel?" Her chair scraped
against the kitchen floor. Donna winced at the sound, and
watched as her daughter left the room.

Donna wasn't sure what to do with herself. She went to the
sink, grabbed a dish cloth and began wiping down the counters.
She wished she could call Gord and find out how Abby was
doing. Maybe after this, Gord would want to invest in a cell

phone. Everything would be so much easier if everyone just had phones. What was happening at the hospital? Someone would have to go into Abby and Al's place to look for all their necessary documents. What could she be doing to get things ready? She walked down to the front room and looked out at the dark yard. The trees in the yard moved a little in the breeze. Allyson had hated the trees when she was young, and begged to trade rooms with Colton. She said the branches looked like fingers reaching for the house.

Donna went back to the kitchen, opened the fridge and started taking things out. When was the last time she had cleaned the fridge? She returned to the sink, wet the dish cloth and began wiping down the condiments, starting with the peanut butter, the jams and the syrup. She wiped down Linda's preserves, the ones she dropped off but no one ever ate, and ended with the plastic squeeze tubes of Co-op mustard and ketchup. The jar of hot peppers at the back of the fridge was cloudy, the vegetables inside swollen with liquid. Clay was the only one who liked hot peppers and he hadn't visited for a while. Unscrewing the lid, she put her nose over it and sniffed, inhaling the spicy brine. The peppers had probably gone off. She screwed the lid back on and dumped the whole jar into the metal trashcan in the corner.

The door opened again. Donna heard shoes getting kicked off, the shuffle of Chloe's feet. That girl had never learned how to pick up her feet properly. Chloe poked her head into the kitchen.

"I'm going to bed now," she said.

Donna looked at her niece. She had washed her face and scrubbed off the mascara streaks. Her face was clean, almost shiny, but the area around her eyes was puffy and swollen. She had changed into a long floral nightgown that brushed the tops of her ankles. The neckline of the nightgown had a light blue ribbon around it. The ends of the ribbon were frayed, as though Chloe had chewed on it a few times. Donna always wondered why her sister-in-law and niece insisted on such nun-like sleepwear. Donna wanted to cry, just slump into the chair and start weeping, but that wouldn't do any good. Before she could help herself, Donna pictured tiny Abby with her cleft chin and bright eyes, lying in a hospital bed, bloody and bruised. How would they tell her that Al was dead? Did she even know what had happened?

"It's okay," Donna heard and Chloe's arms were around her. Her niece smelled like Neutrogena soap.

Donna heard the sound of the tap. Allyson was in the kitchen, filling a glass with water. Donna opened her mouth to tell her daughter to come for a hug, but the only thing that came out of her mouth was a sob. Allyson looked at the two of them and walked out of the kitchen. Donna let go of her niece.

"We should probably all go to bed."

Chloe ran her sleeve under her nose, a childish gesture Donna hadn't seen her do in years.

"Night, Aunty Donna," she said.

She shuffled up the stairs to Clay's room. Donna followed her. Her niece entered the room, flopped down on the bed and rolled over to lie on her back.

"Do you need anything, Chlo? You going to be okay?"

Her niece stared at the ceiling and nodded.

"We'll just be down the hallway if you need anything. Do you want me to turn off the light?"

Chloe nodded again and Donna flicked the switch.

"Thanks for letting me stay here," she said.

"Of course, sweetie," Donna said.

She had no doubt her niece would be dead to the world in a few minutes. Linda and Craig marvelled at what an easy baby she'd been, how she was a perfect child designed to entice every new parent to have more babies. Linda had tried and tried, lost a few and hadn't been able to have any more.

There was no way Allyson would be sleeping yet. Down the hall, her daughter's door was closed. Donna knocked and then opened it once she heard her daughter's muffled voice tell her to come in. Allyson was under the covers. Her bedside lamp was on, and she lay on her stomach, a book open on the pillow in front of her.

"You okay, sweetie?" Donna asked, moving into the room. She sat down on her daughter's bed, taking care not to sit on her outstretched legs. Allyson's hair was cool against her hand as she smoothed it down.

"I can't talk about it," Allyson said. "I just need to think about something else."

"I know," Donna said. She looked down at her daughter's book; a dog-eared copy of *Harry Potter*. She wasn't sure how many times Allyson had read the story of the boy wizard. Comfort reading. Donna understood.

"If you can't sleep, you're welcome to crawl in," she said. "It's okay tonight."

Allyson flipped a page. "Thanks," she said, without looking up. "Can I be alone now?"

Donna ruffled her daughter's hair with the back of her hand and stood up. "I love you," she said.

"You too."

She left her daughter's room and walked down the hall. What could she do to calm herself down? Should she run the tub, fill it with the lavender-scented bath balls she'd bought during her last trip to Saskatoon and have a soak? What if someone called and needed her? What if she had to go to the hospital? She couldn't do that. She walked to the kitchen and inspected everything, checking to see if there was anything she could clean. But the kitchen was spotless, as was the front room. Maybe she should have a drink. A screwdriver would hit the spot right now, or maybe a rye and coke. But what if someone needed her in the city? What if she needed to find something in Abby or Al's house and she was too buzzed to do it? The smartest thing she could do was try and sleep. She didn't think she would be able to sleep, but maybe if she lay down, it would just happen. There was a bottle of sleeping pills in the medicine cabinet that could help her, but she couldn't be out of it if someone called. Best to lie in bed, watch TV and try to make herself sleep so she could help everyone tomorrow.

Donna left the lights on for Colton and went to her bedroom. She hoped he'd be home soon. She wanted him to come home so she could see he was alive and all in one piece. Things would be better once everyone in the family knew what had happened.

She put on her old Saskatchewan Roughriders T-shirt and a pair of pyjama pants, washed her face and brushed her teeth. When she looked in the mirror, she saw her eyes were puffy and red, the skin around them dark. It would be good to have another glass of water before she went to bed, but she didn't want to walk to the kitchen again. Instead, she climbed into bed and turned on the TV. Her fingers pressed the buttons, surfing through channels, trying to find something worthwhile to watch. She flipped across Leonardo DiCaprio and Kate Winslet romancing each other on the deck of the Titanic. She had seen the movie when it came out. She, Abby, Linda, Chloe and Allyson drove into the city for a girl's night. They cried so hard they ran out of Kleenex. Donna tried not to think about that day, to concentrate on Kate and Leo falling in love. She watched until the boat hit the iceberg and then changed channels. There was no way she could watch a sinking ship and a final deathly declaration of love tonight.

Eventually she settled on a cooking show. She just wanted to listen to something she wouldn't have to concentrate on. Closing her eyes, she willed herself to relax, trying to remember the things her therapist had taught her when she had gone for counselling for her postpartum depression. The therapist worked with her on her breathing when she had panic attacks, made her concentrate on taking deep breaths, and calming her mind. She still used these skills fourteen years later. Her depression had been an abyss that had sucked everyone in the house into it. Even Abby, who thought a person should be able to pull themselves out of anything by sheer will and determination, told her to go to the hospital and see somebody, talk to somebody so she could care about her baby again, and pay attention to the two children she already had. When Donna thought back to that time, she felt embarrassed. How she let Linda and Abby take care of the kids, while she lay in bed sleeping or staring at the ceiling. Her fear of the terrible blues she had experienced after Allyson's birth was one of the reasons why she had never had another baby, even though she would have loved to have another child. Gord had been great, rubbing her back, trying to help with the kids, pulling his weight. He stepped into her world, even though she had never been able to step into his. God knows, she had tried to force herself into this life. She never regretted that she'd ended up with Gord, or had his children. It was her own damn fault. She had been looking for a handsome cowboy, hanging out in country bars. The night she met Gord, he taught her how to two-step. He was still living on the ranch, saving up to go to school in the fall. She'd ended up pregnant, dropped out of university and moved out to the farm. Her parents and Pam thought she had lost her mind. But she loved Gord and the matter-of-fact way he talked, his calmness around cattle, his strong hands and back. Most of all, she liked the way he looked at her. Whenever she entered a room, he turned his entire body towards her.

She and Gord built their house close to Al and Abby's and Craig and Linda's, because Al wanted it that way. He wanted all the Klassen family members to be able to look out and see each other's places.

"We're family," he said. 'We're real neighbours, not like those people in the city."

The second Donna saw the plus sign on her pregnancy test, she knew was ready to move to the ranch. She'd fallen in love with beautiful Paul Newman and Robert Redford in *Butch Cassidy and the Sundance Kid*. Now she had her own good-looking, real-life cowboy, just like in the movies.

"I know you wanted to leave Saskatoon after you were done your degree. I know you dreamed of backpacking around Europe," he said in the minutes after she slipped the ring over her swollen finger. "But I'm going to give you and our baby the best life. You'll love the ranch as much as I do."

She smiled. "It's not the order we planned. But I love you."

Those first few years she had been so occupied with Clay, falling in love with being his mom and learning how to be a good wife to Gord. Clay was an easy baby and she loved being a mom so much that they had Colton a few years later. She remembered the smell of her boys' heads, their milky grins and the joy she'd felt at each milestone. Over the years, she mastered cooking by reading the *Best of Bridge* cookbooks, *Company's Coming,*

Chatelaine magazine and Abby's handwritten recipe cards. Her house was immaculate. But she failed at farming. She tried to love farming, the farming life and helping with the animals, but she had been a colossal failure. If she'd been a homesteader or a pioneer, she would have died. Been eaten by wolves. Or she would have gone crazy, been one of those women who just walked off into the bald prairie, marching off like one of those penguins that walked off into the Antarctic alone, determined to die. She took care of the house and the kids, while everyone else ran the farm. How many times did they have family meetings to discuss the farm business while she sat there, listening, wanting to ask what they were talking about because she didn't understand the markets. She was a city girl and always would be, even though she'd been out on the ranch for twenty-five years.

Donna wondered what would happen now. Al had been the head of the farm. There was going to be a huge shift. This thought exhausted her and made her head hurt. It was better to think about the past and things that had already happened. Things that she didn't have to worry about because she couldn't do anything to fix them.

She heard the front door open and bang shut. The glowing arms on the clock beside Gord's side of the bed told her it was almost one. There was a loud thump of a boot, the sound of Colton dropping one of the heavy, scuffed-up Doc Marten boots that he always wore. He was finally home. Thank God.

Donna got out of bed and walked down the stairs to the front door. Colton leaned against the wall. The scent of cigarettes and pot wafted off of him. He must have been at J. D.'s saloon in town. She caught a whiff of campfire. Maybe he'd been at a bush party. It didn't matter. What mattered what that he was here, standing in front of her, alive.

"Colton," she said, rushing forward to hug him.

"Mom?" He was drunk. He looked at her, and she could tell that even through the haze of alcohol coursing through his veins, he knew something was wrong.

"There was a car accident," she said. She hugged him tight, feeling the solidness of his shoulders under his bunny hug. "Your Grandpa is dead. Your Gramma was injured pretty badly."

"What?" Colton cried. "Jesus, fuck. No."

He staggered a bit, pulled away from her, and leaned against the wall again, bracing himself. He sobbed a loud, angry cry. She hadn't heard him cry like that in years.

"I know," Donna said. "I know."

"What happened?" he asked, pulling his head away from the wall. She grabbed his arm and steadied him.

"Let's go to the kitchen," she said. "You need a glass of water. Do you want to hear the details now? Or do you need to sober up?"

"Are you the only one here?" he asked.

"Allyson is in bed and Chloe is sleeping in Clay's room," she said. "Everyone else is in the hospital at the city."

"Is Gramma going to make it?" Colton's nose was running. His eyes were half closed. He looked much younger than his nineteen years right now.

Donna sighed. "Hope so."

She took her son's hand and led him to the kitchen. "Sit there," she said, pointing to the table. She got a glass from the cupboard. Maybe she should make him some coffee. But the best thing he could do was go to bed and sleep it off. Colton flopped down into the chair, and crumpled forward, laying his head down on the table. He mumbled something against the table's surface.

"I don't know what you're saying," she said as she stood at the kitchen sink. He mumbled again and then lifted his head.

"Was Grandpa in pain when he died?" he asked.

Donna held her hand underneath the water faucet. The cool water flowed over her fingers.

"We don't know," she said. She pictured Al lying in the ditch, his face down, his broad back facing the sky. She took a deep breath, and pictured herself shaking the image out of her head, the way her therapist had taught her. Her son sat at the table, waiting for her answer. *I need you*, his face said. *I need my mommy.*

She placed the glass of water in front of Colton. He looked at it, and with a jerky movement of his arm, he hit the water glass. It flew across the table, spraying water everywhere. He sobbed, stood up and ran out of the room. Donna watched the glass roll across the table. She took the dishtowel and wiped up the water, which had soaked into a copy of *The Western Producer*.

When the table was dry, she walked up the stairs to Colton's room. She knocked on the closed door.

"Go away," he said.

Colton wailed again from the other side of the door, screaming like someone had stabbed him. Donna opened the door. Her son sat on the floor in the middle of his bedroom. There were piles of clothes everywhere. He was rifling through a drawer. She heard the crinkle of plastic in his hand. As she watched, he pulled his hand out of the drawer, slammed it shut and turned around, looking guilty. He probably had dope in there. Or some sort of drugs. She wasn't going to get into that now. Her son could be a druggie, but now wasn't the time to discuss it. She heard footsteps and turned to see Allyson standing behind her.

"He probably drove home drunk," she said. "Just like those people who hit Gramma and Grandpa."

"Allyson," Donna said, her voice tired. "Don't talk like that right now."

"Colton's still drunk," Allyson said. "And he was probably driving."

"We're all upset," Donna said.

"You're not even going to ask him how he got home?" Allyson asked. "He could have killed someone."

Colton stood in front of his dresser, swaying back and forth. His face was red, streaked with tears and his hair was lank and greasy around his face. Donna resisted the urge to tell her daughter to shut up. Of course, her son had gotten behind the wheel after too many beers. But she hated talking about that stuff with him, hated having these discussions. Now was not the time.

"We need to get through this," she said to Allyson.

Colton stopped looking at the ground, raised his head and spoke. "Does Clay know yet?" he asked.

Donna was glad her son was thinking about what was actually happening. "We'll let him know tomorrow. I haven't had a chance to call Aunty Pam yet either," she said. She looked from Allyson to Colton. "I'll need you both to get up early and do the chores. Now why don't we all go to bed?"

Colton nodded, swaying a little.

Donna smelled the rank perfume of alcohol on him.

"Colton, why don't you go take a shower first?"

He nodded and left the room, heading towards the bathroom.

"I need to sleep with you," Allyson said. "I don't want to be alone."

"Okay," Donna said. "Let's go to bed."

She put her hand on her daughter's shoulder and followed Allyson as she left the room.

CHAPTER 3

It was light out when Allyson got up, and her room was cold. When she sat up in bed, her mother stirred. Donna always smelled warm and moist after she had been sleeping. Allyson could never describe the smell to anyone else, but she noticed it every time she woke up next to her mother.

"You slept," her mother said. "On and off, but you still slept."

"Did you?" she asked.

"Barely," her mother said. "But I have to get up now. I think they'll want me at the hospital. I've got a lot to do."

Donna got up and walked in the direction of the bathroom. Allyson got out of bed, went to her own room and put on a pair of jeans with a hole in the knee. She slipped on socks and an old hoodie that used to be Clay's. After pulling her hair back into a ponytail, she walked down the hall to Clay's room. She stood outside her cousin's door, trying to decide if she wanted to knock. After a minute, she walked down to Colton's room and rapped on the door.

There was the sound of rustling and Colton mumbling.

"Chores," she said.

"Be right out," Colton said. His voice sounded raspy. That's what happened when he smoked a lot. She heard a large thump from the other side of the door, and quiet again.

In the kitchen, her mother brewed coffee. Allyson grabbed a mug from the cupboard and waited for the brown liquid to spill down, pulling out the carafe so she could stick her mug underneath.

"When did you start drinking coffee?" her mother asked.

"When I turned fourteen. Jeff is always drinking it. Clay got me hooked on it the last time he was here."

Her mother shook her head as if trying to clear it. "I wonder if I should just go to the hospital," she said. "I can't stand this waiting around."

Allyson looked at the clock. It was seven.

Her mother took a mug and poured herself some coffee. "I wish I could call Clay," she said. "I might just call him and wake him up. I'll feel better once he knows."

Allyson didn't answer. Her mother often talked through things out loud.

"Thanks for doing the chores, honey."

Allyson drank her coffee as her mother opened the cupboard and started looking through the mugs.

"Some of these we don't even use," she muttered, taking a few of them out and putting them on the counter.

"What are you doing?" Allyson asked.

"Why do we have so many mugs?" her mother asked, grouping four mugs together in a pile. "I'm going to take these to Goodwill."

Allyson saw Clay's favourite blue pottery mug, the one he always used when he was home, in the group to be discarded. She walked over and put it back in the cupboard.

"That's Clay's," she said, finishing up her cup of coffee. Her mother always made weak coffee. Her parents should stop buying Maxwell House and get the good stuff. Maybe she'd make her mom stop at Tim Hortons the next time they were in Saskatoon or Edmonton and pick up a bag of good coffee. They might live out in the country, but they didn't have to act like backwoods hicks.

"Is Chloe going to help?" Donna asked.

"I thought I'd let her sleep. Colton should be down soon."

Allyson finished her coffee, left the mug next to the sink, and went down the stairs to put on her barn boots. The screen door slammed behind her as she went out to the yard into the crisp air. Morning dew coated the blades of grass and she could smell spring. The quads sat right near the barn, where her dad and grandpa had left them. It was hard for her to believe she wasn't going to see Grandpa Al again, that he would never be out near the barn he had built before she was born.

She heard footsteps and turned to see Colton. He shuffled along, a ball cap pulled low over his face, unbrushed puffs of hair spilling out from below it. As he approached and stood by her, she smelled the staleness of day-old booze and unwashed sleep. There was a patch of dried toothpaste by the corner of his mouth.

"Hey," she said, heading into the barn.

Colton grunted in her direction. Maybe he was still drunk. He squinted as he looked at the sky. He grabbed a bale and took it over to the bull pen. Allyson broke a bale into pieces and threw it over the fence. Her dad's favourite bull, Fully Loaded, leaned against the other side of the fence and scratched his face. His name suited him because he made fine calves. His father, Git'R'Dun, had been a champion, worth a lot of money. There was something about the routine, about just doing simple things like taking care of cattle, that made Allyson feel better. She had done all of these things so many times. Her grandfather was dead and her Gramma was in the hospital, but the world kept on going. The animals still needed to be fed.

"Let's go out to the pasture," Colton said. She nodded, wondering if Chloe would be out to join them. The sky was a bluish grey and it was starting to warm up. Maybe it would be warm today, hot for the beginning of June.

"I'll take Grandpa's quad," Colton said.

Allyson finished feeding the bulls before walking to the quads. Colton got on Grandpa Al's quad and started it, leaving Allyson with Gord's quad. They drove through the yard, up to the gate. Donna hated it when the kids drove the quads; said she'd heard too many stories of kids flipping them, running into rocks and dying. Gord scoffed, saying most of those stories about people getting hurt were about city people who drank too much while quadding at the lake. Donna always countered him. "It's not city people who are dying," she said. "I read about it in a newspaper article about farm safety."

Allyson tried not to think about that as she and Colton drove the quads out to the summer pasture. It was easy to die. She'd seen so many things die on their farm. Now the sceptre of death was even closer. You planned a date to go into the city to see a movie, and next thing you knew, someone hit your car and you bought the farm. The past week before the accident had been so strange. All the adults were talking about the border, and why it had closed, and how they might not be able to sell their cows. Things seemed normal, but in some ways, they didn't. She could tell something was up.

When they arrived in the pasture, Colton stopped his quad and Allyson turned hers off as well. Allyson was glad Colton had helped the day before and knew where the cattle were. Allyson watched the cows, and wondered how everything would change, now that Grandpa Al was dead. She shook her head as if trying to shake the thought out, mimicking the movements of the cows as they shook their heads, trying to get rid of the flies buzzing around their ears. Everyone looked good, chewing their cuds, looking at her with big, curious eyes. The calm of the animals soothed her. They were just chewing, walking, pissing and shitting. Regular cow stuff. Some of the cows moved away from the quad as she got off and walked over to a small group of them. As she approached, one cow raced down the field, kicking out her back legs, frolicking a little as she ran. Her dad would have said the cow was having her own private rodeo. The cow reached the bluff and turned to look at Colton and Allyson before putting her head down to take a bite of grass.

Colton broke off a piece of tall grass, stuck it in his mouth to chew and kicked a bit of dirt. He put his arms over his head, stretched and yawned.

"Colton," Allyson said. She wanted to ask him how he felt and what he was thinking about Gramma and Grandpa. Had it even hit him that Grandpa was dead? It still didn't feel real. She half expected to turn around and see Grandpa Al there, smiling.

"Huh?" Colton said. He coughed, horked and spit into the dirt.

"Gross," she said. Colton pulled a pack of cigarettes out of the pocket of his Mack jacket and lit up.

"Let me have this smoke before we head back," he said, exhaling.

"Gross," she said again. She no longer wanted to ask him anything. He might pretend everything was okay. He'd never been good in a crisis. When her dad cut his hand with a band saw, Colton took off as soon as he'd seen the blood. When he came back hours later, they found out he'd been at Cal's in town, shooting pool and playing video games.

"Gramma is going to be okay," he said. "She's tough. She's not going to die on us. She'd make sure we're okay before she checked out."

Allyson didn't answer. She kept staring at the cattle, then turned to watch as Colton finished his cigarette and stubbed it out on the ground, taking care to grind the butt down under his heel.

"Let's go back," Colton said. She nodded and they got back on their quads and rode towards the house. The wind felt good on her face. Even though everything was different, some things were the same. She and Colton parked the quads by the barn. When she stopped to listen, Allyson heard rustling. Chloe was inside the barn, scooping kibble out of a big bin to feed the barn cats and the dogs. Maggie and Rascal stood beside her, tails wagging. Chloe brushed her hair back from her face.

"Clay knows," she said. "And Dad called. Uncle Gord's on his way home."

Chloe finished filling the dishes and set them down. The dogs crowded around to eat.

"Got any smokes?" she asked Colton.

He patted his pocket. "If your parents catch me, I'll be in shit," he said. "Just don't let them know that you got them from me." He held the red, banged-up cigarette pack out to Chloe and she pulled out a cigarette.

"Got a light?" she asked. Colton pulled out his lighter and gave it to her.

"Just be careful you don't light anything on fire," Allyson said. "That's the last thing we need right now."

She couldn't believe they were both smoking together. How gross. And in a time like this. Just acting normal, when Grandpa

Al was dead, and Gramma Abby was in the hospital. She left her brother and cousin inside the barn and started towards the horse pen. When she got near their pen, she saw Chloe had already fed them. Of course. The horses were her cousin's domain. Chloe had been the one who had been in pony club, the one who spent hours in the barn or near the corrals, talking to the horses, brushing their manes, reading books like *Summer Goes Riding* or *Black Beauty*. She would never neglect the horses. She was probably getting ready to go for a ride later on. Crow and Temple were the working horses, and Cassidy was hers, the one Chloe used most for riding.

Inside the house, it was too quiet. "Mom," she called. "Where are you?"

"Upstairs," her mother called back. Allyson walked up the stairs to the bathroom and stood outside her parents' bedroom before going in. Her mother sat slumped on the bed. The television blared and the sounds of a cooking show filled the room. Donna was dressed and had make-up on, but her eyes were red, her face blotchy and puffy.

"I'm going to the hospital right away," she said. "Your dad is on his way home. Clay has to juggle a few shifts and pack and then he'll be on his way out."

"Can I go to the hospital with you?"

Donna shook her head. "Gramma woke up in the middle of the night. Your dad doesn't want you to see her yet. She's banged up and confused. He wants everyone to wait until she's stronger. She's probably going to be paralyzed. And they think she has a concussion."

"Paralyzed?" Allyson said. She thought of a television show she'd seen years ago, about a guy who could only move things with his mouth. He had a wheelchair he operated with a stick he moved with his lips and teeth. Would Gramma be like that? It would kill her.

"They don't know how bad it is yet," Donna said. "It looks like she's lost the use of her legs and her left hand. We don't know what will happen. But she won't be able to manage all the stairs in her house."

The bed creaked as Donna rose. "I should have waited until Colton and Chloe were here before I told you all that," she said, starting for the door. "Where are they?"

"Out in the yard," said Allyson. She thought about telling her mom they were in the barn smoking.

"Can I do something to help?" she asked.

"Take a shower," Donna said. "Get dressed. Make coffee for your dad. I'll let you know if I think of anything else you can do. There are people we need to phone."

★

Linda must have phoned people from the hospital, because food started to arrive that afternoon. Mabel Jacobson, a Métis woman who lived in town, brought over a tub of butter tarts and Anita, Donna's boss, drove up the long driveway with a tin of date squares. Some of the wives of the Elks club members dropped off casseroles and stews and expressed their condolences. Mary Anne, Donna's good friend, came over and hugged the kids. She brought a card, a couple of her newly published romance books, a big bouquet of gerbera daisies, a box of chocolate and a casserole in a blue Pyrex dish. Donna was still at the hospital.

"Tell your mother she can call me any time," Mary Anne said, sticking her head out of the window of her PT cruiser as she started her car and drove away. As Allyson watched her, she wished she could drive away too. Just drive away from her family, and all of the sadness on the farm. Allyson's friend Amber called to say she was sorry, but Allyson felt bad about tying up the line, and let her go after a couple of minutes. Besides, she had nothing to say. The whole thing didn't seem real yet. It felt as though she was running through the motions, performing some sort of elaborate dance. If she did the rituals correctly, perhaps this would turn out to be some mistake, and Grandpa Al and Abby would appear back at the farm. She almost wished that she was back at the coffee shop, listening to the men talk about cattle. Anything but this.

Allyson and Colton greeted visitors and accepted food. None of them spoke about the accident. Allyson was in the kitchen alone when her father came in. When she looked at him, she was struck by his face, the visible mask of pain he wore. His wrinkles stood out even more, as if they'd been etched into his face with a knife. In the kitchen, Gord put his arms around Allyson and hugged her tight. She didn't say anything, just willed herself not to cry, breathing in her dad's familiar smell of dirt and Old Spice, a musty smell she associated with the hospital, and the faint scent of B.O.

"I need to take a shower and have a lie down," he said. "I'm going to wait until Clay is here to tell everyone what's happening. Your mom isn't going to be gone for long."

"Can I do anything to help?" Allyson asked.

"Go read or draw or watch TV," he said. "Try to pretend everything is normal."

Allyson went to her bedroom and tried to read Harry Potter, but she couldn't concentrate. She went to the family room and turned on the TV, flipping through channels. After a while, Colton joined her. Chloe had gone home, back across the yard to her own house. But after a few hours, she came back and the three of them sat in the room in the dark. Normally Donna or Linda would have made them go out and work in the yard. They generally weren't allowed to sit inside in the dark, watching the boob tube. When Donna came home, she walked into the family room.

"Linda's home," she said. "Is your dad upstairs?"

Colton looked up from his Gameboy.

"He's sleeping," said Allyson. "How's Gramma?"

"Rough," Donna said. "She was sleeping when I got there. She knows Grandpa's gone. Rita says Gramma is going to be okay. Rita has been really great. Even Linda said so. She was there when they brought Grandpa and Gramma in last night and then she was there again this morning."

Rita's name was notorious among the Klassens. Rita Dennis had been Craig's high school sweetheart. But Rita wanted to move to Calgary, and Craig had wanted to go to school in Vermilion before returning to the farm, so they broke up. Rita got her nursing degree and lived in Calgary for a few years before moving to Lloydminster with her four kids after the divorce. Her parents were still in town, so she showed up at the odd town function with her rag tag kids in tow. Chloe called Rita the prairie prune because her face was wrinkled and she wore bright coloured lipstick that ran outside her lips. She had big hair, as if she believed that the bigger her hair was, the closer she was to God. A silver cross sat nestled within her ample, suntanned cleavage. Even though she was the same age as Craig, she looked much older, with lines from years of cigarette smoking around her mouth.

"Dad made the right choice," Chloe muttered as she watched Rita walk away on teetering high heels, her toes flashing bright orange nail polish. Rita always came up to talk to them whenever she saw them, and Abby always hugged her. Linda bristled every time Rita came around. Craig was polite, but never said much around her.

"Clay should be here soon," Donna said. "I'm going over to Linda's to see who she's phoned, and then to Gramma and Grandpa's house to pick up a few things to take to the hospital."

Allyson sprawled out on the couch and watched her brother flip the channels. At one point, Colton left the room, leaving her alone. She could have turned off the television, but didn't. The nattering voices were comforting. Chloe came back and sat down on the couch. Allyson handed her the remote. Uncle Craig didn't believe in satellite television, so Chloe lived with peasant vision—only four channels. Whenever she could, she came over to watch MuchMusic, YTV and everything else she couldn't get at home. Craig came over to watch the news when something important happened. Donna asked him why he just didn't get satellite, but Gord said Craig was too cheap.

"I don't want to be at home right now," Chloe said. "Mom just phoned the paper to place an obit."

She flopped down on the couch and lay on her side, her arm dangling down. "I think they're going to send a reporter out here to talk to everyone. Everybody in town will want to talk about Grandpa's death."

"You can watch whatever you want," Allyson said.

Chloe flipped channels until she landed on a Justin Timberlake video.

"He's so hot," Chloe said. "And such a good dancer. Just look at him."

Allyson zoned out and didn't even hear Donna's footsteps.

"Do you girls want anything to eat?" she asked. "I made sandwiches."

The sandwiches were cut in diagonals, just the way Allyson liked them. She took a ham, lettuce and mustard sandwich off the plate and took a huge bite. The bread was dry, but it still tasted good.

"I got hold of Aunty Pam," Donna said. "Finally."

"Is she going to come out?"

"She is," Donna said. All of them heard the sound of the front door open and bang shut.

"Hello?" It was Linda's voice.

"You must be exhausted," Donna said, as she left the family room and walked towards the door.

"I'm running on adrenaline," Linda said from the other room. Allyson could hear her mother and aunt talking but she couldn't make out what they were saying. She went back to her room. About an hour later, she heard the sound of a vehicle out in the yard and saw Clay's blue Ford Ranger. She ran down the stairs, happy her brother was home. Everything would be better because he was here. Clay's presence always calmed her parents. He had rarely broken his curfew and only stumbled home drunk a few times when he lived at home. He was the sturdy one, the responsible one, while Colton was the wild child.

Outside, Clay hopped out of his truck and grabbed a big blue duffel bag from the back.

"Hey, kid," he said, ruffling her hair. He was ten years old when she was born. Clay was the one she thought of as her big brother, not Colton.

"I'm so glad you're home," she said, giving him a hug. He smelled like Calvin Klein Eternity. He referred to it as his signature scent, until Colton told him that sounded gay. Clay wore the Roughriders T-shirt Donna had bought him for Christmas. He'd cheered for the Riders his whole life. As a joke for Christmas one year, Al had bought him Edmonton Eskimos gear and souvenirs: a mug, a hat, a key chain and a pennant. Clay left all of these gifts piled in the top of his closet, until Craig liberated everything and took it all over to his place.

"How is everyone holding up?" Clay asked.

"Mom's upset. Aunty Linda's been a rock."

"Of course," Clay said. "She gets things done."

Over the next few days, Allyson, Chloe and Colton spent hours watching television, sitting in the dark, saying hello to whoever showed up at the house. Sometimes Allyson went to her room and cried, thinking about how she would never see Grandpa Al again. The phone kept ringing and people kept coming, Tupperware in their hands. They piled tins of food on the table and filled the fridge.

When Chloe wasn't sitting with them or out with Jamie, she was sleeping or out on the trails riding Cassidy. Colton stayed out with friends, returning late at night. Clay helped out with the chores and seemed to be doing a lot to help the adults. Whenever Allyson asked if there was anything she could do, she was told to go sit in the family room and watch TV. She stayed in her room and doodled on her sketch pad. She drew pictures of characters from Harry Potter.

One day, she watched out the window as Chloe drove off into town. She should have asked Chloe for a ride. Things would be different once she could drive legally. She knew how to drive, of course. Her dad had taught her how to drive the truck when she was eleven so she could help out around the farm. He wanted all his kids to know how to drive in case of an emergency. The RCMP had caught a couple of kids driving without licenses before, so no one would let her drive into town. Even though everyone had been getting ready for the funeral and visiting Abby in the hospital, Gord and Craig were still obsessed with the news. The border was still closed and cattle weren't moving. When the border closed, Craig had been down south, about to take a liner of cattle to the States. The border guards had stopped him. Said he couldn't cross, that they weren't letting anyone in. He'd had to drive the whole liner back, which meant he wouldn't get paid. Since the cows couldn't cross, no one was going to get paid.

No one knew when the United States would start buying cattle again. Gord and Craig worried and talked about it, their voices low and murmuring.

"Dad would have hated this," Allyson heard Craig say late one night. "This uncertainty and not knowing would have driven him nuts. He would be in here every night, yelling at the TV, telling people to get some answers and get things done."

"I think the government boys and Shirley are trying. They're not going to let us choke here," Gord said.

"We're going to have to look at Dad's finances," Craig said. "Figure out what's what and get everything settled."

Allyson tuned them out and went back to reading *Harry Potter and the Chamber of Secrets*.

She just didn't want to hear more talk about markets or any of that other crap everyone was always talking about. She bet people who lived in cities didn't talk like this. One day, she would be one of them. She couldn't wait to get out of here, to have another life, to escape the claustrophobic walls of the farm. In school, they'd had to read *As for Me and My House*, a book about a preacher and his wife and a small town. The preacher and his wife were suffocating in their town, closed in by the townspeople, their religion and all the things they couldn't do in the town. Allyson knew exactly how they felt.

The next day, Craig had to do some carpentry work in town. Colton had gone in to work at the shop. Her dad came into her room that morning, and woke her up.

"I need you," he said, his voice still rusty with sleep. "We're going to try and take some cattle to the auction mart."

Normally, Allyson would have moaned and groaned, or asked him to get someone else to do it, but there was no complaining these days. No one had told her that she had to suck it up and help out, that was just what she knew she needed to do. That was the only way they were going to get through this, whatever this was.

"Clay's coming with us," her dad said.

"I'll be there in a second," she said. "Just give me a few minutes."

Her dad stood in the doorway and nodded. When she was younger, he had been the one who put her to bed, who read her the Sandra Boynton books about mooing, and baaing and going to bed. She liked it better when he brushed her hair than when her mom did. But all of that ended as soon as she turned twelve.

She sat up, and swung her legs down off the bed and nestled her toes into the blue carpet. If they were just going to the auction mart, it wasn't worth taking a shower. She put on Clay's old sweatshirt and some jeans, and pulled on a pair of socks that were mismatched, but clean. They were hauling cattle. It wasn't a beauty pageant.

She went into the kitchen. Her dad had already left, but there was a pot of hot coffee sitting on the burner. She drank a cup, and made herself some buttered toast, and walked down to the front door. After shoving her feet into her barn boots and putting on a green Roughriders cap, she pushed open the front door, picked up the toast again, and headed across the yard, chewing on the bread as she walked.

Her dad and Clay were already at the pen. Unlike Allyson, Clay looked like he'd been up for a long time, and had had a shower. His shirt even looked like he'd managed to pass an iron over it.

"Do you even know if the auction is buying cows?" Clay said, turning to his dad. "Did you check?"

Gord studied a heifer. "This girl is so pretty," he said. "Nice looking cow. Shame she's open. We can't afford to keep her."

He turned to his son. "Border's still not open, but we'll head down and check," he said. "There are just a few cows to load up. Even if we have to come back, it won't be a lot of trouble."

"Did you try calling?" Clay asked.

"Called yesterday, but that was no answer," Gord said. "But that doesn't mean nothing. Could be busy if it's a sale day."

Right after the border closed, the auction mart shut its doors and no one could sell anything. When Donna drove past the building on the way into town, the parking lot was empty and deserted, except for Marty Valleau's black pickup. Gord and Craig talked at the table one morning about how Marty had shut the doors of the auction mart and turned away all the people who had driven in with their cattle that day, sending them back to their homes.

"Allyson, you stand in the pen," her dad said. "Clay, you go get the truck."

Clay nodded and tipped his cowboy hat. Allyson sometimes wondered if he'd been born wearing one. Out on the farm, he always wore his white Stetson, brim a bit discoloured from dirt and the sun.

Clay backed the truck and the liner up near the gate. The cattle balked a little when they saw the vehicle approach, but Gord made calming noises. They trusted him, and would follow where he wanted them to go. He opened the door to the liner, and the pen. Allyson stood with her boots in the manure. She wouldn't push the cattle from the rear, but from the side. They'd all clump up, and head towards the liner. Cattle didn't like to go into a dark area from a light area, but her dad, with her help, was able to load them up.

"Nice work," he said, when the last little red heifer was inside the liner. He swung the door shut and bolted it.

"Okay, let's go," he said.

Allyson thought about asking if she really had to go to the auction mart, but one look at her Dad's face told her not to bother asking. Why should she leave him and her brother alone at this time? He needed her. He needed some semblance of normal.

The three of them hopped in the truck, and drove to the auction mart. The truck cabin was filled with the scent of manure from their boots, hay, and cattle. She wondered if her own unshowered scent was in there somewhere, blending with all the other smells. And over all of this earthy farm scent, she could smell Clay's CK One Eternity. She concentrated on breathing that in. A little bit of city life permeating the wildness of their truck.

There were trucks in the auction mart parking lot when they pulled into town.

"This is a good sign," Gord said, mainly to himself, as if he had forgotten that his children were with him.

"I'll go check things out," Clay said, once they had stopped. He jumped out of the truck, and strode over to the back door of the auction mart. Gord and Allyson watched as he yanked on the door handle. Perhaps the auction mart was closed, even though there were trucks in the lot. But finally, Clay pulled open the door and went inside.

Gord jumped out of the truck and started pacing around. "I don't recognize any of these trucks," he said. "Just Marty's. I don't think any of the regulars are here."

Allyson opened the truck door to get some air, and dangled her legs down off the side of the seat. The air was chilly and tasted like dust. They were going to have a bad grasshopper problem this year, Gord said. She hated grasshoppers, and always had. The things jumped out of nowhere, zig zagging, and erratic, gnashing their teeth. Chloe always laughed at Allyson's fear. "They're teeny tiny insects," she said. "They can't hurt you."

Her dad walked down the rows of trucks, as if he was looking for something. The door to the front of the auction mart opened, and Clay came out.

"I don't know if you're going to want to sell today," he said. "The border's still closed and the prices are way too low. It's not even worth it."

"Like how low?" Gord said.

Clay glanced at Allyson. And in that moment, she saw that things had changed somehow between Gord and Clay. They weren't talking to each other like father and son any more. At some point, their interactions had become a conversation between two men.

"She can hear," Gord said. "It's okay."

"It's not worth it," Clay said. "It's probably cheaper to feed them. Wait until things get better. We'll have some green grass soon. Better just take them home and keep them for a while, and then sell them at a later date."

Gord sighed. "Damn, I hope this thing doesn't go on too long," he said. "Nobody in this industry can afford a wreck."

Gord stood in front of his son, looking up at his face, shielded by his cowboy hat. Gord's shoulders were hunched, and Clay looked so much stronger and younger.

Clay touched his dad on the shoulder.

"Yeah, it's really better if we don't sell now," he said. "I talked to Marty. Most of the guys who are selling today are guys who hauled from up north. They just don't want to haul back and pay freight. They're going to take the low prices."

"Okay," Gord said. "Let's go."

They got back into the truck, and drove back to the farm without speaking. Gord didn't even turn on the radio. Allyson helped her brother and father unload the cattle back into the same pen, and then went back to the house, abandoning them once they'd gotten into a heated discussion about body scoring cattle.

*

That night, Allyson woke up to get a drink in the middle of the night and went downstairs for a glass of water. Even though the hallway was dark, it was familiar, and she didn't need to turn the lights on, feeling her way with the soles of her feet. She stayed close to the wall, dragging her fingers along its coolness. But as she descended the stairs she realized that someone was in the kitchen, even though the lights weren't on. She walked a few steps closer, then stopped to listen. As she got closer, she realized that the horrible, guttural sounds she was hearing belong to her dad. Her dad, the one who calmed and soothed her. Her dad, who fully believed in cowboying up, getting back on the horse. He was in the kitchen crying like a little girl.

She didn't know what to do. Should she go in and comfort him? Or would he be embarrassed to know that she was there, that she'd heard him crying? He didn't like to look weak in front of her. Until the accident, she'd never seen him cry. She didn't really need that glass of water. She turned, crept back into bed and put on her headphones to listen to Eminem until she felt relaxed enough to sleep. Something about the anger and swearing in the music soothed her and brought her back from all the sadness and the image of her dad, sitting alone, crying at the kitchen table. She could lose herself in his angry voice.

★

About ten days after Al's death, Allyson lay in bed, reading *Alice, I Think* when she heard the front door open. It was late, and her parents had gone to bed. Clay had gone back into the city. He'd been home for a while to help out, but he was worried about taking too much time off work. Footsteps creaked on the stairs, but she didn't pay any attention to them. Why should she, when her book was so good? She kept reading, entranced in the novel, when her bedroom door swung open and Chloe, Colton and Jamie stumbled in.

"What are you doing?" Allyson said, embarrassed as everyone piled into her room. She had her retainer in, and wore her pyjamas with teddy bears on them. Jamie was the only one of them who seemed sober. Colton dumped Chloe onto Allyson's bed, almost squishing Allyson in the process. Chloe moved close so she lay beside her cousin. Colton and Jamie sat down on the bed, trapping Allyson with their warm bodies.

"She needed to come home," Colton said. "Let her sleep here. Uncle Craig and Auntie Linda will flip if they see or smell her right now. She can go home in the morning."

"I love you, cousin," Chloe said, running her hand through Allyson's hair, her voice a singsong. She stunk like rotten grapes, like the inside of the wine bottle at Colton's graduation. Allyson tried to move away so Chloe could have more room on the bed. Her cousin veered towards her again, her movements floppy and loose. If she stood up, she'd be as wobbly as a newborn calf toddling after its mother.

"You're such a nerd," Chloe said, still stroking her cousin's hair. "Who stays in to read on a Saturday night where there are good parties going on? Everything you do is so nerdy. All that drawing and reading. Cartoons."

Allyson considered pushing her cousin off the bed. It wouldn't take much to shove Chloe onto the floor. But if she fell, she'd make a loud noise. And if she screamed, there was a possibility that she could wake up Donna and Gord.

Jamie laughed, a loud laugh that came from the pit of her stomach.

"Pipe down," Colton said, elbowing Jamie in the ribs. "You'll wake everyone else up."

He looked at Allyson. "Chloe's just drunk," he said. "Just let her sleep here. Tell everyone you decided to have a sleepover."

Chloe sprawled across the bed like a starfish, pushing Allyson closer to the edge of her single bed. She'd shared beds with her cousin before, but they hadn't slept in a single bed together for years.

"So tired," Chloe said, closing her eyes. Colton got up and started towards the door.

"We gotta get out of here," he said to Jamie. "Thanks for driving us home."

Colton and Jamie left, abandoning Allyson with her snoring, sweaty, smelly cousin. Chloe was so hot that Allyson had to get up and go sleep in Clay's room. In the morning, her cousin went to the bathroom to retch. When Donna asked her if she was sick, she said she'd eaten something that didn't agree with her, then trudged across the yard to her home.

That afternoon, Allyson heard Linda tell Donna Chloe had come down with the flu.

That evening, Chloe was in the barn doing chores. Allyson walked up to her as she was scooping kibble out of the bin to feed the dogs.

"Why did you do that to me last night?" Allyson asked.

Chloe stood up and pushed her strawberry blonde hair out of her face.

"Do what?" she asked.

"You were drunk," Allyson said. "I couldn't even sleep in my bed because of you. Why did you have to bring Jamie into my room?"

Chloe turned away from her, and leaned down to put some kibble into Maggie's and Rascal's dishes.

"Here, babies," she said, smiling and patting the dogs' wriggling bodies. "I've got your din din."

Allyson stood in front of Chloe and stared at her cousin until Chloe looked at her.

"You were rude to me," Allyson said. "And I don't even recognize you any more. Why have you become this person?"

"I don't want to talk about it," Chloe said, her face flushing red. "Don't make a big deal out of this. If you bring it up even once, I'll never talk to you again."

She turned, and headed over to the horse corral.

CHAPTER 4

The day of Al's funeral, it was raining and cold. Donna pulled a dress from her closet. Everyone in the Klassen family had found or bought new spring clothes to wear.

"Stupid Alberta weather," Donna said to herself.

Gord came into the room. "Have you seen my tie?" he asked.

"Which one?"

"The navy blue, pale blue and black one."

"Check Colton's room. He was in here a while ago, looking for ties."

Gord sighed. "I probably got something else. No one's going to be looking at my tie anyway. They'll all be looking at our faces, trying to see how we're holding up."

"It feels like it's going to snow again," she said.

"It's June," Gord said.

"Well, it wouldn't be the first time it happened," she said. "And God might just hate us enough to make it snow."

Not only was she crabby because she was going to Al's funeral, she was crabby because her own parents weren't able to make it. Her father had a series of medical tests he couldn't postpone. He'd been on a waiting list for weeks. Donna wasn't close to her parents. They lived in Victoria and rarely visited. Pam was the diligent, reliable daughter who kept in touch. Donna's mother Joyce pretended everything was sunny and light, and she never told the truth about what was happening. When Donna had postpartum depression, her mother told her to buck up, brush her hair, put on her makeup and revel in her newborn daughter's beauty.

Abby, who had become a bit stronger, told Donna she wanted them to have the funeral without her. That was the reason they'd waited so long before holding it. The Klassens wanted Abby to be strong enough to attend if she wanted.

"I know what a good man Al was," Abby said. "I don't need to celebrate him. I do that every day by myself."

Abby could sit up, drink fluids and eat small bits of food. Normally she was a talkative woman who didn't sleep a lot, but these days she just slept. When she wasn't sleeping, she stared into space. When someone came into the room, she tried to smile at them, but it looked like it hurt her face, straining the patches on her cheeks where broken glass had left cuts and bruises.

Clay had taken some time off work to come back home for a while. He was a waiter at Earls in Edmonton. Gord was always bugging him to come back home for the summer to help out, but he said he could make good money in the city and he didn't want to give up his apartment, which he shared with his roommate, Arjun. The two of them had been roommates for three years. Now that Al was dead and Abby wasn't able to work, Clay might need to help out on the farm. Even though she didn't think it would happen, Donna hoped he would quit his city job and move home for the summer. Colton was still going out a lot, but even he had been spending more time at home, checking everyone's cars and making sure all the machinery on the farm was up to par. He'd tinkered with the farm vehicles since he had been small. Gord and Al always joked that if anyone found out how much machinery he had fixed when he was a child, they'd be reported for violation of child labour standards.

At the church, Donna and the rest of the family members filed in last, sitting at the front. The funeral was held at the same church Abby and Al were married in. Donna kept her head down. She didn't want to see all those sad eyes and sniffling faces. She'd been on the other side before, knew how people talked when someone died. How people shook their heads and talked about what a shame it was, and how dear dead so-and-so deserved to live another twenty or forty or fifty years. How everyone pretended the dead was the best person who ever lived, when really they were an alcoholic wife beater who had been having an affair for fifteen years.

Donna glanced over at Pam, who sat with Linda's parents. They'd arrived yesterday from Vermilion. Linda asked them if they wanted to stay in Abby and Al's since it was empty. Linda's parents were nice enough. They had a grain farm and a few cattle and hogs before Linda's dad, Barry, decided he didn't like running after things and sold all the livestock. Donna couldn't stand the idea of them staying in Abby and Al's house, going through their linens, taking baths in Abby's pristine bathtub. The thought made her feel dirty and violated. This was Abby's sanctuary, her palace. How could Linda let them stay there? Donna had been polite to them, but inside she seethed, even though she knew Abby probably wouldn't mind. Gord told Abby the Eilers were staying in her house, but she'd just nodded, and asked if she could watch *Wheel of Fortune*.

Ray Sharp sat in the pew behind Donna. She turned around to give him a small smile. He put his hand out and she took it. The two of them held hands for a few seconds, and he gave her hand a squeeze. She remembered when Ray's wife, April, had died and how broken he had been. Donna had brought him food. She couldn't help him with the cattle, but she could stop by and make sure his house was clean and he had enough to eat.

Donna couldn't remember the last time she had been to a Catholic funeral. Maybe the Catholics in this town had some sort of secret, because they never seemed to die. Donna looked over at Mabel Jacobson, whose husband had died a few years ago. She was sobbing into a handful of Kleenex. What did she have to cry about? She wasn't close to Al or Abby.

Donna had seen Al's body at a small, private viewing at the funeral home. It hadn't looked like him. The body was too small, broken and frail. Gord asked her if she needed a few minutes alone with the body, but she shook her head. As far as she was concerned, Al was gone the second he died. Donna hadn't wanted the kids to see him and Clay was the only one who had asked. She allowed her oldest son to go into the room alone. When he came out of the room, he cried and she hugged him and smoothed his hair, reminded of the years when he was small and vulnerable. Now he was a tall man who looked more like his grandfather than his parents, with his reddish hair and broad shoulders.

Father Murray was talking about Al and what a strong family man he had been. What a pillar of the community. A man with a big smile and an easy laugh. He talked about Al's height, the constant butt of jokes in town. People always compared him to Howard Keel, the actor who played the oldest brother on *Seven Brides for Seven Brothers*. And Abby's small size just made Al's towering presence even more apparent. Donna could feel tears coming as she listened to Father Murray, so she distracted herself by looking at her family. Linda was crying, wiping tears away from her face with the corner of a Kleenex. She always looked so pretty when she cried, like someone in a movie, her cheeks rosy and fresh. When Donna cried, her nose ran. One time, after Gord comforted her and held her, (which he always tried to do when she cried), he asked her if she wanted a pressure washer for her face.

Craig was stoic, staring ahead, his body angled towards Linda. Chloe was on the aisle, on the other side of them. Donna couldn't see her face without twisting and leaning. Clay was mimicking his uncle, staring straight ahead, face calm, eyes on Father Murray. Colton stared into space, eyes transfixed on the spot above the crucifix. Linda, on a night when she had had too much wine, said she sometimes stared at the cross during a boring sermon because the Jesus on the cross reminded her of Brad Pitt.

Now, she was scared to look at Gord. If she shared eye contact with him, one of them might start sobbing. The night before the funeral, he told her that he was scared of his own grief.

"Dad's death hurts," he whispered to her. "It hurts like a wound, like I've been punched in the chest."

The two of them lay in bed, facing each other, the way they always did before falling asleep. This was one of Donna's favourite moments, the minutes when they talked about the tiny details of their days, the things they had been too busy to tell each other in the years when Gord was out in the pasture tending to cattle, and Donna was wiping sticky fingers and cooking for everyone. When the kids were small, those conversations were even more precious.

"I'm scared of how I feel," Gord said. The room was dark. She couldn't see his face when they had these conversations.

"I'm not sure what we're going to do on the farm. The border's still not open. Dad would have a plan. Dad would know what to do." He sighed and she could feel the ocean of worry between them. "We need to figure out new ways to work together. Need to figure out how to do all the things Dad did."

Al took care of all the books and bank accounts. Gord had never even seen the books because his dad didn't want anyone else to mess with his system. "I know what I'm doing," Al said. "Don't worry about it. Just keep on raising good beef."

Craig hauled cattle and did carpentry work on the side. He'd been saving up to add a pool to the house, and for Chloe to go to school. He couldn't read the cattle the way Gord could. Gord took care of the cattle, Al handled the business end of things, and Craig did his own thing and helped out with everything else.

When Gord admitted he was scared of how he felt, Donna knew the words he didn't have the strength to say. He cried, turning away from her, putting the pillow over his head to muffle his sobs. She sat in the dark and patted his back, rubbing it the way she rubbed the backs of her children when they skinned their knees. This was not simply mourning for Al. This was the fear of everything that was going to come, the fear of change and the question of what would happen on the farm. And underneath it all, the uncertainty of mad cow and the whole border closure. She didn't understand what that whole thing was about.

"I know the border is closed," she said. "But I want you to tell me why. Did someone eat a mad cow?"

"Not here," he said. "Not yet. But that happened in Britain years ago. People are worried it could happen in North America. And don't call it mad cow. It's bad for the industry. Call it BSE. You need to read the papers. Follow the news. This is important stuff. If you pay attention, you'll see that Canada is being punished." He had an anger in his voice that made her glad they were talking about this, and that he was thinking about something other than his parents. "They're not taking our meat any more. Who knows how long this is going to go on? Just because of one damn cow."

She listened to the passion and urgency in his voice, the voice of a man she had fallen in love with so many years ago. Then she leaned in and kissed his neck, and moved her kisses to his warm mouth and they tenderly but desperately made love, the way they had when the children were young, stealing a few minutes before one of the children woke from a bad dream, needing a drink of water. The whole experience, both the talking and the sex, calmed them both.

Now, in the church, Donna couldn't bear to look at Gord's face, but she grabbed his hand, held it tight and squeezed. His hand was a bit sweaty, but he squeezed back. She could feel waves of emotion coming off of him. People stood up to sing, Al's favourite hymn, "Be Not Afraid." Donna could hear Allyson's soprano coming from the other side of Gord. Gord never sang; he had a terrible voice. But Allyson, that girl could sing. So could Chloe. Chloe was in choir when she was younger, but then she dropped out. The older she got, the more things she quit.

People were moving, filing out of pews, heading out of the room towards the church basement. Donna didn't want to meet their eyes, so she looked down and admired the women's shoes. Most of them wore sensible flats or high heels. But one woman wore flashy green open-toed sandals with bright orange toenail polish. When Donna looked up to see who the shoes belonged to, Rita Dennis looked back at her.

"I'm so sorry," Rita said, and there was something in her tone and the way she looked Donna in the eye that made Donna believe her. "He was such a good man. I always liked him."

Down in the church basement, a crowd of over a hundred gathered.

Mabel Jacobson was the first to approach. She leaned over, and hugged Donna tight. Donna inhaled the scent of cloying, old lady lavender. Mabel must have marinated in her perfume that morning.

"How are you holding up?" Mabel asked. "I remember how it was when my John died. It hurt so much I felt like I was going to die too."

Donna didn't have the words or the energy to say anything, so she just let Mabel hug her and tried not to get a headache from her perfume.

She spotted her friend Mary Anne across the room over Mabel's shoulder and raised her eyebrows at her. Mary Anne nodded and started to make her way through the throngs of people.

"How's Abby?" Mabel Jacobson asked. "I heard she wasn't doing so great. Is she ever going to get out of there?"

This was a question Donna wondered herself. They still weren't sure if Abby would come back to the farm. Before she could answer, Mabel prattled on, "And this whole border thing. Have you been able to sell any cows? You must be so worried about your money."

Donna searched for Mary Anne again. She could see that she'd been sidelined by Rita Dennis. Rita would understand if Mary Anne had to bolt. She was a strange woman, but she'd get it. She'd done right by the Klassen family.

"This whole border is just a mess," Mabel said. "Al would have hated it. John would have hated it too. Who knows how much longer this could go on?"

Mabel was a close-talker with sour, coffee-smelling breath. Donna had the urge to just turn on her heel and walk away. Could a person do that at their father in law's funeral, or did they have to pretend to be nice, smile and nod along? She was debating this, when she felt a tap at her side.

"I need to talk to you in private," Ray Sharp said. "Let's go out front for some air."

He took her hand, the same way that Al would have taken it, in a friendly way, like an uncle, and he led her outside, out into the hall. In the hallway, he let go of her hand and they walked past some bulletin boards, down an empty hallway. The only other people that Donna saw were her daughter, and Joe Chin's son, Jeff.

"I could see she was bugging you," Ray said. "I guess she's forgotten what it's like, to have everyone staring at you and asking all those questions. I remember that when April died. I just felt like I was on display. But you were one of the people who helped me through it. You didn't ask too many questions. Just brought me those pies and cakes, and came over to watch tv. Sometimes you need quiet after someone dies. We can just sit here for a bit." He patted her hand, and the two of them sat in silence on uncomfortable wooden chairs.

"We better go face the music," Donna said after a few minutes. "I can't just hide out and leave the rest of my family to deal with the hordes."

"You're going to make it through this," Ray said as he stood up. "This'll be over before you know it."

Inside the hall, the sound system was playing Al's favourites: Johnny Cash, Dolly Parton, Kenny Rogers and Roger Miller. People talked and drank coffee out of Styrofoam cups and ate beef on a bun that was soft and tender from simmering in slow cookers for hours. Tables were covered with mountains of coleslaw, ambrosia salad, bean salad, potato salad and Jell-O with fruit in it. Some of the women brought homemade buns. There were matrimonial squares, cookies, rice krispie treats, Nanaimo bars, peanut-butter marshmallow squares. Plates of cookies covered every bit of the coffee service area at the back of the church basement. People laughed as they told stories about Al. He would have loved his own wake. Mary Anne stood beside Donna and didn't leave her side for the rest of the event. She was able to deflect anyone else who wanted to come up and ask questions.

When the family had thanked everyone, they were finally allowed to leave. Al would be buried next to his parents, and the child Linda had lost. The burial was just for family members and they would be doing that tomorrow. There were spaces for all the family members in the family plot. Abby would be buried beside her husband. Donna didn't like to think about her place in the plot. She didn't mind being beside Gord or his relatives, but the gravesite had always bothered her because three churches loomed over head. Just her luck. A non-church goer, she'd be surrounded by churches for the rest of eternity. The church women and the Royal Purple promised to clean up. The Klassens piled into their vehicles to go home.

Donna closed her eyes, pretending to sleep as they drove back toward the farm.

"Can you turn up the heat?" Allyson asked. She was in the back seat of Gord and Donna's truck; Colton and Clay were in Clay's truck. Linda, Craig and Chloe had driven up together.

Donna closed her eyes and concentrated on the heat coming from the vents. The heat was something real, something that reminded her she was still alive.

CHAPTER 5

The night after the funeral, the immediate family huddled around Donna and Gord's kitchen table. Gord said they had celebrated Al with everyone else, and now it was time to celebrate by themselves. They were the ones soldiering on, while everyone else could escape back to their lives. The eight of them played crib and canasta in memory of Grandpa Al. He loved a good game of cards, and they always played during holidays. Craig brought out a bottle of rye, and poured rye and Cokes for himself and Gord. Clay and Colton drank beers. Colton had turned eighteen a few months ago. Colton gave Chloe a sip of his beer. This was just for show. Everyone in the room knew she drank.

"You can have a beer," Craig said to Chloe. "Or you can have some rye and Coke."

"I'll try some rye," Chloe said.

"I'll make it light for her," Gord said. He poured a thimbleful of rye into a tall glass and filled the rest with Coke before handing it to Chloe. "Allyson, you want some?"

Allyson shook her head.

"Just try a sip in honour of Grandpa," said Gord.

Allyson had tried the odd sip of beer before and found the taste reminded her of the smell of cow urine. There was nothing appealing about it. She didn't understand why people drank. Maybe she'd eventually try Baby Duck or Boone's or a vodka slime or some of the other drinks she heard people talk about in the hallways of school. Someday. When she was older. She had better things to do then get drunk and barf every weekend. She knew stories of the girls who drank too much, who said stupid things and made out with guys they didn't even like on Monday. Maybe Chloe was turning into one of those girls. After all, she'd been drunk last week, and was hanging out with a crowd of partiers. Sooner or later, Allyson would probably hear a nasty story about her cousin in that rumour mill they called a school.

Gord poured glasses of Al's favourite rye and Coke for everyone. The family sat around the table and raised their glasses. Allyson wished she could pour the booze out and just drink the Coke.

"Dad was a class act," Gord said.

He looked around the table, glancing at Donna and his children before turning to face his brother, Linda and Chloe.

"He was so proud of all of you and everything he worked so hard to build. He loved you all. He may not have said those words very often, but he didn't need to. He lived those words. He believed in trying to make the world a better place. He was all about family."

At this point, Donna started to cry. Allyson looked away. Her mother was such a bawl baby. Grandpa Al had said all you had to do was wait for the weather to change and Donna would start snivelling. Donna reached for the box of Kleenex on the table. There were Kleenex boxes in every room of the house. Right after the accident, someone had gone down to the I.D.A. in town and bought a 12-pack of Kleenex.

Through her tears, Donna said, "Here's to Al. One of the best."

"Let's make him proud," said Craig. "Cheers."

They raised their glasses high, clinked them together and downed their drinks. Donna sniffled and wiped her tears. Allyson felt like crying, but she held back. Al would have wanted the tears to stop. Whenever Allyson cried when she was younger, he clasped her to his big chest, stroked the back of her hair with his hands and told her she had to stop because Grandpa didn't like it. He was softer with her and Chloe, but really enforced his "no crying" philosophy on Colton and Clay. Even Donna learned not to complain around him. He was always telling people to "Git'r done" or "Cowboy up." When Craig refilled Allyson's drink, she snuck off, took it into the bathroom and dumped it down the toilet. She went to bed early, but the rest of the family

stayed up late, playing cards, drinking and laughing. Al would
have approved.

                                    ★

     As she lay in bed, Allyson wondered who would take over
the farm, and what would happen between her and Chloe.
Clay would be first in line to take over the farm after Craig or
Gord. In 2025 the farm would be a hundred years old. The
Klassens had watched as some of the other farms in the area
became century farmers, and had plaques erected near the gates
of their front yards. The plate that read *Klassen Family Farm, estab-
lished 1925,* had been erected near the gate at the end of the
driveway, fastened to a large rock Al hauled there. When other
farms turned a hundred years old, generations of the family posed
for photographs in *The Messenger.* Awards were presented during
lavish ceremonies put on by the county. The reeve and local MD
councillors gave out plaques, and spoke about the history of the
farm, the strength of the family and the drive and passion it took
to work and keep the land.
     When she was younger, around eight or nine, Allyson had
been dragged to several of these ceremonies, even though she
begged to stay home and told her parents Clay was old enough
to look after her and Colton. But her grandparents and father
insisted, and she endured several of these events. Sometimes
she and Chloe wandered away to slip into cloak rooms, where
they examined everyone's coats, going through the pockets
when no one was watching. You could find some weird things
in peoples' coats. There were always gloves, coins and packs of
gum. When Allyson was ten and Chloe was twelve, they'd
found a condom in the pockets of a plaid dress coat. Chloe was
the one whose fingers landed on the plastic-wrapped circle of
latex. She pulled her hand back as if she was burned. Then she
came over to Allyson, who was looking through another coat
pocket. She whispered to Allyson that she should stick her
hand in the pocket of the plaid dress coat. Allyson felt the thin
packet of the condom and pulled it out to look at it. When

Chloe saw her pull it out, she stage whispered at Allyson to stick it back inside.

"What if someone sees us?" she said.

The two of them started laughing. Mabel Jacobson walked by, and they jumped away from the coats and ran back to their seats. Allyson missed having secret adventures with her cousin. Chloe stopped looking through the coats when she turned fourteen. Allyson never understood why, but one day, she asked Chloe if they were going to sneak into the cloak room and Chloe gave her a look of disdain, took a long, hard pull on the straw stuck in her Sprite, and turned away from her.

During the ceremonies themselves, Allyson slumped on her chair, bored out of her skull as people talked about the joys and hardships of farming. The family of the hour gathered at the front of the hall, grinning grandparents holding themselves up with canes, proud middle-aged fathers wearing plaid shirts, boots and shiny belt buckets, young women cradling chubby, drooling babies. They all lined up for photos. Maybe it was the closest any of them would ever be to a red carpet. The only redeeming thing about these ceremonies was that Allyson got to have Coke.

"That'll be us in twenty-five years," Al always said, when they attended these affairs. He said it every year, in a tone that was both hopeful and proud. The number of years until their farm turned one hundred changed, but Al's tone of voice and his hope, conviction and dogged determination never wavered.

Allyson never thought she or Chloe would take over the farm. They were girls and far down the line. They could get married and come back to the farm with their husbands. Maybe Chloe would want to live out on the land. When she was younger, she loved doing everything on the farm, riding quads, helping out in the barn. Craig was always after her for taking the dogs and cats into the house, calling her a city kid just like her Aunty Donna, who believed cats and dogs should be allowed indoors. Chloe used to be the perfect farm girl. All the adults used to joke that one day she'd be crowned Rodeo Queen.

Colton was more interested in machinery than cattle and even though none of the adults said anything, no one thought he was reliable enough to take anything on. Besides, Clay was the oldest. He was the one who helped out and understood the most about the operation, even though he was in the city right now. He'd been gone from the farm for years, encouraged by Donna and Gord. They wanted him to get an education, experience the city, know what it was like to live somewhere else. Clay boarded a plane, bussed tables in England and worked cattle farms in Australia. He sent colourful postcards from every place he visited. Now he was in his third year of animal science at the University of Alberta. Sometimes he talked about going to Saskatoon to go to vet school, but his marks might not be good enough. Clay was smart, but there was so much competition.

There had been no talks about who would take over the farm if Al died. There hadn't been any family meetings about it. Al had gone to some sort of farm workshop years ago. The advisor at the workshops recommended farm families have business meetings and sit down and discuss things like a real business. Donna opted out, saying she didn't understand what was happening on the farm, so why should she attend? Chloe decided she was too young to be involved in farm decisions and left to go brush the dogs. Al tried to guide the rest of them through the agenda he had written out in his scrawl. He called the meeting to order, rapping on the kitchen table with his big knuckles, which made Colton and Allyson laugh.

"Are we pretending to be big city lawyers or something?" Craig asked. "Why so official?"

"This is business," Al said. "In today's farming world we need to hold family meetings like business people. We can't just holler at each other when we're out in the yard. We need to have agendas, plan and assess where we are going. I might die someday and you'll need to know where I'm at and how to understand my bookkeeping. Need to make sure everything is clear as mud."

"We've got lots of time," Gord said. "You're not going anywhere any time soon. Donna's watching the game. I hate to think of her cheering those Riders on by herself, jinxing our precious Esks."

Craig pushed his chair back from the table and followed Gord as he left the room.

Allyson remembered this all, remembered her grandfather's face, and cried herself to sleep. She had too many questions in her head, and none of them could be answered.

★

After the night of cards, everyone in the family stayed away from each other for a few days, trying to get back to their regular work lives. They were sick of each other, and of each other's grief. Clay went back to the city and Chloe hung out with Jamie all the time. Colton was gone a lot too, probably hanging out with Lily Stevens. Lily had a wild reputation. She'd disappeared for a few months when she was in Grade 10. It was rumoured her disappearance had to do with her parents' divorce, but some speculated she'd been sent away to have a baby. Lily worked at Joe's or at the Husky truck stop in town. Some people said Lily turned tricks for money. Everyone in town knew there were prostitutes from the city who came to service rig workers. Sometimes big cars with dark tinted windows drove through town. People said they were full of hookers for the rig workers. But there were also a couple of town girls, like Lily Stevens, who were rumoured to give blow jobs or more for extra cash.

The first day back at school after the funeral was the worst. Allyson woke up in the morning, and stared at the ceiling. How would she deal with all the questions, all the curious stares? Would it be like the day of the funeral, when she'd had to smile and nod and listen to everyone reminisce about her grandpa?

When she was in the kitchen, eating soggy Cheerios while reading *"A Wrinkle in Time"* Chloe walked into the house and up the stairs.

"Morning," Donna said, as she poured herself a cup of coffee.

Without looking at Allyson, Chloe went over to the coffee pot and poured herself a cup.

"Do you want a ride?" Chloe asked. "I can wait for a bit if you want to go with me."

She stared deep into the cup, rather than at her cousin.

"Yeah," Allyson said. She'd been hoping her dad would give her a ride to school, the way he had before the accident. "Just let me get dressed."

She hadn't really spent any time alone with her cousin since her cousin had crawled into her bed. Maybe this was a chance to start talking again. Maybe they could walk into the school together, instead of alone.

When Allyson finished getting ready, Chloe was already sitting in the driver's seat of her Celica. "This is going to suck," Chloe said as Allyson opened the door. "So hard."

During the ride, Allyson stayed quiet. She searched her mind for topics to talk about with her cousin, but she was too nervous to say anything. They hadn't talked for so long, and she was feeling anxious about going to school. It was easier just to say nothing, and stare out the window. When the school came into view, Chloe parked the car and turned to Allyson before she got out.

"Everyone is going to be talking about us," she said, leaning toward her cousin. "They're going to whisper and ask questions and stare. They did the same thing when Jamie's grandpa died. She told me the best thing we can do is just ignore it. People are going to tell you how sorry they are. They'll be really nice to us for a few days. People you've never talked to will smile at you. Don't try and take advantage of their sympathy. Something else will happen and they'll forget all about us."

Chloe stood up and got out of the car. Allyson followed. She expected her cousin to walk ahead of her, to pretend that she didn't know her, but Chloe walked beside her. For a second, Allyson had a flash of how things used to be, when they were friends. Chloe pushed the heavy doors of the school open, and waited for Allyson to pass through.

"I'll see you later," she said, as she turned to go to her locker, which was in the opposite direction from Allyson's. "Stay strong. It'll be okay." She gave her cousin an affectionate little punch in the shoulder and walked away. Allyson smiled in spite of herself. Maybe things with her cousin would be back to normal. She walked along the hallway to her own locker. By the time she got to the end of the hall, she could see someone standing in front of it. Was someone blocking her locker? Was she going to have to ask them to move? As she got closer, she saw it was Jeff.

She felt her face growing hot. She had apologized and talked with him a few times since she'd opened his notebook and seen all the drawings of naked people and the drawings he'd done of her.

"Are you waiting for me or just hanging out?" she asked. She swung her head a little so her hair fell in her face. That way she could hide her cheeks if they started to turn red.

"I brought you a present," Jeff said. "I've been waiting here every day before first period. I figured you had to come back eventually."

He held his hand out to her and pressed a graphic novel collection in her hand.

"What is this?" she asked, studying the cover.

"It's the first few issues of *Sandman,*" said Jeff. "Neil Gaiman. It's good stuff. I got it for you when we went into the city last week. Thought you could use something to read. Something to take your mind off everything that is happening around you. I knew you hadn't read it yet."

"Thank you," she said, looking up at him. "That was really nice of you."

He scratched his head and look away. "Um, it's not really light reading. It's a bit heavy. But I know you'll like it."

He moved toward her, and opened the page. "See, just look at this art. It's amazing stuff. And well, there's no one who can tell a story like Gaiman."

He pointed to a goth girl with black hair. "That character's called Death," he said. "I hope that's okay."

She shrugged. "Can't really avoid it."

"Anyway," he said. "I remember what it was like when my grandma died. I would just wake up in the morning, and there would be a couple minutes when I would forget she was dead. And then I would remember, would know that I wasn't going to see her that day, and that I'd have to see my mom dragging her ass through the day, trying not to cry. It was rough. I know what you're going through right now."

The bell rang.

"Can I walk you to your class?" Jeff said. "You've got Mrs. Henshaw, right?"

Allyson nodded. "Just let me get my binder out of my locker."

Jeff moved aside. "I think you'll really like this," he said. "It's such a great collection."

She closed her locker. He moved a few steps away, and waited for her.

"Does it feel like everyone is staring at you?" he asked. "I felt like that after my grandma died. But they're not really. They're all too worried about themselves."

When they got to her classroom, she stopped before going in the door, not sure what to say. She was just grateful she hadn't had to walk through the halls alone.

"I'll talk to you later," Jeff said. "I hope you like the book."

"Thank you," she said, and turned into her classroom. She walked to her desk and put her head down, no wanting to look at anyone until the class started and she could look up and stare at the teacher.

It turned out Chloe was right. On that first day, everyone wanted to come and say something to Allyson about the Klassen family loss. Every student, teacher and their dog had a memory of Al they wanted to share. Thank god for Amber. She came and met Allyson after her first class, and stayed with her between every class that first day.

"I would have met you at your locker, but Booger was late driving me this morning," Amber said, when they saw each other in the hall after English class. "Honestly, I don't know why I bother getting rides with him. I would be better off walking."

As the day progressed, Allyson stopped listening when people talked to her about Al and Abby. When a person told her a story about her grandpa, she stared at the space between their eyebrows, nodded and smiled like she was listening. After they'd had a chance to express their condolences and share their memory, Amber changed the subject.

But two days later, people were excited about grad and the end of the year. Talking about someone's dead grandpa and injured grandmother was less exciting than grad dresses, bush parties and summer vacation. Allyson couldn't have been more relieved by everyone's short attention span.

★

A couple weekends after Al's funeral, Craig tried to hold another family meeting. Chloe, Colton, Allyson and Clay were all in Donna's kitchen when it started. The visits, phone calls and food from the neighbours had mostly stopped, although cards still arrived in the mail. Donna opened the cards, commenting every time she recognized one from *Memorable Moments*, the card shop she worked at on Main Street.

"Maybe you kids should go watch TV or something," Gord said. There was something about the way he spoke that told Allyson the adults were about to discuss something important. Colton and Chloe moved out of the room, taking their drinks to the TV room. Clay didn't move away from the counter. Donna stood beside him, her arm brushing against his. Gord gave Allyson the look and she left the room. If she snuck into Clay's room, she would be able to hear everything through the vents. Doing her best not to make the stairs creak, she hurried up the stairs, grateful she didn't have any jangling coins or keys in her pockets. No one was going to notice her.

Clay's room was still tidy, even though his duffel bags and suitcase were on the floor. A pair of socks were draped over the clothes hamper. He'd even made the bed. She grabbed a pair of clean socks from the top of his suitcase and tossed them from hand to hand. When she heard the sounds of voices from the kitchen, she leaned down on the floor, and put her head beside the vent, butt up in the air.

"We weren't prepared for this," Uncle Craig said. "We've got to change what we're doing. Dad was always going on about how we should update the succession plan, trying to get us to figure it all out. Too bad we didn't listen to him."

The room was silent for a moment, and Allyson listened hard, trying not to breathe. She worried her family would hear the sound of her breath, her heart beating fast inside her chest.

"There were always things to do," Gord said. "Always some damn thing. I didn't worry about it because Dad didn't want to retire. I thought he had a lot of life left."

"We'll be okay," Linda said. "We've saved up all the money to build the swimming pool."

"Has anyone talked to Abby about this?" Gord asked. "Has she said anything?"

Allyson doubted Gramma had anything to contribute. She was working with occupational and physical therapists to regain the use of her hand. She would never walk again. Allyson had gone to visit her in the hospital with Donna one time, and with Clay another time. Gramma had been pretty with it, and she'd even asked about Clay's roommate, Arjun. He'd come out to the farm once. Abby had asked him about his turban and he'd been really open and honest with her. She had a soft spot for him, and always asked about him.

"We were so dumb about never insisting that Dad show his books," Craig said. "All those times. We might as well be shovelling shit now."

"Can't we just keep going and wait until Mom is better?" Gord asked.

Linda's voice was clear, almost as if she was in the room with Allyson. It must be an effect based on where she was standing in the kitchen.

"We need to do this soon. We need to figure out what we're going to do with Abby. Rita and I have discussed some possibilities. She thinks it would be good to move Abby into town. She could do okay at the lodge."

"You discussed things with Rita?" Craig said. Allyson could hear the disdain.

"She's been good to us," Linda said. Her tone was firm, no-nonsense. "She's been good to Abby."

"Can't we have Abby here?" Gord asked. "She might do better in her own place."

Someone sighed. Allyson couldn't tell who.

"There are all those stairs," Craig said. "And who will look after her?"

"I could do it," Donna said.

Allyson couldn't hear anything for a minute. Maybe they were being quiet while they figured things out.

"It's too much," Linda said. "Do you really want to quit your job? Abby is going to need a lot of rehab and help. Plus, she's confused. I don't even know what to think about half of the things that come out of her mouth. A couple days ago, she told me she didn't even want to come back to the farm without Al here."

"She said that to me too," Donna said.

Allyson heard the scrape of a chair as someone stood up from the table.

Then her mother's voice again. "The kids all need to visit her more. She seems to brighten up when they're there."

"We need to split up the visits," Linda said. "Make sure someone goes out there every day. It can't just be me and Donna out there all the time."

"I could take some time off," Donna said. There was the sound of a cupboard closing, the shuffling of feet. The squeak of the fridge door and the clink of bottles.

"No, no," Linda said. "Think of all the money you'd lose. You're going to have another kid in university in a few years. Besides, who knows when the border will open?"

"I just keep on thinking about all those stories you read about the old people who die after their husband or wife passes."

Allyson trembled. She hadn't even thought of that. Could Gramma Abby die too? She was so frail and tired. Would she just close her eyes, start thinking about Grandpa and never wake up? She had better go see her tomorrow. Say all the things she had never said to her. Show her all the drawings she'd never shown her; the drawings of the farm yard trees, the poplar bluffs in the back quarter that Abby loved. She would go see her tomorrow.

She had band practice, but she could skip it. Gramma was more important.

She hated walking past Gramma and Grandpa's empty house. She was so used it to seeing it with the lights on, being able to wave at Gramma or Grandpa if they were standing at one of the windows. One time, she'd looked up and seen them making out in the upstairs bedroom window. She looked away when Grandpa started to pull up Gramma's shirt. That wasn't something she wanted to see. The windows on the front of her grandparents' house looked like a smiling face, the roof like a hat. When Gramma and Grandpa moved around the house, their lights would go on and off, brightening up the different parts of the face. But now, the face was downcast and sullen. She hated the way the empty house loomed, silent and abandoned, looking over the rest of the farm yard. The three houses were giant heads staring at each other with big round eyes and mouths. Her grandparents' house was silent, the doors locked tight and the curtains drawn. Uncle Craig's house and her dad's were still alive, blinds going up and down and doors opening and closing. She avoided looking at Gramma and Grandpa's house when she was out in the yard.

The adults started talking again. What were they going to do with Gramma?

"You went into the house?" Donna said.

"You went to the bank?" Gord said. "Without talking to me about it?"

"Hold on," Uncle Craig said. He was talking in a rush, his voice louder and his words faster than his normal easy-going drawl. "Linda and I didn't want to upset you. So we just did it. We found all the shoe boxes and receipts. I couldn't make heads or tails out of Dad's shoebox system. So I took it to the bank so they could tell me what's what. They gave us some insight."

"Why didn't you talk to me about this?" Gord asked. "Why did you just go ahead and do it all yourself? This isn't just your business."

"You two were just so upset," Linda said, her voice low and calm. Allyson wondered where she was standing. It was like she was speaking in a microphone, while the rest of the family sounded farther away, as if their voices were travelling through a decrepit television set. "We just got the stuff out of the house after my parents stayed there. I needed to clean up."

Everyone was silent. Then Gord spoke. "I'm perfectly capable of taking care of things," he said. "I wish you'd mentioned this to me and hadn't just gone ahead and done it. I'm older. I should have been the one to go to the bank."

Linda's voice was quiet. "I saw you out in the field that one day, out by yourself in the morning. Snowflake came up to you and you stroked her nose, and then you leaned down, and it looked like you were crying. We couldn't ask you to do anything that day."

"What about the border?" Craig asked. "I can't make any money hauling. The markets aren't moving. What are we going to do? We don't know how much longer this is going to go on. We need to figure out how to make some money."

She heard footsteps behind her and jumped.

"Are you listening to all of this?" Clay asked.

He stood in the doorway of his room. She moved away from the vent and Clay sat down on the bed.

"I feel like they're completely lost down there," he said. "No one knows what to do."

"You were listening," she said. "Why can you listen when I can't?"

"Because I'm nine years older," he said. "I need to know this stuff. You don't need to know this right now."

"But it seems important," she said.

"It's finances," Clay said. "Adult stuff."

Why didn't anyone want to talk about money, she wondered. Shouldn't people know how much money other people had? Wasn't that important? She was saving up for a band trip next year. How could she save and budget for new art supplies and books if she didn't know how much money was in her account? Why didn't the adults see that?

She heard the low murmur of voices, and leaned down towards the vent again, even though she knew Clay didn't want her to listen.

"Don't," he said, coming over to pull her back up to standing. "I had to get away from it. It'll just make you feel bad."

"Things aren't great," she heard Craig say. She heard the low sounds of her mother crying. "This whole border thing will just make everything worse. We're really going to have to watch it."

"I want to hear," she said, yanking her arm out of Clay's.

"This is not for you," he said. "Come away from the vent. I'll play you some of the new music Arjun loaned me. Have you ever heard of Moby?"

Clay moved in front of her and put his sock foot over the vent.

"Just come with me," he said. "You don't need to think about this."

She looked at his face. He wasn't going to move.

CHAPTER 6

The summer sped by and then it was fall. The old grain elevator was about to come down. Everyone had been hearing about the demolition for weeks, since the beginning of August. Donna's friend Mary Anne asked if she wanted to go watch the elevator fall. The destruction of the grain elevator was an event, like the town parade, a rodeo or fireworks. *The Messenger* ran several stories about it, their three-person newsroom scrambling around for interviews. The radio, newspapers and television ran constant news about BSE, SARS and Iraq. Donna was scared to watch television or read the news, because every single thing depressed her. The world was falling apart. People were dying in Iraq, Toronto was full of SARS, and in town, people were going to lose their shirts if the border didn't open soon.

The border closure was weighing on Gord. The auction mart opened a week or so after the border closed, but the prices were so low it wasn't even worth trying to sell.

The other day at breakfast, Gord told Donna about Phil's bull. Phil raised purebred bulls and had sent one of his champions down to the States. He couldn't get the animal back since the border was closed, and they wouldn't let cattle through. Fortunately, one of his American cattle buds was looking after the bull, but Phil wasn't sure when he would get it back.

Just that morning, when Donna and Gord were in their bedroom, Gord looked in the mirror and examined the greys on his head.

"I think there are more," he said. "But at least it's not falling out. I don't think I could handle losing my looks right now."

Gord was lucky to have a full head of hair. Craig was balding. His forehead got bigger every week, and the back of his head got shinier. Linda loved the reddish tint of Craig's hair. Donna knew that secretly, Linda hated that Craig's hair was falling out, even though she'd never say anything about it to him. A man could control his weight and how big his belly got. But no man, not even a man who ate only steamed vegetables and worked out on a treadmill every day, could control his own hairline.

"You've still got your looks," Donna said, putting her arms around her husband. He was a good-looking man, even if he had a few wrinkles and the start of a spare tire. He had big brown eyes, nice white teeth and the same strong hands, nice arms and muscular back she had fallen in love with. He was her cowboy. They had a pile of good-looking children, and two of them were growing up nicely.

"Don't worry about this mad cow stuff," she said, letting go of Gord to pick up a pile of laundry. Ever since the funeral, she was falling behind. Things needed to be done around the house, and she hadn't gotten to them yet. She was treading water, on the verge of losing her ability to keep afloat. She had piles of stuff to wash. Gord's barn clothes were starting to smell, which drove her completely crazy. "We'll be fine," she said. "You just keep doing what you're doing. We've always been fine."

His body stiffened, the way the bodies of their dogs did when they saw a coyote in the yard.

"Don't call it mad cow," he said. "You need to call it BSE."

"Why?" she said, her arms full of laundry.

"If you say mad cow, it sounds like something is wrong with the meat. People need to know that they can't get sick from eating beef."

Donna sighed. BSE was another bunch of letters, like the rest of farming. Phil Hill was on the board of Alberta Beef Producers, known as ABP. ABP and CCA had constant meetings. Their grain farming neighbours talked about the CWB, and ACPC and going to pick up things at UFA. These people just loved the alphabet. They'd use any excuse to stick three or four letters together.

"I have to put this in the wash," Donna said as she left the room.

★

She got off work early because of the grain elevator. Anita, the owner of *Memorable Moments*, thought about keeping the store open so she could make money off the people coming downtown to watch the grain elevator fall at the end of the street.

"I feel sick thinking about it," Anita said. "But hey, the store could use the business. We have to keep up our sales, so that we're top of mind when Wal-Mart comes."

Anita Babchuk had lived in town all her life and was now in her fifties. Sometimes Donna wondered how she could stand it, living her entire life in one place. Didn't Anita ever wonder what other places were like? She and her husband Kelly used to run the video store in town too, but they sold it when Kelly got into inventing. He started out making those wooden silhouettes of cowboys and wagon wheels that people put in front of their homes. His cut-outs were immensely popular, so Kelly started travelling to farm trade shows and rodeos. He had also invented some kind of watering system for cattle to drink out of when it got cold. The Babchuks were in the money now.

Donna didn't know how someone could be as happy as Anita. No one in town ever said anything bad about her. She was the best with customers and could always help anyone find the right card for any occasion. The card she sent the Klassens after the accident still sat on the mantle in Donna and Gord's house, even though many of the other cards had been thrown out. Anita's card was beautiful; purple, pink and orange just like a prairie sunset. On the front of the card, a couple wearing cowboy hats stood on a ledge, looking out into a valley. The inside of the card said, *Together, we can get through the roughest of times. Wishing you and your family strength and courage during this difficult period.*

Anita eventually decided town pride was worth more than commerce and she announced they would close the store early.

"I can't bear to watch the elevator fall," Anita said, as they locked up for the night. "I'm going to go home, sit on my back porch and have a glass of wine. When I wake up in the morning, the town will be different."

Mary Anne knocked on the window of the store. Donna waved at her.

"Go ahead," Anita said. "I'll finish up."

Mary Anne was one of Donna's oldest friends in town. She was a few years older, but moved to town a few years after Donna did. Clay and Mary Anne's daughter, Naomi, had been in the same swim class at the town pool when they were little. Mary Anne grew up in Red Deer, and met her ex-husband, John, at Red Deer College before he went to med school. She had worked as an elementary school teacher, but didn't like it, so she turned to writing. She was now a successful romance author and was known for a series of steamy cowboy romance books that took place in Texas. She spent most of her days in the purple writing studio at the back of her house, staring at a computer screen, her Boston terrier Henry snoring at her feet. Naomi was the same age as Clay and lived in Vancouver.

"I didn't want to have sex with John for a long time because I thought he was cheating," Mary Anne confessed late one night, when she and Donna had had a few too many wine coolers on her back porch. "We were staying together because of Naomi. But then one night, he rented *The Magnificent Seven*, and I don't know, there was something about Yul Brynner in a cowboy hat that did it for me."

Mary Anne's other daughter, Bryn, was born nine months after *The Magnificent Seven* incident. John started sleeping with the receptionist at his clinic when Bryn was five. John and Mary Anne split up and he moved to Ottawa. Mary Anne stayed in town because she didn't want to take Bryn out of school, and she loved her sprawling bungalow, which she painted purple after the divorce.

Donna read all of Mary Anne's books. They were steamy and delicious, focussing on how good a man could look in a Stetson, hoisting himself onto a beautiful, well-muscled horse. It was enough to make any woman need a cold drink. Mary Anne wrote love stories between city girls and ranchers. One time, Donna asked Mary Anne why she didn't set any of her books in Alberta.

"Books set in Alberta or Saskatchewan don't sell," Mary Anne said, taking a sip of her wine. "Have you ever noticed that none of the cows or horses ever shit in any of my books? These cowboys live in shitless worlds. It's all about the fantasy."

Donna understood this better than anybody. She had always had a thing for cowboys. She loved all the old westerns, just like everyone else in the Klassen family. Al had called them "dusters". He didn't have to teach Donna about westerns when she moved to the farm. She'd known them all already. *The Good, the Bad and the Ugly*. Gorgeous red-haired Robert Redford and handsome Paul Newman in *Butch Cassidy and the Sundance Kid*. John Travolta as *The Urban Cowboy*. Before she moved to the farm, she'd been obsessed with *Dallas* and Dolly Parton and the fancy, shiny sequin dresses Dolly wore, especially when she was singing with Kenny. Islands in the stream, how could they be wrong? It was still one of Donna's favourite songs.

Donna went outside to meet Mary Anne.

"Do you need to eat anything?" Mary Anne said. "Did you have supper?"

"I'm good," Donna said. She was a bit peckish, but she hadn't felt like eating much lately. Every time she sat down to eat, all she could think about was poor Abby. Abby, who still had a great figure in her sixties, had loved a good home-cooked meal. She always insisted on having everyone sit down to eat at the table. Her tablecloths were pressed and the knives on the table settings faced inward. When they had holiday dinners at Al and Abby's, Abby used the good china.

Donna had been visiting Abby a few times a week. Abby was trying to teach her to knit. Donna hated knitting and was really bad at it, but doing it around Abby helped engage her. Rita Dennis suggested it. Rita was usually on the desk when the Klassens came into the hospital. She'd been so great, just telling them all what was actually happening, cutting past the bullshit of the doctors to give them the plain truth. Even Linda said she'd been wrong about Rita.

"That woman has terrible hair, but a great big heart," Linda said.

Abby was doing better, but still not great. She was eating bits of Jell-O and soup, and looking more like herself, but she was still sleeping a lot. The doctors talked about putting her on antidepressants, but no one had decided anything yet. Abby said she dreamed about Al, but couldn't remember her dreams when she woke up.

One night when they were visiting, Rita sat Linda and Donna down in an empty room and told them they needed to look out for a few things.

"I don't want to alarm you because she seems to be doing well," Rita said. "But when people experience trauma like this, the way Abby has, they often show personality changes. And these changes are generally not for the better."

Donna and Linda looked at each other. Sure, Abby was tired and listless. She was sleeping a lot. But she'd lost the use of one of her hands, she was paralyzed from the waist down and her husband was dead.

"Aren't her reactions pretty normal?" Donna asked.

Rita nodded. "So far, she seems okay. But you need to watch her."

"She's been watching a lot of Judge Judy," Linda said. "Maybe we can get her one of those books-on-tape things."

"I just wanted to let you know," Rita said as she stood up and left the room, abandoning the two Klassen women.

Craig, Donna, Linda and Gord had a family meeting about Abby and decided to move her to the lodge in town so she would be closer to her house and the kids. Donna was glad she'd be moving to town. Ever since the accident, she'd felt nervous driving on that highway. When she came to the intersection where Abby and Al had been hit, she felt like throwing up. One time, she passed through the intersection and realized she'd been holding her breath the entire time. The next time, she forced herself to count her breaths as she drove down that part of the highway. Thank God Abby would be in the lodge before winter. Donna couldn't have handled a whole winter of crossing that intersection several times a week. Craig and Linda asked Donna and Gord if they wanted to put a cross at the intersection to mark the spot where Al died, but Donna refused. She thought highway memorials were sad and creepy, and she felt empty every time she saw one. There was no way she could have handled driving past a cross that marked the last place Al had been alive.

"You're a million miles away," Mary Anne said. "You doing okay?"

"Just stressed," Donna said. "So many things happening. There's not much for me to say that you don't already know."

"You can still vent if you want to," Mary Anne said. "I understand grief."

Donna wanted to ask Mary Anne how booting a lying, cheating, pig of a man out of the house, enjoying freedom and getting a pile of money was the same as losing a great father-in-law and having a mother-in-law who now sat in a hospital bed, watching reality TV and staring at the walls. She stopped that train of thought. Of course Mary Anne suffered when she and John divorced. It couldn't have been easy when the entire town was gossiping about you, saying that maybe your husband wouldn't have cheated on you if you lost a little weight.

"I parked my car around back and I got the lawn chairs inside," Mary Anne said. "Also I have a screwdriver inside a thermos if you feel like having a nip or two."

"Sounds good," Donna said, even though she didn't want to drink. She felt weird about drinking ever since a drunk driver hit Al and Abby. All people in this town did was drink or talk about drinking.

Mary Anne and Donna went around back to Mary Anne's purple PT Cruiser and picked up the chairs. A small crowd had gathered at the end of the street. PJ the hot dog vendor had set up his cart. PJ and his mother had been selling hot dogs for years. Everyone knew PJ was touched in the head, so they all bought hot dogs from him. He was allowed to drop the puck during Mustang games too.

"Hi, PJ," Donna said, waving to him. He waved back, smiling his awkward too big smile.

"I'm so glad summer is here," Mary Anne said as she sat down. "Naomi will be coming back soon and the three of us are going to take some girls' trips. We'll go down to Red Deer and visit my folks. I made some good money off *The Bride, The Outlaw and The Baby*, so we'll probably be able to go to Banff and stay in the Fairmont. I think it's time to take Bryn for a pedicure in a real spa."

As Mary Anne said this, she looked down at her sandaled feet and inspected her purple nail polish. Donna, who had already sat down in her lawn chair, tucked her feet under her, glad she was wearing closed-toed shoes. She should probably get a pedicure at some point in her life. This town was starting to get to her. She was turning into a country bumpkin. In a couple of years, no one would even be able to tell she had grown up in the city.

Donna looked around to see who else was there. She spotted her own daughter a few rows ahead, hanging out with Amber and that Jeff Chin from Joe's. She thought Allyson might have a crush on him, the way she was always mooning around him, asking Gord if he could take her to Joe's with him. It wasn't because she liked hanging out with the men while they were having their coffee and talking cattle. Tim Coates walked by and Mary Anne didn't even try to conceal her gawking.

"Look at that tall drink of water," she said. "I'm getting thirsty." She leaned over, pulled the thermos out of her purple purse and took a big sip.

Donna looked at him, and then looked away. She'd never been able to stomach Mary Anne's ability to look at teenagers. She couldn't do it. She was the mother of two sons, for God's sake. One time Mary Anne commented on Clay's arms, and said how he was growing up to be a fine, strapping, good-looking man. Donna changed the subject. "Do you want to make something for the school bake sale?" she asked, shutting the conversation down.

But this time, Mary Anne kept staring at Tim for so long that Donna's curiosity got the better of her. Tim's pants sat low around his boyish hips. She could see a line of checked boxer shorts rising above his belt as he leaned down to talk to a blonde-haired girl Donna didn't know. She was old enough to be his mother. So was Mary Anne. How could she not feel dirty looking at these young guys?

"That kid needs to have a party and invite his pants to meet his waist," she whispered to Mary Anne. Mary Anne laughed, a sharp bark, before she took another sip from her thermos. Donna thought about going up to say hi to Allyson, but she knew better. One time she had gone up to talk to Colton at a public event, and he hadn't even looked at her. If Allyson wanted to talk, she'd approach her. Donna felt around for her purse. "Shit," she said. "I left my purse back at the store."

She stood up. "Just wait. I'll be right back."

Mary Anne nodded without taking her eyes off from the crowd. She was probably writing in her head, figuring out a crowd scene for her next novel. Maybe the cowboy in Mary Anne's next book would have longish, floppy hair and a lanky body like Tim Coates. Donna wouldn't put that past her.

She started down the street, patting her pockets for her keys. Thank God her keys were in her pockets and not in her bag. Donna passed a few people on the street on the way back to *Memorable Moments*. She kept her head down, so she wouldn't have to talk to anyone. She was tired of people asking how she was doing. Everyone wanted to ask her about Abby or the kids and how they were holding up. People kept looking at her face, searching for signs of grief. People in town were talking about the Klassen family, wondering how they were doing with the recent tragedy and this mad cow thing that was putting so much stress on people. She'd done her own share of gossiping over the years, and she knew the drill.

When she got to the front door of *Memorable Moments*, she took the keys out of her pockets and unlocked the door. The door was sticky so she shoved her weight against it to open it. Gord knew she had to do this, so he often massaged that hip, saying she was wearing her hip down every time she shoved the door open.

"Don't flatten out your hips," he would say, running his hands across her hips and lower back. "Don't want to ruin your great shape."

Gord hadn't given her a massage since Al and Abby's accident. She'd barely rubbed his back either. She should take better care of him. He needed her. Her man was stressed. She didn't need anyone to tell her that. She should be there for him. That's what a real farm wife would do.

"Stand by your man," Donna sang to herself as she walked to the lunchroom at the back of *Memorable Moments*. She liked to sing, but normally didn't sing in front of others. In the back room, Donna spotted her purse on the back of a chair. Pam had bought it a few years ago on one of her trips to the United States. She'd got it in Texas. It was a purse made out of a pink, shiny cowboy boot.

"You're the only person who is country enough to use this," Pam said when she gave her the present. "I think it's a one-of-a-kind item."

When she was a young girl, Donna dreamed of being a country star and living in Nashville. She wanted to dress like she was in Nashville the first few years living on the farm, but there was no way to make that work. Who could dress like that when they were trying to run a farm? Who wanted shit on their sequins? Who had the time to do their make up all the time or put on false eyelashes? She'd been too busy taking care of her family to make her hair big. She was comfortable in jeans, bunnyhugs and t-shirts. She had a nice pair of boots she wore when she went to town, along with a couple of Western shirts and a nice Stetson.

Donna grabbed her purse, locked the front door to *Memorable Moments*, pulled on the lock to make sure the door was shut and started back up the street. The crowd at the end of the street had grown. She tried to remember why they were knocking down the elevator in the first place. Times were changing, the article in the newspaper said. It cost a lot of money to maintain the old elevators and this one was barely used. It was cheaper to knock it down.

Donna passed by *The Messenger* office and looked in the windows, hoping to catch a glimpse of Julie Taylor, a reporter who had been working there for a couple of years. She was around

Clay's age. Donna hoped she could set the two of them up. She'd even shown Clay Julie's picture in the paper.

"Not my type, Mom," Clay said as he flipped through the paper and took a sip of his coffee.

Julie sometimes came into *Memorable Moments* to chin wag with Donna. She had grown up in Saskatoon too. She'd gone to journalism school in Montreal and had moved back west to be with her boyfriend, who was still in Saskatoon. Donna met him once before they'd called it quits. When she had looked at his face, she knew he wasn't good enough for Julie. He mumbled when he talked and couldn't look Donna in the eye. Julie wouldn't be in town for much longer. Town reporters never stayed for long. They were all city kids who cut their teeth writing news about fourth-grade plays, special event dinners, town anniversaries and petty crime. After they'd got some experience under their belts, they moved on to greener pastures. One of the reporters who had been at *The Messenger* was now at *The Edmonton Sun*. And another had moved on to *The Calgary Herald*. Julie would probably move on soon. She was young. She would move, travel the world, meet interesting people and write about them.

There was no sign of Julie at the office. She was probably down at the elevator already. Funny how this street seemed so much longer when you were walking it alone. When you were walking along Main Street talking to someone else, the street was just a blip.

She admired the door knocker on the front of Carver and Sons law office. She'd only been in there once with Gord, and the office had been open. She loved that knocker. One night, when she'd been alone, she'd walked up, and grabbed the brass knocker and sneaked a few good knocks in. As she was admiring the knocker, the door opened and Linda and Craig walked out.

"Oh," Donna said, before she could stop herself. "What are you doing here? Are you trying to sell some chocolate covered almonds?"

The entire Klassen family had been trying to sell chocolate covered almonds to help Allyson raise money for next year's band trip. Donna had put a little box on the counter at *Memorable Moments* to try and rack up sales, but Linda was the one who had been selling the most, just because she was always buzzing around town.

Linda's face was red. She gave her sister-in-law a smile and looked down. Her smile looked plastered and fake, like a smile worn by a girl in a Miss American pageant.

"We had some business," Craig said. "Just trying to sort out a few things. We had some questions Ken could help us with. You going to watch the elevator?"

Linda had moved ahead and was looking in the planter boxes up the street. She bent down and fiddled with her shoe.

"Yeah," Donna said. "Mary Anne's waiting for me over there."

"Well," Craig said. He wasn't wearing his Stetson or his John Deere hat. Donna looked at his hairline. He would be bald as a cue ball in a couple of years. The thought gave her a shiver of joy.

Craig walked up to his truck. Linda opened the door of the truck and got in.

"Donna," Craig said. "Promise you won't tell Gord you saw us at the lawyer's. I don't want him to worry."

Donna nodded, but inside she seethed. Of course she was going to tell her husband. Why would she keep that secret from him? What kind of wife did they think she was?

Craig started the truck. The engine sounded old and tired. As she watched them go, she wondered if the truck would die soon, if it just wanted to sit and rest and not have to work so hard. After she watched them go, she thought about going back to *Memorable Moments* to call Gord and let him know that she'd seen Craig and Linda acting cagy at the lawyer's. But Gord probably wouldn't answer. He might be out in the yard, in a pasture or in the barn. She was dying to know why Craig and Linda had been at the lawyer. And if this was something family-related, why hadn't she and Gord been invited? Were they sneaking around with Abby and Al's estate? She took a deep breath, willed herself to calm down and started walking. It was hard for anyone to keep secrets in this town. How could Craig ask her not to tell her husband what she had seen, even if she didn't know all the details? She was going to let Gord know, that was for god damn sure.

More people gathered at the end of the street. Mary Anne was talking to the mayor, Barb McGuinty. Barb had been the town mayor for about five years now. She grew up in town, and her dad was the mayor years ago. He passed away before Donna had moved to town, but he was a legend, because of his golf game, charitable work and his legacy as a great mayor. People were pretty happy with Barb as mayor. Her husband Paul worked in the patch and he was often away. Barb's mother, Faye, stood on the other side of Mary Anne.

"Are you okay?" Mary Anne said as Donna walked up to join them. "You look as though something's wrong."

Barb and Faye turned their heads. Donna might have told Mary Anne that she'd seen Craig and Linda coming out of the lawyer's office, but she certainly wasn't going to mention it in front of the mayor and her mother.

"Just tired," Donna said. "A lot going on."

"I haven't seen you since the funeral," Barb said. "How are you holding up?"

"Okay," Donna said. "Everybody's okay."

Faye leaned in towards Donna and gave her a quick, fast hug. Faye was the town hugger. The good thing about her hugs was that she didn't hold on too long.

"I've been out to see Abby," Faye said. "But I know what it's like. You feel like hell when you lose your other half."

Faye's husband had died in a tragic farming accident. Donna couldn't remember the details, but she was pretty sure it involved a grain auger.

"It'll be good when she gets into town," Faye said. "You're moving her next week, yes?"

God, Faye was a talker. Was Abby getting moved next week? Donna didn't even know if they'd made all the arrangements for that yet. Donna must have looked worried, because Faye patted her arm and hugged her again. "I shouldn't be talking about these kinds of things," she said. "I should sit down and let you enjoy the event."

Donna walked back to her lawn chair and sank down into it. After Mary Anne settled herself too, she passed the thermos to Donna, who took a sip. Faye and Barb moved away to talk to Mabel Jacobson. Mary Anne looked at Faye and then closed her fingers and thumbs together in quick succession, imitating Faye's flapping lips. Donna swirled the orange juice and vodka around in her mouth and smirked. Everyone in town knew Faye couldn't shut up. If you ever wanted someone in town to know something, you told her. She spread news faster than *The Messenger*.

"Want some popcorn?" Mary Anne asked, holding a brown paper out to Donna. Donna put her hand into the greasy, butter-covered bag and took a handful.

"Where did you get this?" she asked as she crunched the kernels.

"The theatre," Mary Anne said, pointing with her purple nails. "I guess they've got a cart now."

Donna hadn't been to the town theatre in months. The last time she'd been, the projector had acted up. She, Abby, Linda, Chloe and Allyson had come into town to see *Chicago*. The theatre was almost empty. The film kept slipping up, cutting off Catherine Zeta-Jones and Renee Zellweger's heads as they danced. Donna went to tell the staff at the front of the theatre what was happening, and they fixed the problem for a while. The last straw had been when Richard Gere's beautiful face disappeared from the screen for a few minutes. Donna made a promise to herself to boycott the theatre until things improved. She wanted to ask for a refund but Abby wouldn't let her.

"Who needs to see the top of someone's head anyway?" Abby said in the car on the way home. "All I'm really interested in is the dancing."

"What did you pay for this?" Donna asked, pointing to the popcorn bag.

"Nothing," Mary Anne said around a mouth full of corn. "They're giving it away."

If that crap theatre was giving it away, Donna was going to take advantage.

"I'll be right back," she said, as she stood up to go over to the cart.

Donna came back with the popcorn in hand, and sat down next to Mary Anne, who was searching through her purse. Her purse was so big that Donna was always amazed by what came out of it. There were probably entire meals in there. Mary Anne pulled out a small purple notebook and started scribbling.

"Sorry," she said, her pen still moving across the page. "I just had a few ideas. Came up with a new name for the hero. The cowboy's name is going to be Lance Fairley."

"Nice one," Donna said. She'd seen Mary Anne do this before. She lived in perpetual fear that she was going to forget her ideas, so she tried to write them down as soon as she could.

The crowd had been sitting for over half an hour, and nothing had happened yet. She watched as the bulldozer started towards the elevator. There were lots of young boys in the crowd, excited to see a wrecking ball in action. Her boys would have loved to see this when they were young, Colton especially.

"It's about to happen," Mary Anne said. "Got to freshen my drink."

She reached into her voluminous purse and pulled out a flask. Hiding her hands behind her purse, she poured the vodka into the thermos.

"It's been a rough week," Mary Anne said. "I had copy edits from hell and one of my characters is mad at another and won't tell me why. I'm just trying to get them into bed with each other."

She passed the thermos to Donna. "Bottoms up," she said.

Donna handed it back to her without taking a sip. The crowd had stopped moving and was staring ahead, waiting for something to happen. A team of volunteer firemen stood at the front of the group, preventing the crowd from getting too close.

People are so dumb, Donna thought. They like to get close to danger. Thank God she and Mary Anne were sitting far away. Donna looked over at her daughter. She was still off to the side with Jeff and Amber. She was drawing in a notebook. That girl was so talented.

The bulldozer wound up, the wrecking ball ready. The crowd leaned forward, watching. Donna looked at Barb and Faye. The two women were holding hands. Tears streamed down Barb's face. That woman loved the town. It was a good thing she was mayor. As Donna watched, the wrecking ball hit the wood of the elevator with a sharp crack. A few people in the crowd cheered. The wrecking ball swung back out and hit the structure again. The elevator began to crumple and topple. As the wrecking ball hit the elevator for the third time, a huge cloud of dust burst forth from the elevator walls and enveloped the crowd. When Donna opened her eyes again, everything was hazy and covered with dirt. She tasted grit in her teeth and could feel it in her ears. Mary Anne wiped her face with a large purple handkerchief. The crowd, which had screamed when the giant dust ball enveloped them, was now quiet. Donna looked ahead, at the pile of rubble, lumber and cement that had once been the town's grain elevator.

CHAPTER 7

As she approached the door of her house, Allyson heard her parents' voices through the screen. The tone of their voices told her something was up. She'd just seen her mom a few hours ago, watching the grain elevator fall. After the crowd had dispersed, she'd gone to Husky House with Amber and Jeff. Amber's mom had picked them up and given her a ride home. Now Allyson opened the door with a slow, careful motion, letting it close behind her without a sound. She stood in the doorway with her shoes on. If she moved, they might hear her.

"They were coming out of the lawyer's," her mother said.

Her father sighed. "I think I have an idea why they went there."

Her father told her mother he'd looked through Al's shoeboxes, trying to decipher Al's records over the years. He was angry that he was the second one to do it, trying to follow up after Craig and Linda had already looked at it.

"It should have been done together," Gord muttered, but Allyson could still hear him. Some of the notes he understood and some of them he couldn't make heads or tails of. He searched through Abby and Al's entire house until he found a ledger in the nightstand next to Al's side of the bed. He took the red Hilroy notebook to the hospital to show to Abby.

"She told me that she didn't want to look at it," Gord said. "She said he was the one in charge of the books, and she had no head for figures."

Everyone in the family knew about Abby's slight number dyslexia. When she dialled phone numbers, she said the numbers out loud to make sure she got them right. Abby hated making phone calls and would try to get anyone, even her grandchildren, to dial a number for her.

"I'm still trying to understand what Dad was doing," Gord said. "I went to the bank today and tried to get them to sort it all out. They told me I had to go to a lawyer. I guess Craig went first. He tried to take the notebook away from me, but I told him I needed to do this," said Gord. "I'm the one who is supposed to be in charge here."

"You're the oldest," Donna said. "And you're more involved with the farm any way. Craig's always off trucking or doing work for other people."

Gord sighed. "Ever since this BSE stuff happened and Dad died, I can't concentrate on anything. I haven't even picked up a book in weeks. Any time I have a spare minute, I'm watching the news and trying to figure out what's happening with the border and whether we'll be making good money with cattle sales soon. I can't remember anything. I'm just so tired all the time, so tired I can barely stand it."

There was a long silence. Allyson's leg itched, but she worried that if she leaned down to scratch it, they might hear her move. She didn't want them to know she was there.

"What are you trying to say, Gord?" Donna said. "Spit it out."

"Our money situation is not great," he said. "We're not doing well. In fact, I thought we were doing a lot better. If we can't sell our cows for a good price, we might be screwed."

"How bad is it?"

Allyson strained her ears, trying to hear her dad's answer. If he knew she was listening, he wouldn't be happy.

"Dad did so many things wrong," Gord said. "He didn't take out life insurance. It was like he didn't want to think about dying, so he never even made any plans for it. And now we're screwed. Things could have been so much easier. We might actually end up in trouble," he said. "We're going to have to dip into our savings. Do you think Anita could give you more hours at the store?"

"I'll see," Donna said. "But I can't cut into Bonnie's shifts. She's got four kids at home."

"I'm having a hard time getting everything done," Gord said. "Balancing this workload without Dad is tricky."

"Ask for help," Donna said. "Craig could be doing more around here, couldn't he? And what about the kids?"

Gord coughed a little. "Colton might be able to help out a bit more. Same with Allyson. Chloe's got that job," he said. "Craig said she's picking up lots of hours. She needs to have money for school next year."

They said a few sentences, but all Allyson heard was mumbling and her name. She'd probably missed the most important part.

"I'm going to talk to Craig," Gord said. "Find out exactly why he was at the lawyer's. I think I know, but confirmation doesn't hurt."

"What day is Abby getting moved?"

"Sunday," Gord said. "They'll bring her to the lodge in one of those handi-buses. Maybe we can go there and get some flowers and bring some of her quilts. Make her room seem nice and homey."

"Why didn't you tell me she was being moved?" Donna asked.

"I thought I did," Gord said. "Must have forgot. I got to take a piss."

Allyson heard the shift of a chair and the sound of her father walking out of the room. If he looked down when he crossed the hall, he might see her. When her dad wanted to end a conversation, he needed to pee. Either that or he'd go out into the yard and check the animals.

She opened the front door and went out into the yard herself, eager to look at their bottle baby. The red calf had been so small when its mother died. She was living in a pen with a couple steers and some heifers Gord wanted to sell at the auction mart. The calf was a few months old now. She liked people and wasn't too weird because she had been raised with other cattle.

Allyson reached her hands through the fence and petted the calf on its head. The calf brought its wet mouth up and tried to suckle on her fingers. Allyson tried not to look toward her grandparents' house. Whenever she was out in the yard, she expected Grandpa Al to step out of the house, wearing his shit-covered boots and a big grin on his face. The memories kept sneaking up on her. A few years ago, he'd taken her out in the truck and taught her how to drive. When she was small, he had called her "my girl" and gave her piggy-back rides. He always told that since she spent so much time studying and reading and worked so hard, she was going to blow the rest of the family out of the water.

"A man would be lucky to marry a girl that's as pretty and smart as you," he said. "You're a prize."

Grandpa Al was never stingy with hugs. He liked to take his granddaughters into town for hot chocolate with whipped cream on top. At the town parade, they'd sit and watch the floats go by and half of the town would come up and say hi to Al.

"These are my girls," he would say, patting her and Chloe on the head. "My pretty, smart girls. Aren't I the luckiest man in the world?"

If Hollywood could have seen Grandpa Al's smile, they would have made him a movie star, Gramma Abby said. He was better looking than Clint Eastwood. Better looking than Gary Cooper.

"I fell in love with that smile," she said. "I still get a tickle every time he smiles at me."

Allyson visited Gramma Abby about once a week in the hospital. It was too hard to see her grandma so listless. Besides, she needed to rest. Gramma Abby would talk, but then she'd go back to sleep. They could only visit her for short periods. She was out of bed now, sitting up in a wheelchair. They could push her around the hospital and put her chair near the window so she could look out. Her room faced the parking lot, which wasn't the best view, especially for someone who loved the country, but it was something. The nurses said Abby's rehabilitation was going well and she had more mobility in her right hand. But she would never walk again.

Allyson pulled her fingers out of the calf's mouth. The calf's eyes widened and it strained forward, reaching for her fingers again.

"You're not getting anything from me now," she said, her voice soft. She started thinking about Jeff. She'd had a good time with him and Amber at the elevator. He'd given her another graphic novel, a collection of stories about "Tank Girl," a tough girl who was in love with a kangaroo and drove around in a tank. The comics were wild, a little too sexual in a way. When Allyson sat up in her room late at night, reading them, she felt uneasy, as if she was reading something that she shouldn't be reading.

Jeff had been so kind to her lately. There were several mornings when he had come by her locker to give her books or just to say hi. Sometimes she thought about him when she went to sleep, thinking about what she would say to him if he was at her locker the next day. Did he like her? She thought he might, but the whole thing was confusing. Should she ask him? Should she ask Amber what to do? She'd never talked about boys with Amber. It just wasn't one of the things they talked about. Was Jeff just being nice to her because he was her friend? Or did he want something more?

Allyson heard the sound of a truck on gravel, and looked up to see Chloe and Colton in Colton's black truck. He always kept his car clean and shiny, and had paid a lot of money buying flashy rims for his wheels.

She took her hands off the calf's head, wiped her sticky fingers on her jeans and walked away from the fence. The calf, unsure what to do, followed her along the fence line for a minute. Chloe and Colton got out of the truck and went into their respective houses. Allyson started back to her own house, kicking up dust with her shoes as she walked. She opened the door to her home and went inside. The sound of the television blared from downstairs. Colton was in the kitchen, rummaging around for something to eat. The fridge door closed and the cupboards banged, and Colton stomped downstairs to the television room. She poked her head into the kitchen. A mustard covered knife sat next to a pile of crumbs on the side of the sink. Her mother was going to have a bird if she saw his mess. Allyson thought about cleaning it up, but didn't. Let Colton face up to it. God knows he got away with enough stuff around here.

She climbed the stairs to her room and pulled her trumpet out of its case, admiring its gold shininess and the curve of its bell.

She should draw a soldier with a trumpet. Or maybe she'd just sketch the trumpet itself, all its golden lines and the white mother-of-pearl on the keys.

She heard footsteps outside the door.

"Did you have a good time at the elevator?" her mother asked.

Allyson nodded.

"There's some hamburger soup in the fridge if you want some dinner," her mother said.

Ever since the border closed, her mother had been cooking beef all the time, even more than normal. Everybody in town was cooking and eating beef. Joe's was selling more steaks and hamburgers than ever before, as people tried to show their support for the ranchers in the area.

Her mother walked into the room and ran her fingers over her daughter's hair.

"You okay, sweetie?" she asked. "So much has happened and we haven't really talked about it."

"I'm fine," Allyson said, pulling her head away from her mother's hand.

"You sleeping okay?"

"I sleep. I have to read a lot before I fall asleep, but I'm sleeping," she said.

"Well, if you want to talk," her mother started.

"I need to practice," Allyson said, cutting her off.

"All right," her mother said. She turned to leave the room. "You're a good girl," she said, as she stood in the doorway. "The best."

Allyson didn't say anything. Instead, she raised her trumpet to her lips and started to play. Afterward, she put on her pyjamas and slipped down under the covers. Tonight she was going to re-read *The Wizard of Oz*. It was one of her favourite movies, and the book was almost as good. Grandpa Al had bought this copy for her. It was a beautiful hardcover with illustrations, pristine except for the small coffee stain on the back where Colton had put a coffee cup on top of it. She opened the pages and smelled the book. She could always lose herself in a book.

There was one thing that always bugged her about *The Wizard of Oz*. She could never understand why Dorothy would want to go back to Kansas, back to a boring farm. In Oz, she had friends and adventures. Sure, she might miss Aunty Em and Uncle Henry, but she would get over it. Why would she want to go back to a farm where nothing happened? Allyson would pick Oz over Kansas any day.

★

A week after the family moved Abby into the lodge, they brought her home for a Sunday dinner. She refused to go into her own house, and wouldn't have been able to manage all the stairs in Gord and Donna's house, so they decided to have dinner at Craig and Linda's. Allyson watched from Craig and Linda's front window as her dad lifted Gramma down from the truck. Gramma looked so small and broken in his arms, like a tiny bird. Gramma Abby was in her late sixties, which was impossibly old, but ever since the accident, she looked ancient. When she moved her hand or her head, her movements were slow, as if she was pushing her limbs through water. Allyson wondered how such big people like her dad and Craig could have emerged from such a small woman.

Her dad put Gramma Abby in the wheelchair and rolled her across the yard. When they got to the steps, her dad lifted Gramma out of the wheelchair again and carried her up the steps while Craig carried the wheelchair. Linda, who was waiting by the window, went to open the door.

"So glad you're here," she said, watching as Abby was carried past her. "Dinner is almost ready."

"Nice to see you, Gramma," Allyson said. Colton and Chloe were in the TV room. Her mother was in the kitchen. Craig and Gord settled Abby back into the wheelchair. Then they placed a striped blue and white afghan over her lap. She clutched at it with her good hand as they wheeled her into the dining room.

"Might as well get you set up right away," Craig said.

"Maybe we can start taking you around to see some of your friends for visits," Gord said, sitting down at the table. Abby didn't say anything. Allyson stood in the doorway of the dining room, watching everyone.

"Why bother?" Abby said. "Anybody wants to see me, they can just come to the lodge." She looked down at her hands. "Not too many people want to come see a cripple."

Gord put his hand on her shoulder. "Don't talk like that, Mom."

"It'll just be a few minutes until dinner," Linda called from the kitchen. "Donna is just mashing the potatoes."

Gord walked into the kitchen, away from his mother. Craig left too, leaving Allyson alone with her grandma.

She thought about leaving the room, but that seemed awkward. So she sat down at the table, across from her grandma. The two of them sat in silence.

"Go wash your hands," Donna called from the kitchen. "Dinner is in two minutes."

Gord came in from the kitchen, carrying a carton of milk and a basket of buns.

Linda walked into the dining room, hands full with a ceramic dish full of green beans. "Don't you like the new table cloth I bought?" she asked, setting the beans down and stroking the yellow and blue plaid cloth. "It's so sunny and cheerful."

Abby just grunted. Allyson stared at her. Who was this person?

There was the clatter of feet as Chloe and Colton entered the room.

"Hi, Gramma," Chloe said. She walked over and kissed her gramma on the cheek. Colton jerked his head at her in a nod, and sat down at the table. He poured himself a glass of milk and gulped it down.

"I'll sit beside her in case she needs anything," Donna said. "I can help her out."

"I'll be okay," Abby said, her voice hoarse and raspy.

Allyson wished this wasn't happening. This was not the homecoming that she wanted for her grandma. It was as if her dad had wheeled in a corpse, not the chatty, smiling, busy woman Allyson remembered. She tried to remember if she'd

ever been to a family dinner where Abby had been the one waiting at the table. She hadn't. Abby was always the one in the
kitchen, carrying things out, making sure the kids had milk, that
everyone had everything they needed. If Grandpa Al stopped by
the stove to taste something, she swatted him on the behind with
a tea towel.

"Are you glad to be home, Gramma?" Allyson asked, touching her Gramma's good hand. Abby pulled it back. "I'm not
home," she said. "Home is next door, with Al. And I can't go
back there again."

Before Allyson could answer, Gord came in from the kitchen
with a platter of roast beef. Donna followed behind, carrying
mashed potatoes. Craig entered the dining room, a beer in each
hand.

"I got one for you," he said to Gord, putting it in front of
him. The family assembled themselves around the table. Donna
sat on one side of Abby and Linda on the other.

"Do you need me to cut up your meat for you?" Linda said.

Abby looked at her. "I can only use one of my hands properly," she said. "What do you think?"

Linda drew back, as if surprised by the way Abby had spoken
to her.

"I'll make you up a plate," Donna said, patting her mother
in law on the shoulder.

The family was quiet for a few minutes, passing dishes
around the table, loading up on food.

"So, Colton," Craig said. "How is the repair business
going?"

"Good," Colton said, as he took a bite of homemade bun.
"It's a little slower though. Boss says everything has slowed down
since the border closed. They see it everywhere. A lot of people
don't have money to spend."

Abby picked up her fork and speared a piece of roast beef.
"The whole thing is a damn shame," she said.

"Oh, I forgot," Linda said and she bounced up from the
table and left the room. She returned a few minutes later with a
pair of knitted yellow and green slippers.

"Mabel Jacobson gave me these for you," she said, holding them in front of Abby. The colour combination reminded Allyson of the time she looked into a Kleenex when she had a sinus infection. "She thought you might like them. Are your feet cold? Do you want me to put them on you now?"

Abby shook her head. Allyson wondered if her gramma thought they were ugly too. She might be biting her tongue to keep from saying something.

"How are the cows?" Abby said.

"A bull got out a couple days ago," Craig said. "We had to chase him all over to try and get him back in. We lost a few hours of work."

"Which one?" Abby asked.

"Top Gun."

"That boy's got a temper," Abby said. "Al didn't like him. You should sell him."

"Maybe we will," Gord said. "If we could get any money for him. That's just not happening right now."

"Well," Abby said. "Just hang onto the farm. Just keep it up and running. That's what Al would want. This is his legacy. He's built this whole place."

She stared down at her plate. She poked at the roast beef and green beans.

"Is everything okay?" Donna asked. "Do you need any-thing?"

Abby started to cry. "It feels wrong to be here without Al," she said. "I don't think I've ever had dinner with all of you with-out him. And I didn't even like seeing my house, knowing he's not going to be there."

Donna stood up and stroked Abby's back. "Shh," she said. "It's okay."

Allyson couldn't remember the last time she'd ever seen Gramma Abby cry. She had no patience for tears. She always mocked Donna, the bawl baby of the family, whenever she cried at a tear-jerker movie.

"What's up with Clay?" Linda asked. "He still thinking about becoming a vet?"

She was trying to change the subject. Clay was her gramma's favourite and she stopped crying and perked up at the mention of his name. She tried to pretend that he wasn't her favourite, but they all knew he was.

"His marks aren't good enough," Donna said.

Donna was still rubbing Abby's back. Abby turned to look at her, annoyed and Donna stopped, and sat back down. Her fork lay on a mound of mashed potatoes, untouched.

"Guess you're our last hope for a vet in this family," Linda said with a smile, looking at her daughter. "You've got the marks."

Allyson wasn't offended. If anyone in the family would be a vet it would be Chloe, since she loved animals more than anyone.

Abby, who had stopped crying, snorted. "She's your last hope for everything." Her voice turned dark and mean. "That's what happens when you only have one kid."

Linda's face turned red. She turned her head down, as if she wanted to bury herself in her plate. She slouched forward, as if she had been punched.

"Too bad you couldn't have any more babies," Abby said.

Craig stood up. "Mom, that's enough."

Allyson looked across the table at Chloe. Her cousin looked back at her, her eyebrows raised. If Chloe had spoken out loud, she would have said, "Holy shit, I can't believe this is happening."

Allyson had heard about the dead babies, especially about the son who had been born after Chloe, before she herself had been born. He only lived a short while and died from something called Sudden Infant Death Syndrome. Chloe's brother had been named James Albert. Allyson had never seen a picture of him, but Clay told her the baby had red hair, like Grandpa Al. He was buried in the family plot too. He was one of those things you didn't talk about.

"And you," Abby said, turning to Donna. There were little bits of white saliva flecks around Abby's mouth. Her pink lipstick smudged around her lips. In the past, Abby would have never appeared with makeup that was less than perfect. "You can't do anything right."

Chloe stood up.

"What the fuck is wrong with you?" she said to her grandma.

"Chloe," Craig said, his voice a sharp bark. "Go to your room."

"You can't order me to my room," Chloe said. "I'm seventeen."

"Don't talk back to your grandma," Craig said. "And sit back down or go to your room."

"I don't know why we're all pretending everything is normal," Chloe said. "Because it's not. This isn't normal."

Allyson caught her brother's eye. She didn't dare move. Colton's eyes usually looked heavy-lidded, as if he'd smoked a bunch of weed, but right now, they were wide open.

Chloe left the room.

"You're grounded," Craig called. "Don't you dare leave the house."

Allyson heard the sound of her cousin's feet as she stomped up the stairs. She looked down at her plate. Her food no longer looked appealing at all.

Colton and Gord kept on eating, as if they were trying to pretend a hell mouth hadn't opened up around them.

"I want to go back to the lodge," Abby said. "I'm tired."

"Why don't we take you upstairs?" Gord said. "I can carry you up and you can have a little lie down."

"Why don't you finish your dinner first?" Craig said.

"Just take me home," Abby said. "It's too hard for me to be here."

Donna looked at her husband. "Maybe you should just take her," she said.

Gord stood up. "Come on, Mom," he said. "Let's go."

Linda started towards the kitchen. "I'll put together a doggie bag for her," she said. "She can take some of that back to the lodge."

Gord turned to his brother. "Come on," he said. "I'm going to need your help here."

Allyson faced her mother, wondering what was going to happen. Her mother glanced first at her, and then at Colton. "Just keep eating your dinner," she said. "Some of us might as well enjoy it." She wasn't eating either.

Allyson kept her head down while her dad wheeled Abby out of the room. Linda was already in the kitchen. Allyson heard the bang of cupboard doors and the clatter of dishes as her aunt moved around. Colton picked up his fork. When he stabbed a few green beans, the tines of his fork scraped across the plate. Allyson looked at her mother, wanting to ask to be excused. But when she saw the expression on her mother's face, she knew better than to speak.

★

The next day, Allyson ran into her cousin in the barn. Chloe sat on some hay bales, scratching the tortoise shell cat she called Buffy. Willow, the orange cat, sat on her lap, purring.

"Come sit with me," Chloe said.

Chloe hadn't asked her to do anything like that in months. Allyson sat down next to her cousin. Her hoodie rode up and a piece of hay poked her in the back. It was chilly. The snow would be coming soon. Maggie was curled up behind Chloe, sleeping.

"I'm so glad I'm getting out of here," said Chloe. "I can't wait to leave. It's going to be so nice to be in Edmonton."

Maggie stood up and came over to Allyson. Her doggy smell was soothing and familiar. Her calm brown eyes studied Allyson.

"I can't believe Gramma Abby," Chloe said. "Pretty soon everyone is just going to start blurting out shit. It's like Grandpa Al used to say. You can bury something, but it never stays buried. It doesn't go into the ground. Eventually, it all comes to the surface."

This was the most Chloe had said to her in a long time. Maybe, if she just listened, her cousin would tell her why she barely talked to her any more. Soon her cousin would leave the farm and would have a whole other life, just like Clay.

When Clay came home, he talked to her about his friends. About how he'd gone to the Sikh temple with his roommate, Arjun, and how Arjun's dad wore a turban and his mom had a long black braid that hung down her back. He had gone to their house and eaten something called samosas. Soon Chloe would have a whole different life like that too. Chloe would take the LRT by herself and go shopping on Whyte Avenue. Maybe eventually she'd have an apartment, and buy wines with intricate designs on the labels. She would never come back to the farm.

"You're not listening to me, are you?" Chloe said. Willow jumped off her lap and ran across the barn.

"I am listening," Allyson said.

"You're daydreaming again," said Chloe. "That's probably the only way you can stand being here. I don't know what you've been hearing from your parents, but shit is about to get ugly. Last night was just the start of it. We're sitting on a powder keg."

"What do you mean?" Allyson said. She was lost. Chloe was talking another language, an adult language, walking around in the adult world like she owned it.

"Grandpa Al didn't have a will," said Chloe. "He owned everything. Dad and Uncle Gord worked for him like employees. That's why Dad has always been trying to do so much off the farm. Get some of his own money. Save up for me to go to school. We're not scrambling around like you guys."

Allyson's face was hot and her stomach hurt. She curled her fingers in Maggie's fur, digging down deep.

"I know it's hard to hear this," Chloe said. She leaned over, rustled around in her purse and found a pack of cigarettes. She pulled a single cigarette out of the crumpled red pack, stuck it between her lips and lit it with a lighter. She inhaled, then exhaled with a deep sigh.

"Smoking is so bad for you," Allyson said. How had Chloe forgotten the pact they had made years ago, the promise they had made to each other not to smoke?

"Makes me feel kind of alive right now," Chloe said.

"How do you know all this stuff?" Allyson said. "I mean, all the stuff with the family."

"I just listen," Chloe said, exhaling. "If you pay attention, someone flaps their gums at some point."

Chloe finished smoking and stubbed out the cigarette, taking care to put the dead butt in her pocket.

"I feel sorry for you," Chloe said, as she stood up. "I'm counting down the days until I leave."

She picked up her purse and walked out of the barn.

CHAPTER 8

Gord came into the house, slammed the door behind him and clomped up the stairs to the kitchen.

"God damn it," he said. "Donna, I finally found out what Craig is doing."

It was the day after the family dinner that ended with Abby's outburst. Donna pulled a sheet of chocolate chip cookies out of the oven and placed it on the stove to cool. The chips were swollen and misshapen, like clods of dirt. They would probably taste okay. She couldn't eat much these days, but everyone else seemed to be eating more.

"What?" she asked, as Gord came into the kitchen.

"Craig told me why they were at the lawyer's when we were talking about what happened with Mom last night." He grabbed a glass out of the cupboard, turned on the tap and filled the glass with water.

Donna waited for him to speak. He walked over to the oven and put his finger on a cookie.

"Careful," she said. But it was too late. Gord pulled his hand back as a stray chocolate chip stuck to his fingers.

"They were checking the land title," he said. "They did it without us."

Gord gulped down some water, filled his glass again and drank some more. She took a cloth from the sink and wiped the counter, even though she'd wiped it down twice already. The kids always teased her about her constant counter wiping. Colton said he left piles of crumbs behind so Donna had something to wipe up.

"They were talking to the lawyer to see who can get on the title after Mom dies. She's the owner of the land now. So Craig wanted to see if he can own it, or if we have to co-own it."

"Well, it sounds like he's taking care of things," Donna said. "Thinking ahead."

Gord set his glass down on the table and stared at her. "God damn," he said. "It's like you have been living somewhere else for over twenty years. You've been on the farm for over half your life, but you don't pay attention to what's happening. It's frustrating."

"I don't want a lecture right now," Donna said.

"He didn't bother to ask me about going to the lawyer. He could be trying to get it all in his name. I feel like they're playing us, doing all this stuff without telling me," Gord said. His face was red and sweaty.

Donna felt as though she was swimming through deep water, unable to get to the surface. Every time she tried to understand something happening at the farm, with the money or the cows, she just sunk deeper into the murk. Lately, when people talked about the simplest things in their lives, it sounded like noise to her. Even when people came into the store to chit chat with her, she found herself growing annoyed with them, wishing they would leave her alone.

"What does this mean for us?" she asked.

"I don't know," Gord said. He slumped down into the chair, his water glass in front of him. "I need a drink." He walked to the liquor cabinet and took out a bottle of Crown Royal. Lifting the bottle up, he peered at the amber liquid.

"This looks a lot lower," he said. "Has Colton been drinking this?"

"He's barely been around," Donna said.

Gord took out a shot glass, poured himself a shot and downed it. "I just need something to take the edge off," he said, pouring another. When he was finished it, he shuffled the empty glass back and forth between dirty fingers.

"You need to pay more attention to what is happening around here. We shouldn't have let Mom and Dad take care of everything. You weren't involved in the business decisions, and that's all coming to a head. Dad and I were working together and Craig was off doing his thing. Now you and I are paying for it.

And unless we can start moving cows for a good price, we'll be paying for it in other ways."

He gripped the glass. He had such big hands, and the glass was so small. What if he crushed it between his fingers? She had never doubted his toughness and his abilities, but she worried about him since Al died. Gord used to be young, strong and invincible, like the cowboys in the movies. Now he was older, tired and broken. His paunch was rounder and there were more lines around his eyes.

Gord poured himself another shot, but didn't drink it.

"If the border stays closed, it'll push our retirement back years. But I'd rather dip into that money than spend the money we've saved for Allyson's university."

Donna put her hands on her husband's and wrestled the glass away from him. "Enough," she said. "Stop talking like that." She took the bottle of Crown Royal and put it on the counter. "It's the middle of the day."

"It's the only way I can keep from exploding," Gord said. "Drinking takes the edge off."

"Does this have anything to do with last night?" she asked.

"I don't know," Gord said. "Mom's really not herself. It's upsetting."

"You can't start drinking every time you feel bad," she said. "That's how people end up alcoholics. You need to do something else. Drink some tea, listen to music, take a shower. Go for a walk. Go visit somebody. Don't hide in a bottle."

"You've been watching too much Oprah," he said.

"Just trying to tell it like it is," she said. "You lost your dad. You think I don't miss him too? You think I haven't noticed you out in the yard, moping around, crying when you don't think anyone is looking. I've seen you," she said. Everything was coming out in a rush, like water spilling out of the tap.

Gord studied his hands. "You don't know how bad things are," he said. "They keep saying on the news that the border could be closed for months. I talked to Phil Hill, and he tried to sell a bull and got pennies for it. After he paid the commission, he couldn't even afford to get two hamburgers from A & W. How can we live like this? We got two mouths to feed and a kid that will be going off to university soon. I'm working my ass off here trying to make up for everything that Dad did. And my mom is going to live out the rest of her life in the lodge as a cripple."

He grabbed her hand. "I just wish you could get this. I know that there's a big part of you that hates this farm and that you moved here. I know you hate it here. I've known that for years. But I need you to understand what we're dealing with. Because this problem is bigger than this ranch. The entire beef industry could go down if things don't get better."

Gord was right. She was a failure. She should pay more attention to what was happening on the ranch. She'd been a child, relying on Abby and Al to take care of everything. And now they were gone, right in the middle of a cattle crisis, and everything was falling apart around them.

"What can I do?" she asked. Gord's tone grated her, the way he'd spoken to her in such a condescending way. Other things in her life had sucked over the years, but things between her and Gord had generally been good. If she hadn't loved him, her in-laws, and the kids, she never would have stayed. She would have hightailed it back to Saskatoon at the first opportunity.

"You're going to need to find some ways that we can get some more money," he said. "And close your wallet as much as you can. We need to be frugal."

He leaned in close to her, as if he was going to tell her a secret.

"Keep your eye on Linda and Craig. We need to make sure they don't do anything else."

He cleared his throat and coughed. She could smell the warmth of the whiskey on his breath. There was a sourness to the smell of his body. She wondered what was happening to him. Maybe he was starting to decay on the inside, as worry ate away at him.

She held his hand in hers, squeezing the familiar width of his hand. Ran her fingers along the backside of his hands, felt the spots on his knuckles where cuts had healed over, leaving little ridges on his hands. She loved his rough, imperfect hands, like a real cowboy's.

Gord stood up.

"I'm going to go watch TV," he said. "Do we have any chips?"

She pointed to a cupboard and watched as he took a bag of Hawkins Cheezies and shuffled out of the room. Cheezies were gross, but the boys, Gord and Allyson had always loved them. Gord left orange fingerprints on things after he'd been eating Cheezies, and blamed it on the kids.

Gord's back had a slight hunch, as if he was too tired to stand up. Did aging happen that fast? Maybe it was happening to her too. The cookies were cool now. She picked one up and ate it. It tasted good, sweet and rich. Using a spatula, she scooped up the cookies into a cookie tin that Abby had given her. The cookie tin had a Holstein cow on it and was dented where one of the kids had dropped it.

Donna picked the whiskey bottle up off the counter and went to put it in the cupboard. Then she thought better of it. Gord had been taking too many nips out of the bottle. She should hide it. If he asked, she could blame it on Colton. She took the bottle and glanced towards the family room. She could hear Ian Hanomansing talking. She couldn't make out all the words, but there was a sense of urgency in his voice. He was probably talking about Iraq or the border closure. Maybe an update on SARS. When she thought about everything that was happening in the world, she had trouble breathing. It was such a scary place. Even things that seemed innocent, like cows chewing their cuds in a field, could turn dangerous, wild and unwieldy if provoked. Who knows what would happen next? Two years ago, she watched the news as planes slammed into the Twin Towers. Anita, always a sensitive soul, had been so affected by the news that she closed the store and gave Donna and Bonnie time off. Even when they'd opened the store days later, it had been quiet. No one wanted to come in to buy wedding, anniversary or birthday cards. They couldn't imagine the world could just go on, that things could continue happening in the face of tragedy. Donna saw this with her own family after Al's death. It felt like though things should stop, but they just kept on going.

But her entire family had gotten older and more worn. Allyson seemed to have retreated even further into her books and drawings. Colton was gone all the time, out with Lily Stevens. Donna didn't trust her. She knew all about that type of girl. Always thinking with her pants down, trying to get ahead by using her tits. Donna had met women like her before. She'd even been friends with one of them in university, a girl named Rebecca. But when she started dating Gord, she and Rebecca lost touch. Rebeca didn't even come to the wedding. Some of Donna's other friends had come, but she hadn't been able to maintain friendships with her city friends after Clay was born. Sometimes she wondered what would have happened to her if she hadn't met Gord, hadn't gotten pregnant, hadn't left Saskatoon when she was so young. Would she have a good group of girlfriends in the city? Would they dress in stylish clothes and go to movies, plays and concerts? Who would this other her be? She would have finished school. Maybe she would be in a big city somewhere, living a glamorous life, working in an office and wearing suits. But even when she imagined these other lives, her chest tightened when she thought about life without Gord and her kids. When her children were born, she leaned over their cribs, surveying the rise and fall of their tiny chests. *Keep breathing*, she would whisper to them. *Stay in this world.*

The whiskey bottle was a weight in her hand. She debated where to hide it. She didn't want to hide it in the house, but she couldn't just throw it out. It was such a waste to dump it. Maybe she could hide it in the barn, behind the hay bales. If anyone found it, she'd blame it on Al and his fondness for taking a nip while he looked at the cattle. He always said there was nothing better than standing out on his land, looking at all he'd built and all they had created, while enjoying a sip of whiskey.

She walked towards the door and put on her cowboy boots. She closed the door with a click behind her, careful not to bang it. No need to make Gord come down and see her going out into the yard with a bottle of booze.

As she started towards the barn, Maggie and Rascal came up to greet her. Their doggy scent and wagging tails were comforting. She would have loved to have a house dog, but Al always teased her and Gord never would have allowed it. The air outside was crisp.

As she continued towards the barn, she glanced over at Abby and Al's house, looming like a sentinel over the yard. If she didn't know better, she would have sworn the house was watching her. Out of the corner of her eye, she saw the door open. Her breath caught in her chest. Even though Donna knew Abby and Al were gone, she half expected to see one of them in the doorway. But it was Linda, emerging from the house with plastic bags in her hands. As Donna watched, she closed the door behind her.

As soon as she saw Linda, Donna felt both irritable and enraged. Linda was trespassing. Donna stopped moving and stood still. The hand holding the whiskey bottle rested against her leg.

"What are you doing in the house?" she asked as Linda came down the steps. "Why do you keep going in there?"

"Cleaning," Linda said. "If I didn't, everything would be covered in dust. Besides, someone needs to check it. We don't want to get mice in there."

It was just like Linda, trying to take care of things without asking anybody, trying to control everything.

"What's in the bags?" she asked.

"A few quilts and a couple of blouses. Maybe some things that Abby would want at the lodge."

"You going to visit her?" Donna asked.

"In a while," Linda said. "Not today. Not after last night."

"I hear you and Craig are looking into the title."

Linda shuffled her weight from foot to foot, and transferred one of the plastic bags to her other hand. The bags looked heavy. Linda wore pink Converse high tops. She must have borrowed Chloe's shoes.

Linda stared off into the distance, searching for something out on the land, tempting Donna to look in the same direction.

"We can't do this anymore," Donna said. "We need to work together. There are only four adults here now."

"The farm is Abby's and she can decide what she wants to do with it. And I should tell you, Craig was the one who insisted we go to the lawyer's alone. I wanted to bring you two."

"Why didn't you say something to him?"

Linda snorted. "I can barely talk to him. He just works all the time. He's been a stone since Al's death. Hasn't even cried. Barely sleeps. He's been trying to get as much work as possible. It's like he's afraid that if he stops moving, he might have feelings."

Donna's voice got small. "How is your money situation?"

Linda glared at her. Her gaze was so intense that Donna felt herself wilt.

"I'm not going to tell you that. That's private," she said.

She took a gulp of air. "I swear, Donna, you don't pay attention to anything that happens out here. You're not a country person and you never have been. You just like to pretend you are, with your boots and your Dolly Parton CDs and your love of cowboy movies. But now you're going to have to get real. You're going to have to saddle up and help us out now that Abby and Al are gone. You're going to have to be a real farm wife."

"I live here, don't I?" Donna said. "I'm not acting on my own. I'm trying to help everyone. Al would be rolling in his grave if he knew how you two were behaving."

"No, you're wrong," Linda said. "He'd say the exact same thing."

Donna could feel tears behind her eyes. She hated being the family bawl baby. When she started to cry in the middle of a fight, she felt like a child.

"We're all hurting and we're all trying to figure out what we need to do. And everyone is stressed because of the whole cattle thing," she said.

"You're telling me," Linda said. "You're the one who is walking around oblivious to everything."

Donna could feel a harsh knot building in her chest. All the ugliness inside Linda had unleashed itself and landed on her.

"I'm not oblivious," she said. She put her hand in Maggie's fur. She concentrated on the sound of the dog's panting, their pink tongues and bright eyes. She was okay. The dogs wouldn't be around her if she weren't a good person.

"I see what's happening to us," she said. "We're all on our way to some dark place."

She willed herself not to cry; she was so sick of crying. Tired of fighting. She looked at her sister-in-law and saw fear on her face. Her features, which had been pinched and closed a few seconds ago, softened. This was the same woman who had helped her with her newborn babies. The same woman who cheered alongside her as the kids took their first steps. They had been so close when the kids were small. But then Linda started teaching, and they stopped hanging out with each other as much.

"I gotta go," Linda said, adjusting her bags again. The handles of the bags left red marks on her skin.

"Want me to take one of those?" Donna asked.

"I'm okay," said Linda.

"Let me know if you decide to do anything else," Donna said. "You guys can't keep sneaking around. We all need to be on the same page."

Linda nodded, turned her back and started towards the house. Then she turned around and called over her shoulder.

"I just gotta ask," she said. "Why are you carrying around a half empty bottle of Crown Royal?"

★

The winter was long and uneventful. When Donna thought of it, all she could think of was a long stretch of highway and grey and worry. Visits to the lodge to see Abby. Gord monitoring the news every day to see if the border had opened. The family tiptoeing around one another, going through the motions, trying to pretend things were normal when they weren't. Donna worried about money. The farmers waited for the border to open, but nothing happened. They waited for aid packages and government money and nothing came. There was just an endless space of grief, and grey and not knowing and waiting. And then it was summer time again.

CHAPTER 9

"Holy crap, Dad, look at Spirit," Allyson said, pointing as Gord drove past. Spirit was the large, black bronco statue that a local artist had built and donated to the town when the town was created.

"Can you stop the truck?"

Her father idled the truck near a crowd of people gathered around Spirit. Spirit was the town mascot. The local hockey team was called the Mustangs. Town businesses featured Mustangs in their logos. Allyson had asked Gord about the history once, but he couldn't remember if there had been a famous mustang in town, or if it was something the town had just adopted. No one knew why the horse was named Spirit. Spirit's sculptor had made sure the animal was anatomically correct, with a large scrotum and pendulous balls. It was popular for townspeople to get visitors to have their photos snapped beside Spirit's oversized genitalia.

Allyson rolled down her window and leaned out of the truck.

"I can't see," Gord said. "My eyes aren't as good as yours."

"The grads must have done it as a prank," Allyson said. She started to laugh. "If you get out of the truck or drive a little closer, you'll see it," she said. "Spirit's balls are bright gold."

Her father started to laugh too. "It would save us a lot of trouble if good stock had gold balls."

Gord parked the truck. "I need a better look at this."

Mabel Jacobson was among the crowd of people gathered at the base of the statue.

"It's a crying shame," Mabel said as Gord and Allyson approached. "Who would take Spirit's dignity like that?"

"Yes," Gord said, trying to keep a straight face. "How could they do such a thing?"

Allyson couldn't even remember the last time she'd seen her father laugh or smile. The Klassens watched as an RCMP officer joined the crowd. This officer had only been in town for a few months, but there were already rumours flying that he was gay. He was a good-looking single man who lived alone. Allyson had overheard a bunch of women talking about him one day when she'd been at Joe's.

"We better get going," Gord said. "Much as I'd like to stay and watch this, I don't want you to be late for practice."

Allyson nodded. They walked back to the truck and drove towards the school.

"Break a leg," Gord said. "You've been practicing a lot.

"I'll see you soon. I'll be so cleaned up that you won't even recognize me."

Allyson grabbed her trumpet case and unbuckled her seat belt.

"See you in a bit," she said, and started toward the school.

★

The gymnasium was too hot. Allyson could feel sweat gathering under the armpits of her white blouse. She should have listened to her mother and worn short sleeves. It was so warm on the stage. Thank God no one was looking at the band. The audience was all staring at Mr. Warsylewicz, the principal, as he talked to the graduates and their families. The band had finished the overture and only had to play Pomp and Circumstance while the graduates accepted their diplomas from Mr. Walrus. The principal had earned his nickname because of his huge belly and multiple chins. Mr. Walrus had been droning on for several minutes, so Allyson looked at her family in the third row. Her dad was wearing his black Stetson and a red plaid short-sleeved shirt with a black bolo tie. He'd even cleaned his cowboy boots. Her mom looked pretty in her peach dress. She looked less tired than she normally looked. Colton sat beside her, his long legs stretched out in front of him as he leaned back, contemplating the ceiling. Allyson had heard her mother and Colton arguing last night. Colton had wanted to bring Lily Stevens to grad but Donna had forbidden it. Allyson heard the whole argument from upstairs.

"She's my girlfriend, Mom," Colton said.

"I don't care," her mother said, sounding like a petulant child. "She doesn't get to sit with us."

Then Colton started in on how his mother didn't like Lily and didn't accept her. The argument wasn't anything Allyson hadn't heard before. She knew her mother didn't want Lily to become anything serious. It was weird that her mother seemed to want Colton to be single, and Clay to get a girlfriend. When he was in high school, she'd look at the pictures of the girls in the yearbook and point out the pretty ones to Clay.

Clay dated a girl named Nadine for a few months, but it had never gone anywhere. Nadine wore a lot of pink and giggled when she and Clay sat in the TV room, stealing kisses when they thought no one else was around.

Allyson didn't like Lily either. There was something about her that was dark. She looked at people down her nose, with her eyes slightly closed as if she knew something you didn't.

Clay sat on the other side of Colton. His white shirt showed off his arms. He had a bit of reddish stubble and wore a white cowboy hat. Allyson caught his eye and he raised his eyebrows at her and smirked a little with one side of his mouth. Uncle Craig, looking stoic and serious in his tan cowboy hat, sat beside Clay. Allyson looked forward to the day when she could go to an event and not be surrounded by cowboy hats. Seriously, her family looked like a bunch of hicks. It was like they thought they lived in Texas or something.

Aunty Linda dabbed at her eyes with a crumpled pink Kleenex that she had pulled from her purse. It couldn't be easy for Linda, now that her only child would be heading off to Edmonton in the fall. She and Craig would be rattling around their house, just the two of them. Linda's parents were sitting behind the rest of the family, but they weren't doing anything interesting. At that moment, Allyson missed her grandparents. If they had been there, they would have both been beaming at the stage. Linda had asked Abby if she wanted to come, but she said she didn't want to. Chloe hadn't visited her for months. Donna had told Abby they would take lots of pictures for her. She would bring the pictures to the lodge and give Abby a recap of the entire night. Allyson wondered why they kept on pretending that Abby cared about these things, when she clearly didn't. It was like Abby was looking at the world through a very thick pane of glass. She could look if she wanted, but there was no way she could touch or interact with anything, so there was no reason for her to bother.

"This is the time when our children become adults," Mr. Walrus said. "They will be moving forward, growing into men and women. And who knows what these young men and women will become? Do we have a Nobel prize winner in the bunch?"

He gestured his arm, pointing along the rows of graduating students. "Look at this group, ladies and gentlemen," he said. "One of these people could discover the cure for AIDS. We could have future doctors and lawyers in this group. One of these fine young people might write a Pulitzer-Prize-winning novel. Another could be the next Shania Twain."

Oh, please, Allyson thought. Half of the guys would end up in the oil patch. A number of the girls would end up pregnant by next year and would never leave town. They'd be talking about soaps, popping out the next bunch of townies and gossiping about their children and who was screwing who. Some of them would join the parent teacher council, and others would organize the curling bonspiel and decorate floats for the town rodeo parade.

Laura, the trumpet player who sat beside her, nudged her foot. "How much longer?" she whispered, ducking her face behind her music stand. "If he goes on for another ten minutes, I might pass out."

Allyson nodded. She could see Amber's long brown braid a few rows in front of her. Amber and her oboe sat right in the middle of the front row. Like her, Amber would leave town as fast as she could.

Mr. Walrus announced the valedictorian, Emily Chin. As Emily walked to the podium, Allyson scanned the crowd, looking for Jeff and his parents. Jeff sat a few rows from the front. Next to him, Joe and Winnie Chin beamed. Winnie wore a red sundress with white polka dots. Her red lipstick looked elegant. Joe wore a suit. He shuffled a little and hunched his shoulders up and down, adjusting his jacket as if he wasn't quite comfortable in it.

Emily started her speech with a clear, calm voice. Allyson had never really spoken to her. But Emily was well-liked, did well in sports, and got good marks.

Emily was talking about their future, how they were all going to go out into the world and make it this amazing place. Why were grad ceremonies supposed to be life-changing events? After today, the graduating class would take off their gowns and fancy suits and go back to being their pimply, smelly selves. Why did people need to talk about how amazing everyone was? The world wasn't so simple. These people weren't going to change it.

Allyson looked at Jeff. He was bent forward, listening to his sister's words. Emily was headed to the University of Alberta in the fall, Jeff said. She'd be a doctor or a lawyer. She would have degrees that she could hang on her walls. Allyson wanted to be one of those people too.

Jeff caught her eye and winked. She pointed to herself. "Me?" she mouthed. He nodded. She could feel her face getting hot. Did he like her? When people liked each other as boyfriend and girlfriend, things got messy and complicated.

The audience applauded and Emily walked off stage. Her pink sweetheart gown looked beautiful on her. Mr. Walrus came up to the microphone and started calling the graduates to the stand. They each walked to the middle of the stage to shake his hand, and then on to shake hands with Miss Shandler, the vice-principal. There were forty-five students to go through. People in the audience whooped and hollered when Tim Coates got his diploma. He pulled his arm down in a fist pump and yelled "Yeah!" waving at the crowd like he was a movie star. Allyson looked over at Jack, Connie and Tracy Coates. They were laughing and Connie Coates put her head in her hands and shook it like she was embarrassed. It was more of a joke than anything. Everyone loved Tim Coates.

Allyson watched as the rest of graduates paraded by. The Gs went by and then the Hs, including Josh Hutchinson, a guy Chloe had probably made out with. Allyson couldn't understand what her cousin had seen in him. He looked like an ugly, red-headed version of Matt Damon. He was good at hockey, though, and would probably get recruited by the WHL someday.

Chloe's name was called and she walked across the stage, her smile a little too big. Chloe walked like she had a stick up her butt. She did look pretty, though. Her strawberry blonde hair was piled on top of her head in an updo and her blue dress fitted her perfectly. She looked like a real grown-up, like someone who was going to go out and do something. This fall, Chloe was going to be able to floor her car, squeal out of town and leave a cloud of dust behind her.

Uncle Craig and Aunty Linda beamed from the audience. Craig, Linda's mom and Clay stood, cameras in front of their faces as they snapped away. Chloe reached Mr. Walrus and Miss Shandler, shook their hands and walked off stage with her piece of paper.

That was it, Allyson thought. Two minutes to cap off three years of hell. Those minutes on the stage meant that Chloe could leave now. She zoned out as the rest of the grads walked across the stage and took their diplomas. The whole thing reminded Allyson of the Miss America pageant.

As the last grad, Jordan Zebot, accepted his diploma, Mr. Taylor, the band teacher, walked onto the stage and stood in front of the band. He waved his baton around, cueing them. It was time to play "Pomp and Circumstance" as the grads departed.

With her trumpet raised to her mouth, she waited, poised. Mr. Taylor brought his baton up and they started the regal march. Allyson couldn't wait until she could march out of the room with the rest of the group. Once everyone in the auditorium had left, Mr. Taylor stopped them, and the sound of the song faded out, until the band members were left silent and alone in the empty auditorium.

CHAPTER 10

The town's Stampede parade was held two days after grad. The night before the parade, Gord asked Clay if he was willing to move back to the farm for the summer.

"I could really use your help," Gord said. Donna, Gord and Clay were sitting in the family room. Gord leaned back in his La-Z-Boy, waiting for his son's response, showing the same kind of nerves and anticipation of a romantic lead asking a lady on a date.

Donna sat beside Clay on the couch. The TV was on, but no one was watching it.

"I can't," Clay said. "I have things to do in the city."

He'd gotten a good job at the university farm for the summer, helping out with dairy experiments.

"I'm sorry, Dad," Clay said. "But it's about the money. You can't pay me, can you? I need that money for school."

Gord stared at his hands.

"You can't afford it, can you?"

Gord shook his head. "We're not doing so hot," he mumbled.

"I wish I could help you. But the money I can make in the city is just too good for me to pass up right now," Clay said. He walked over to stand next to his father. "It's not your fault. I don't blame you."

Gord looked so small and broken next to Clay. Was Clay still growing? Could you get taller in your mid-twenties? Was Gord already starting to wither and fade? Donna was afraid and she wasn't sure why. Gord reached for the remote and turned the TV on, ending the conversation. Clay left the room without saying anything. Gord started flicking through channels, and his eyes started to glaze over. Donna hated it when people skipped channels, but she said nothing. The stress was getting to Gord. He was trying to run the farm without Al and Abby, and dealing with the financial pressure, what he would do next and where the money would come from. The family hoped Abby would return to her regular self and magically appear as the person she had been before the accident, but this was not happening. She just wanted to stay in her room and stare out the window. Gord had taken to walking the fields, studying the cows. For the millionth time, Donna wished she was a better farm wife and could help. At least school was out and Linda would be around more. Colton hadn't been much help lately. He was getting more hours at the auto shop, which was good. He had barely been at home. Donna suspected he was shacking up with Lily. She needed to talk to Gord about giving Colton the boot, since he wasn't contributing to the house at all. He just came through the house like a tornado, making messes and scavenging through the fridge. He was old enough to move out. Clay had been out of the house by the time he was nineteen. Colton was now almost as old as she was when she'd gotten pregnant with Clay. Donna would have to talk to Gord before she told Colton he had to leave, and she wasn't ready to have that conversation.

Gord flipped past a cooking show and some music videos before landing on Paul Newman's face.

"Ooh, *Hud*," Donna exclaimed. The enthusiasm in her voice made Gord stop changing channels. They watched a few minutes of the movie. Then Donna remembered *Hud's* plotline. It wasn't just about hunky Paul Newman and his white undershirt. It was a movie about cattle, specifically about the death of cattle and the fall of a patriarch. In one of the movie's most disturbing scenes, the rancher, after killing his cattle because they were sick with hoof and mouth disease, crawled along a gravel road through dust and dirt.

"We don't have to watch this," she said. "You can change the channel."

"But you love Paul Newman," Gord said, without looking at her.

"Doesn't matter," she said. "Change the channel."

Pam would be arriving tomorrow to attend Stampede. She hadn't been for a visit for a while and said she wanted to come by and see everyone. Donna suspected that she wanted to see how everyone was doing.

"If money's tight," Pam said, during their weekly phone call. "You don't even have to ask. I'll help you out in any way I can."

"No," Donna said. "We can't take anything from you. Don't mention it again."

But money was tight. A couple days before grad, she'd come downstairs to see Gord, who had never worked off the farm in the entire time she had known him, looking through the classified ads in the newspaper. He sat at the kitchen table, hunched over the paper, his movements furtive as if he was afraid someone was going to catch him. Donna suggested that he ask Craig if anyone needed help with carpentry work, but Gord shook his head.

"I can't go piggy-backing on Craig," he said.

"So what are you going to do?" she asked.

"I'm looking at patch jobs," he said. "Maybe there's something there. Maybe one of the guys knows of something. I'll have to ask. But I thought it would be easier to go to the papers first."

He sighed and ran his hands through his hair. It stuck straight up on his head. He touched the stubble on his chin.

"I'm not sure what I can do," he said. "Would an employer hire some old guy like me when they can hire some kid?"

He looked down. "I'm not even sure how that would work anyway. How could I go to work when I have to do things around the farm?"

"What about trucking?" Donna asked. "Craig's done it. Didn't Phil Hill do it?"

Gord leaned over the table, propping his head up as if it was too heavy to lift. "The thing is, Donna, the trucking industry is hurting too. The cattle business is slowing everything down. There probably aren't any trucking jobs."

The border closure was affecting everyone differently. The Hills had sold some of their cattle during the drought last year, so they had fewer cattle and were doing okay. Because prices were so low and the markets weren't moving fast, a lot of people were planning on keeping their cattle instead of selling them. They had no way to get any money. The government still hadn't figured out any sort of aid package. Everyone was still waiting.

"This whole thing is a mess," Gord said. "The only time I really feel okay is when I'm out in the yard with the cows. I just put my head down, do what I'm supposed to do, and forget about all this nonsense."

After Gord went to bed that night, Donna confronted Clay in his bedroom.

"I'm worried about your dad," she confided, whispering so Gord couldn't hear. She closed Clay's bedroom behind her, and the door to the master bedroom was closed but she was still paranoid.

"I know," Clay said. "I wish I could come home and help," he said. "But Dad can't give me any money and my summer job is a really good opportunity. And I don't want to lose my place. Arjun would never be able to find a roommate on such short notice."

She looked at her son. She wished he could stay home too. "It's not your fault," she said. "But can you just come and visit more? Help out? Relieve some of the stress?"

Clay nodded. He stood up from his bed, where he had been sitting, playing solitaire on his laptop.

"I'll try to do what I can," Clay said. "It'll be okay, Mom."

He stood up and gave her a hug. She let him. When had he become the one to reassure her? And even though he said that everything would be okay, she strongly suspected that it wouldn't. They'd been treading water for months now. Thank God they'd made it through winter to the summer. Things could only get better.

*

Donna hoped the parade would help everyone forget about what they were going through, at least momentarily. Clay, Allyson, Craig, Linda and Gord were all downtown for the parade. Chloe and Colton had been called to work. A group of ranchers had a big float to remind everyone to keep eating beef and support the local cattle industry, even though the border was closed. The men dressed up in full cowboy gear. Some of them were on horseback, while others would sit on the float that Phil Hill and his wife Marian had built out on their farm. The float featured a big barbecue, with the slogans "Eat Alberta Beef", "We Love Beef" and "Save our Ranchers" all over the sides. Allyson was on a float with the other school band members who weren't lucky enough to leave town for summer holidays.

Memorable Moments would be busy, because everyone would be hanging out on Main Street during the parade.

When she arrived at *Memorable Moments*, Donna gave the floor a sweep before opening the front doors. The store was packed with people browsing cards and stationery. No one was buying much. Anita had noticed that a while ago, and mentioned it to Donna almost apologetically.

"It's the whole cattle business," she said. "Everything is slower. Even Kelly's silhouettes aren't selling at the same rate. People are feeling the pinch."

As the parade got ready to start, families lined the streets with their lawn chairs, the little ones dressed in cowboy gear. It was hard for Donna not to feel a little cheerier when she looked at their smiling, excited faces. The kids were ready to dive into the street and pick up candy as people threw it from their parade floats. The whole town went crazy for Stampede. Businesses decorated their offices to look western, and the whole town, even people who had never been on a ranch, brought out their cowboy hats, belt buckles and tight jeans. It was a good time. Donna always liked going to the rodeo. She knew bull riding was stupid and dangerous, and every time she watched it, she thanked her lucky stars that none of the men in her family had ever thought to take it up. But when she was watching it, as she and Pam were going to do that evening, she always felt a thrill of excitement and an almost sexual feeling as the sweating mass of the bull bucked and thrashed and the handsome cowboy on his back held on for dear life. Even though she was glad Gord had never taken up rodeo, she definitely understood the attraction.

It would be good to hang out with Pam tonight. They'd take in the rodeo, watch the chuckwagons, drink in the beer tent, and maybe dance a little. She could take her mind off her troubles for a while. It would do her good to cut loose.

The crowd inside the store filed out as it got closer to 11 o'clock. The parade wouldn't start on time. Nothing ever started on time here. This was a "last-minute town" with people always running late, falling behind and making plans at the last minute.

Eventually, she heard drums off in the distance, and the sound of an air horn signalling the parade was underway. Her kids always loved the town parades when they were little. They'd begged to go to the spring parade in the village next to the town. The village was so small that they just ran the same parade around the village twice so the whole event would last longer. The first time Donna saw this happen, she wondered what sort of hick place she had moved to.

She propped the door open to *Memorable Moments* and stood inside, watching. No one would come into the store while the parade was on. Several RCMP members rode by on their black horses, followed by Barb McGuinty sitting in the car waving at everyone while Faye and several city workers threw candy out into the crowd. The Elks Hall members followed behind. All the older gentlemen sat on a float, wearing funny hats and waving. Cars drove by, and colourful floats filled with smiling and waving people drove down the street. It was amazing how the town could go so western in one week. Even people who had never been near a cow or a horse in their life were able to pull out some western wear. She'd been one of those people when she moved here. She'd always dreamed of the romance of cowboys, watching *The Good, the Bad and The Ugly* and John Wayne movies. Listening to Dolly Parton and Kenny Rogers and Conway Twitty. Then she married a cowboy and moved to small-town Alberta and realized the cowboy dream was created by Hollywood and the reality of it all was a hell of a lot different.

Children squealed as they swooped in to grab the candy thrown from the floats and she smiled.

Her husband and his brother rode by on their horses. As Gord passed, he waved at Donna, winking and smiling as he tipped his hat in her direction. She hadn't seen him smile like that in a while. She watched as he passed by, his horse Temple's head held high. Gord loved that horse so much. He was in his element now. He always looked different, stronger somehow when he was doing something with the cattle or the horses.

"Hey, hot stuff," she heard. Mary Anne came to stand beside her, and started catcalling at the ranchers. Gord saw her and laughed as they passed by. He needed moments to just celebrate who he was, distracting him from having to think about the ranch, and the money, and everything else.

The float passed by. Clay, Doug Miller and some other ranchers stood on it, waving. Clay wore his best western garb, with boots, a hat and some chaps over his jeans. Linda stood on the float too, wearing an apron that said, "Eat Alberta Beef', waving with one hand and throwing candies out of a bucket with the other. Clay walked over to his aunt, reached deep into her bucket and pulled out fistfuls of candy, which he threw to small children lining the sides of the road. He caught Donna's eye and threw a couple candies in her direction. Mary Anne whooped and waved at him. Donna found herself smiling. The weekend would do the entire family good. They would go out to watch the rodeo, and there would be drinking and dancing and maybe she and Gord would even have sex. And she'd get to spend some time with Pam for the first time in months. She used to go visit Pam several times a year, but she hadn't left the farm since Al's accident. As the float passed by, she hoped for a minute that the parade would go past the lodge. Abby had always loved Stampede. Two years ago, Abby would have been on that float herself, laughing, waving and smiling at everyone. Donna felt a pang of guilt. She hadn't been to visit Abby in a while. It was hard to go see her because she didn't seem to want to talk. Donna would try to keep up a steady stream of chatter and ask Abby questions she wouldn't answer. Whenever she went to visit, the two of them just ended up watching television. Donna had stopped bringing knitting. The last time she'd brought it, Abby had tried to help her and got frustrated because she couldn't make her good hand work well enough to help out. That had put a stop to that.

"Good crowd," Mary Anne said. "Should be a good night at the rodeo."

"Maybe you'll get some story ideas," Donna said.

"I've already got a few notes for my next book," Mary Anne said, patting her large purple purse. "But watching the rodeo always fires up the old imagination. What time is Pam coming in?"

"Said she'd be here at five," Donna said.

"Why don't we cab it from my place?" Mary Anne said. "You two can stay over. Have a girl's night."

"God, do I ever need that," Donna said.

Mary Anne squeezed her shoulder. "What you really need is a trip to the spa or a ladies' weekend away."

How she wished she had the money to go away. That couldn't happen now. But tonight Donna would drink with her friend and her sister and watch cowboys.

She heard the sound of the school band and looked for her girl. She spotted her on the back row on the float. She watched as her daughter passed by, her face mostly obscured by the shining golden bell of her trumpet.

There was something about the sunny day, and the parade, and her friend and the crowd and the energy of it all that made Donna feel calmer. Maybe the Klassens were past the worst of it. Maybe things would get better now, and the border would open soon. They'd made it through tough times before. It had been over a year. She was going to try to live in the moment and concentrate on what was happening in front of her. As trick riders trotted by on their horses, they whooped loud "Yee haws!" at the crowd. Donna raised her arms and whooped back.

★

During Stampede week, a couple days after the parade, the Alberta Beef Producers and the town decided to have a barbecue and a rally to support the local cattle ranchers. During the past year, many of the farmers had been to the Legislature in Edmonton to stand in front of the big building, asking government officials to deliver them an aid package. People were going broke, trying to make money any way they could. Some of the men were looking for extra jobs, and some were selling meat to the people in town or in Edmonton, Calgary or Lloydminster, slaughtering up their cattle and selling their meat to anyone who would buy it. They were doing anything they could to make a buck.

Every business in town had posted signs for the barbecue and *The Messenger* had run stories about it. Gord had met with other cattlemen earlier that weekend to organize the event. Donna had made her famous potato salad and baked beans to serve alongside all the beef they planned to sell. She was glad to clear some of the beef out of her freezer and hoped they'd be able to sell it all. Lord knows they needed the money.

Earlier that week, Allyson asked if they could have chicken. They'd been eating so much beef the past year. Ground beef, roast beef, steaks, tenderloin. If there was a beef recipe in her house, Donna had used it in the year since the border closed. Gord had taken cull cows to the slaughterhouse because he had to get rid of them. The cows that he normally would have sold at the auction were on the farm, costing him money.

"We're bleeding money right now," Gord said to her as they lay in bed together one night. A few months ago, Donna had picked up another job doing baking for Carmen Wilson, who owned a catering company in town. The extra money Donna was pulling in made her feel good. But it still wasn't enough.

They needed to kick Colton out. He was an adult after all. He had a job and was earning his own money.

The day of the barbeque, the ranchers drove their trucks up Main Street and parked in front of the museum. Donna watched out the window of *Memorable Moments* as the trucks streamed by. Bonnie and Anita would handle the store and Anita had given her a couple hours off so she could go help out.

"How are you holding up?" Anita asked. "Everything okay?"

Donna felt her cheeks redden. If she started talking, she'd probably tell Anita too much. Tell her how stressed she really was, how her family was hanging on by a thread. She had been very careful not to talk about the things that were happening at home. If you talked about your troubles in town, everyone would know all about it in a few minutes. There were many things she never mentioned, like how hard it was for her to live on the farm, and how some days, she wished she were somewhere else.

"I'm okay," she said. "Just carrying on like usual." She paused, thinking how to broach the question. "Do you think I could pick up more shifts this summer?"

Anita shook her head. "Sorry, business is slow. But Kelly might need help for craft shows. Maybe he can use someone at the booth."

It would be tough for Donna to juggle the booth, catering and the store, but she was willing to try. She looked out the window and watched as Doug Miller's dirty white truck drove up the street.

"I'd appreciate it," she said.

"You better hurry and get out there," Anita said. "Go sell that beef."

Main Street was packed. When she got to the museum, she saw Gord, Craig and Linda and many other cattle ranchers and their wives. Doug Miller and his wife Norma were there, along with Tony Smith and Mary, Marty Valleau, the Hills and Don Salmon and his wife Wendy.

A large banner strung across the door of the museum read, "Save our ranchers." Balloons and ribbons decorated the ends of the banner.

"Here, Donna, we saved one for you," Linda said, pushing an apron into her hand. Linda was wearing an "I love Alberta beef" t-shirt and a cowboy hat. Donna regretted that she'd left her cowboy hat at home.

"Just let me go to the bathroom first," she said to Linda, starting towards the museum. She hadn't been there in months.

Town residents mostly ended up taking out-of-towners to the museum. The museum specialized in town history and oddities. There was a collection of salt and pepper shakers that Mabel Jacobson had donated after her mother died. Patrick Stevens' shoes were displayed in a glass case. He'd been struck by lightning and died. There were displays cases filled with pioneer farming tools and pictures of past Mustangs hockey team members who had gone on to play in the western hockey leagues. Other displays cases and rooms were filled with photographs of people who had gone on to do great things, like Scott Morris, the chuckwagon champion who had grown up in town. The museum's pride and joy, a five-legged squirrel, sat in a dusty room full of taxidermied animals. The squirrel held a peanut in one of his arms while his demonic yellow glass eyes stared at nothing. There was no charge to go into the museum and the kids always wanted to go when they were smaller. When he was young, Clay had been obsessed with the squirrel. Pam, who had been to the museum on several occasions, made fun of it. It pissed Donna off when she made fun of things in town. It was one thing when Donna criticized stuff in her head, but it was another thing entirely when people who didn't live in town made fun of things.

Donna pushed open the heavy museum doors, stopping in the entryway of the museum to check out the paperback bookshelf. You could donate your old paperbacks to the museum and buy new ones for a dollar. Donna spotted a few Stephen King books and a copy of Barbara Kingsolver's *The Poisonwood Bible* in the stacks and picked them up.

Mabel Jacobson sat at the volunteer desk where Donna had to pay. Mabel volunteered for so many things that Donna wondered when she found time to sleep. Maybe that was what you did when you were a widow and your kids moved away. You had to keep busy.

"Thanks, dear," Mabel said, taking Donna's coins from her hands.

Donna went into the bathroom to pee. Inside the stall, she changed into the Alberta Beef t-shirt, folding her other shirt and putting it in her bag. When she came back out, she studied herself in the mirror. She was starting to look squishy around the middle. She shouldn't be so hard on Gord for his gut. She was no spring chicken either. When Donna had turned forty a few years ago, Abby told her the alternative to getting older was dying, so no one should ever complain about aging. Donna washed her hands and dried them before going outside.

Phil Hill, who was on the board of the Alberta Beef Producers, was spreading out "Eat Alberta Beef" stickers, "I love Alberta Beef" bumper stickers and pencils on tables. He gave Donna a smile as she approached.

"At one of the last meetings, we were talking about how we worried that people were going to stop eating beef because they were worried about BSE," said Phil to Donna. "But they haven't stopped. In fact, people have been buying more."

He squeezed Donna's shoulder in a friendly, familiar way. She'd always liked Phil. He was a good man, steady and strong, the type that came to mind when someone said the phrase "good old country boy."

A crowd of people gathered in front of the tables, waiting for the signal to start buying hamburgers and beef on a bun. The ranchers also had coolers of meat for sale. Donna could smell the rich scent of meat as the smoke from the barbecue drifted over the crowd. She stood behind the table as Linda showed her the price list and the cash box. Then the crowd was ready, lined up to buy. The crowd kept the crew busy and the guys talked and laughed as they cooked the meat, served up coleslaw, beans and potato salad, coffee and pop to their customers. All the local businesses had donated goods to help out. Everyone knew how much the ranchers were suffering.

When the crowd had dispersed for a bit and she was taking a breather, Linda sneaked over to talk to her.

"Ray Sharp's not here," she said. "Craig said no one's heard from him today. I'm kind of worried. Maybe someone should go check on him."

"I'll tell Gord to do that on the way home," Donna said. "Ray's not the type to just disappear. If he was sick, he would have called someone."

Linda held onto Donna's arm. Donna hated it when she did this, because she held on so tight that it felt like a pinch.

People had started lining up again and so she broke away from Linda and began smiling and taking people's money. Barb McGuinty made a speech honouring the cattle ranchers, and how it was so important that everyone had showed up to support them and buy their meat. By the end of the day, the ranchers and their families had emptied their coolers of meat. Donna put her hand on a stack of ten-dollar bills in the float. They would all have some money to take home. Every little bit helped.

★

Later that evening, Donna sat at the kitchen table, the copy of *The Poisonwood Bible* in front of her. She didn't feel like cooking supper. The family could fend for themselves. She thought about all the townspeople who had shown up to the barbecue and meat sale. So many people had come out, smiling, offering their support, telling the ranchers that they were doing a noble job. She smiled at and thanked so many people, many of whom she had never seen before. It was enough to make a person feel teary. Sometimes it was surprising to realize how much people really did care.

She heard the sound of the door slam and knew by the sounds that it was her husband. He grunted as he removed his boots and then came up the stairs.

"I got some bad news," he said, slumping down at the table. "They found BSE in one of the cows in Ray's herd."

CHAPTER 11

When Allyson came down into the kitchen that night, she knew something was wrong. Her dad and mom sat close together at the kitchen table. She opened the cupboard to get a glass of milk when she glanced at her father's face. He looked old and tired. Her parents sprang away from each other, as if they'd been caught telling each other a secret.

"I can tell something's up," she said.

Her dad looked up from his coffee cup. "They found BSE in Ray's herd," he said.

"What does that mean?" she asked.

Her dad explained the government had been trying to find the origin of BSE, and they'd been testing the brains of cows that had been slaughtered. They'd been looking for abnormal traits in the brains to try and found out more information about how BSE had gotten into Alberta. They'd found some of those traits in a cow Ray slaughtered a few months ago.

"The government guys are going to come out and take away all Ray's cattle," Gord explained. "We can still go on and off his farm, but it's been quarantined, and he can't move or sell his herd."

Gord shook his head. "Ray said this is going to take him out of the cattle business. They're coming to take the cows away tomorrow."

"Are the cows contagious?" Allyson asked. She knew there was no danger of people getting sick, but she didn't really know how the whole thing worked.

"They just don't want them to get into the food chain," Gord said. "And they need to test the rest of them."

Donna stood up. "I've got some pies and a lasagne in the freezer. I'll get everything together and you can take it to Ray when you go over there tomorrow."

Allyson hadn't wanted to go over to Ray's with her dad to watch the whole thing. But her dad asked her to go. Even though she was old enough to stay alone, the look on her dad's face was enough to make her hop in his truck and sit beside him in silence as they drove to Ray's. Gord had loaded Temple into the trailer they were pulling behind the truck. He'd asked Allyson if she wanted to ride and help round up the cattle but she had a feeling she would probably be in the way.

"Ray doesn't want to watch the men come and take his cows away, but he can't make himself leave," her dad told her as they pulled up to Ray's house. She got out of the truck. Craig, Gord and Phil were mounted on horses, ready to go. Ray trotted up on his own palomino, slowing down as he approached the car.

"This is like watching a man take his last ride," Gord said to Allyson, while Ray was out of earshot.

The two of them sat in silence in the truck and watched Ray approach.

Once her dad put the tack on Temple and mounted her, the four men drove the cattle into a pen, and then up the chute into a cattle liner. The cattle would be trucked to a special slaughter plant, where plant workers would kill them by shooting bolts into their brains. From there, their bodies would be burned down and rendered. The cattle probably weren't sick, but the government couldn't take any chances, so they had to kill them all, separating the infected material, all the spines and the brains— any of the tissue that could possibly infect anyone. Ray had to give the government all his cattle records, so the government could do a trace back on all his animals. The government inspectors would work as though they were solving a mystery, visiting farms and looking through records.

For Ray and the rest of the men, this herd was the only one that mattered now. Ray sat on his horse and watched as the truck drove off with all his steers, bulls, heifers and cows. The men stayed around visiting with him for a bit. They had a few beers, ate some chips and shot the shit. Allyson had a ginger ale. But eventually, they all had to go home and leave Ray alone.

"I don't know what Ray is going to do now," Gord said, when he was back at his kitchen table. "Jackie is coming out to get him. Said she'd take him into the city for a week, so he could hang out with the grandkids."

"So sad," Donna said, sipping on her coffee. "Why do bad things happen to good people?"

It was just the three of them in the house. Who knew where Colton was? As Allyson watched, Gord and Donna both took sips from their coffee, raising mugs to their mouths in unison. How long did it take before a couple adopted each other's mannerisms? Would that kind of thing happen to her someday? Would she eventually look old and tired like her parents? She didn't like that thought.

★

The annual post grad/post Stampede party was coming up. It was a town tradition. For the past few years, Tim and Tracy Coates held parties when their parents were out of town.

"I think you should go to the party," Donna said, leaning into her daughter's room.

Allyson looked up from her copy of *Keeper of the Isis Light*.

"Why?" she asked.

"You need to get out more," her mom said. "It's not good for you to keep moping around your bedroom all the time. You need to hang out with more people. What kind of kid doesn't want to go to a party?"

This one, Allyson thought. She looked up from the pages of her book to her mom's face. Her mom had her no-nonsense look on.

"I can't believe this," Allyson said.

"What kind of life are you going to have if you just sit in your room and read all the time? Besides, you can't spend all your time alone. It's a good way to get depressed."

Allyson opened her mouth to say something and then closed it. She wanted to tell her mom that she was worried about her dad. Both her parents had been somber and quiet through the long, dull, boring winter. Her dad paced around outside all the time. Her dad had always loved spending time in the yard, but now he was out there all the time, wandering around, aimless. Uncle Craig was always off on other jobs, trying to help people with their crops, doing carpentry work. When Clay was home for grad and Stampede, her dad had roped him into helping with fencing. But whenever her dad was in the house, he didn't talk much, just sat slumped in his chair, drinking beer and eating Cheezies. He flipped through TV channels without seeming to watch anything except the news and the odd sports game. *Western Producer* articles piled up next to his chair. He was obsessed with the border closure and the cattle markets. He had taken to cutting out articles about cattle, BSE and cattle markets out of the newspapers with the kitchen scissors. Her mother had thrown some of the articles away a few months ago, and Gord yelled at her. Now she didn't dare touch them.

Everything was different since Grandpa Al died. Even though it was only about twelve months ago, Allyson felt a lot older since the accident. It took more energy to get out of bed in the morning. It was as though someone was sitting on her shoulders, pressing down. Sometimes, when she woke up in the morning, she wondered why she was getting out of bed.

"You should go to the party," Donna said, interrupting her thoughts.

Allyson looked away from her mother and back at her book. She kept reading, ignoring her mother, until she heard the footsteps that indicated her mother had left.

The day of the party, Allyson walked into the barn, looking for a quiet place to read. Chloe was inside, feeding the cats.

"You're coming to the rager tonight?" Chloe asked, as she leaned down to pet Willow.

"Nope," she said.

"You should come with us," Chloe said. "Jamie and I were at Joe's and we asked Jeff if he was going. He asked if you were going to be there."

Allyson thought about the last time she'd seen Jeff, at grad.

"Do you want to go outside?" Jeff had asked her. "I need some air."

She nodded. Had he read her mind? She had been thinking about sneaking out and reading the book she had in her bag, just to deal with her boredom. Jeff stood up and she followed him, wondering if anyone in her family was watching her leave with him. Outside, she and Jeff talked about Princess Mononoke and Frank Miller and the Dark Knight Chronicles. They sat on the bench outside the school. As she watched, Booger's truck pulled into the parking lot. She hadn't even noticed that Colton had left the gym, but now she saw him run over to the truck and lean into Booger's open window. Booger's truck blared loud, angry rock music; Korn or Limp Bizkit or one of those other bands with lead singers who postured like angry roosters. Colton walked over to the passenger side of the truck to talk to someone. Colton climbed inside the truck and the person shifted over. Allyson could tell it was Lily by the long dark hair that hung down the side of her face. Booger gunned the engine and the truck peeled out of the parking lot.

"Weird," Jeff said. For a moment, she had forgotten he was there.

"How are your parents doing?" Jeff asked.

His question sounded so adult, so formal.

"I mean, with everything happening," he said. "When my grandma died, my mom took it really hard."

Jeff's grandma had come over from China and spent her days in the restaurant. She never learned how to speak English, except to say "thank you." His grandma toddled around the restaurant, smiled, wiped the tables with her gnarled hands and cleared away plates when people were done eating. Allyson had never known her name. She was a fixture in the restaurant until one day she was just gone.

"I think my parents are okay," she said. She didn't want to talk about it.

"You should come over and watch a movie with me," Jeff said. "It's been a while since we did that."

He shifted his body next to her on the bench. His arm brushed against hers. The warmth of his body was startling, and she shifted away from him. But then she willed herself to relax. What would she do if he reached out and touched her? What if he put his arm around her? Did he like her?

She became aware of her own breathing. Should she touch him? She could smell him beside her, a faint smell of woody cologne. He smelled different than her brothers. Better somehow. Was this what it felt like to like someone? Or were they just friends?

Jeff was talking. They needed to hire someone in the restaurant that summer. Emily would be leaving soon and they needed someone to pick up extra shifts.

"I should go back inside," he said. "They've probably stopped playing that god-awful country crap."

Allyson stood up with him. "At least you don't have to listen to country all the time," she said. "My mom is crazy about that stuff. If she had her way, we would have moved to Texas. Or Nashville." She laughed. "I should show you some pictures of my parents when they got married. My mom had really big hair, like she wanted to be Tammy Wynette or Dolly Parton. My dad looked like a cowboy out of the movies."

Jeff opened the door to the school. She wasn't sure if he was listening to her. Was she babbling?

"My mom says she fell for my dad because he looked like a cowboy," she said. "She thought she was going to be living in Lonesome Dove. Instead, she ended up here."

Inside the school gym, people had gathered in a circle and were dancing around to Boney M's "Rasputin". There were cheers as someone's dad ventured into the circle, doing high Russian kicks.

"I'll talk to you later," Jeff said. "Maybe we can catch up on IM."

She nodded. Had she done or said something wrong?

"See you," she said, watching him go. Then she went back to the table where her family was sitting, even though they weren't there anymore. She saw her mom and dad on the dance floor. Eventually Clay came back and sat beside her. After a few minutes, she convinced him to give her a ride home.

Chloe cleared her throat. "I asked you a question."

"Sorry," Allyson mumbled. "What did you say?"

"So do you want to come?" Chloe asked. She scooped Willow up into her arms. The orange cat leaned against her chest and purred like a tired motor.

Allyson looked at her cousin's face. Soon Chloe would move to the city. The two of them barely talked any more. Chloe was asking her to do something, and Jeff was going to be there too. She'd have to be around Jamie, but she could suck it up and deal with it.

"Okay," Allyson said. "I'll go."

"Great," Chloe said. "We'll be ready to come get you around nine."

★

After dinner, Allyson changed her clothes. This rager was legendary. Chloe had gone last year and told Allyson about it.

"People were wandering all over the riverbank, making out and drinking beer," Chloe said. "I've never seen anything like it. Cody Turner brought his guitar and was serenading a girl. And Body Count was there."

Body Count was a local death metal band. The lead singer, Brett, was known for his love of metal. He could do a high-pitched scream that sounded like Axl Rose, but his favourite thing to do was a death metal growl. Before Chloe had ditched Allyson for Jamie, she dragged her to see a free all-ages Body Count show at the Royal Canadian Legion in town. The band had played some Metallica covers, a bunch of Guns N' Roses and some originals. For most of the concert, Brett screamed and growled in a way that reminded Allyson of Cookie Monster. She wasn't sure why anyone would pay to listen to that music.

Allyson didn't know what a person wore to the summer rager.

"Are you ready yet?" Chloe asked, poking her head into Allyson's bedroom.

Allyson thought about telling her she didn't want to go, that the whole thing was stupid. But part of her was curious. Wouldn't it be worthwhile to go and see what actually happened? It couldn't be as great as everyone said it was. Even her dad used to tell her about the bush parties he and Craig had gone to back in the day. After-grad parties around Stampede had been a tradition since he was in high school. Her dad, Craig and all the rest of their graduating class had partied at the river. The location of the party changed over the years, but it was a tradition as old as the town.

"Can I wear this?" Allyson asked, pointing down at the black t-shirt and jeans she was wearing.

Chloe nodded. "It doesn't really matter. You'll need to put on a jacket later. It gets cold near the water."

Chloe wore coral-coloured lipstick, and heavy kohl ringed her eyes.

"Jamie is waiting out in the car," Chloe said. "We have to hurry."

Allyson followed her cousin down the stairs. As she left her room, she glanced at the book lying on her bed. They stopped at the front door to put on their shoes. Allyson tied up her favourite red Converse high tops. Chloe said they looked like something an artist would wear, and that made Allyson like them more.

"Bye girls," Donna called from the kitchen. "Have a good time. Drive safe."

Outside, Jamie waited in the passenger seat. Ben, her boyfriend, sat in the driver's seat. Allyson had never really talked to him, but she nodded at him in acknowledgement as she scrambled into the back seat.

"Thanks for the ride," she said. Her voice sounded high and squeaky, like a little kid. She felt like one right now. Even though Jamie and Chloe were only two years older, they looked so much more worldly. Jamie's lips were bright red. Allyson touched a finger to her own unadorned lips. She'd tried wearing lipstick once but she hated the waxy feeling of the lipstick on her mouth. When her lips were outlined in a bright colour, it felt as though her lips were oversized and crooked. She watched Jamie's perfect mouth as she talked.

Allyson reached into her pocket, pulled out her lip chap and ran it over her lips as Ben started the car and drove down the driveway. Jamie leaned over and turned up the stereo, which was playing that Blue song that had been so popular a few years ago. The chorus was something about living in a blue house in a blue window in a blue world. Allyson hated the song because it didn't really mean anything. She knew Chloe hated the song too, because she'd told her so.

"I love this song," Chloe said to Jamie. "Can you turn it up?"

Jamie leaned over the back seat, turning around to face Allyson and Chloe. "Want a smoke?" she asked. Chloe nodded. Jamie lit up and handed the cigarette to Chloe before lighting one up herself. Soon everyone in the car was smoking except Allyson. She was going to smell like an ashtray. If she had had a bottle of perfume, she would have sprayed it all over herself. Her eyes started to burn, so she rolled down a window. The sound of air rushed into the car.

They had to drive through town to get to the Coates' place.

"I need to get some pop for my mix," Ben said, turning into the 7-Eleven parking lot.

He stopped the car and hopped out. "You guys coming?"

Jamie and Chloe got out of the car. Allyson didn't need any-thing, but she didn't want to stay alone in the car. Chloe and Jamie were already a few steps ahead of her, giggling about some-thing. Allyson couldn't hear what they were saying. She looked at their backs and remembered when she and Chloe had giggled together like that.

Inside, Ben filled up a Big Gulp cup with Coke. Jamie and Chloe got Slurpees. Her cousin went from lever to lever, layering coloured ices over top of each other.

"Gross," Jamie said, filling her own large cup up with lime.

Allyson walked to the stand-up coolers and got herself a bot-tle of Fresca before heading to the candy aisle for some sour soothers. You were supposed to use tongs to pull them out, but she never did. The clerk behind the counter was busy helping customers ring through their purchases. When she was satisfied that he wasn't looking, she grabbed the sour keys with her fingers and stuffed them into the baggie.

Chloe, Ben and Jamie were already in line. Jamie looked at Allyson's hands to see what she was buying.

"Fresca," she said. "That's what my grandma drinks."

Allyson paid without saying anything and followed the other three out to the car. As she walked, she pulled a bit of her hair past her nose and took a whiff. Her hair stunk like cigarette smoke. She heard Booger's truck before she even saw it. The loud music sounded like AC/DC, or some of that older rock stuff that Colton listened to.

"Hey," she heard Chloe say. "Are you heading to the party too?"

"Wouldn't miss it," Colton said. She watched as her brother and Lily walked towards the store. Booger stayed in the driver's seat of the truck. Her brother saw her and raised his eyebrows. "You're going to the party?" he asked. "People are going to be doing shit there," he said. "All kinds of things. Are you sure you're ready for that?"

He gave Chloe a look. Allyson ignored him and headed toward the car. Ben was already back in the car by the time Allyson climbed in the back seat. She watched out the window as Booger hopped out of his truck and joined Chloe, Colton and Jamie on the sidewalk. She wanted to go back home more than ever. She couldn't ask Ben to take her home because she'd look like a baby. It was too far for her to walk. Maybe she could fake some sort of illness, call her parents from the 7-Eleven and ask them to pick her up.

Before she could even figure out a plan, Chloe and Jamie were back in the car. Allyson opened the crumpled baggie in her hand and pulled out a sour soother. The candy was hard and acidic in her mouth. She chewed, forcing her teeth down on the stiff shape. She leaned towards the front seat as Ben started the car up again, and passed the bag to Jamie.

"Take some," she said, looking out the window as they drove through town and onto the highway to the Coates'. The Coates family had a long driveway with high hedges leading up to their house. Allyson had been there years before, when she was about eight years old. For her birthday, Tracy Coates hosted a pool party and invited everyone in the class. Then Tracy's mom had served them lemonade and they ate cake and watched Tracy open her presents.

It seemed like forever until they reached the Coates' house. People in town always talked about the house's design. Donna said it was inspired by Tara in "Gone with the Wind." The Coates house was a large, sprawling white mansion that belonged in the deep southern United States, not in rural Alberta.

Cars and pickups were parked all over the property. Ben pulled his car up next to a red truck and killed the engine. Jamie leaned over the front seat and handed the bag of sour keys back to Allyson. Allyson had forgotten that she'd even handed them over. Clutching the bag, she got out of the car, and waited as Chloe and Jamie stood around the trunk of Ben's car, watching him fiddle with the lock.

"Brain freeze," Chloe yelled, putting her hand on her forehead. She was still holding her Slurpee in the other hand.

"Put your tongue on the roof of your mouth," Allyson said. Clay taught her that trick. Chloe looked at her, and Allyson could tell that she didn't believe her. Ben finally popped open the trunk and pulled out two backpacks. He passed a blue backpack to Chloe. From the first backpack, he pulled out a large thermos. He poured a generous amount of vodka into the thermos, followed by a splash of the Coke that he'd bought at the 7-Eleven. Leaning his head back, he took a large swig of his concoction.

"Tastes like a good night," he said, grabbing Jamie's hand. "Let's go."

Off in the distance, Allyson could hear loud music. Jamie and Ben started walking in the direction of the river. Chloe crouched beside the back of the car, fiddling with her shoelace. Allyson kneeled down so her mouth was close to her cousin's ear.

"Isn't Ben driving?" she asked. "Shouldn't he be sober?"

Chloe looked up from her shoe and raised her eyebrow. "We're going to be here a long time," she said. "Ben will be sober by the time we go home. Don't worry about it. He knows what he's doing."

Chloe abandoned her Slurpee cup by the back wheel of Ben's car, stood up and hurried after Jamie and Ben, her backpack slung over one arm. Allyson trudged along alone. She could hear voices in the distance, and the sounds of laughter. It reminded her of a *Buffy* episode, or the horror movies she'd seen. If she were some sort of monster, this was where she would strike. She looked around at all the greenery and shrubs around her. She kept on walking, and caught up to her cousin, who had stopped to fumble around in her backpack.

"Do you want a vodka cooler?" Chloe asked, reaching into the bag. Allyson heard the sound of the cap twist, and the rush of air as her cousin opened the cooler. She shook her head and held up the Fresca she had brought from the car.

"Didn't think so," Chloe said. "But figured I'd offer."

Allyson followed her cousin down the gravel path. There were a few people coming back up, but she didn't recognize any of them. After a few minutes, the narrow path grew wide again. Allyson could smell campfire and saw fire pits scattered in an open area.

Jamie and Ben were already sitting at the nearest campfire. Josh Hutchinson sat beside them, roasting a hot dog.

"Check out his stick," Jamie laughed. Josh's hot dog rested in front of a little wire man, so it looked like the hot dog was the man's giant penis.

"So gross," Chloe giggled. Allyson blushed. Josh was asking what their plans were for the summer, if they were going to go away. Chloe would be working at the feed store, the same place she'd worked last summer. Josh said he was going to see the Tragically Hip concert at Klondike Days. Did Chloe want to go with him? They could go to West Edmonton Mall and go to the water park. They should all go camping this summer. Josh knew a place in Kananaskis that was right near a mountain. They should all have one last hurrah before they went off to university.

"I can't wait to move," Chloe said. "Can't wait to get out of this shit hole," she said.

"Here's to graduating and leaving this dump behind," Jamie said, holding up a can of beer. The four of them clinked bottles and cans while Allyson watched. She wished for the day when she would be them, ready to leave, heading into the city. Jamie stood up and grabbed Ben's hand, pulling him up with her.

"I need to talk to you alone," she said, leaning towards him.

Chloe wiggled her eyebrows at Jamie. "Sure you do," she said, as they moved away. "Go ahead and talk." As they walked away, Ben put his hand in Jamie's back pocket, and Allyson looked away.

"I need to go find the buns and the ketchup," Josh said, pulling his hot dog out of the fire. "Want to come with me?"

Chloe stood up. Allyson wondered what she was supposed to do. Was she invisible? Did they even care that she was here?

"I'm going to see who else is here," she said. "I'll find you in a bit." She hoped she could find Jeff. She just didn't want to be around Chloe if her cousin was just going to ignore her. She walked away from the fire, towards small groups of people scattered around the open area. Was Amber here? Probably not. Amber had better things to do. She was probably at home reading or practicing the piano, or sleeping. Maybe there would be some other people from band that she could talk to. She wandered over to one of the other fires and sat down next to it for a while, staring at other groups of people sitting with friends and laughing. She recognized lots of people but they were all older. They were people she had never spoken to. All the groups of people talking, laughing and drinking around her made her feel even more alone. Why had she even come to this party? She wasn't made for parties. Not this kind. Maybe the kind you had in the city, where people talked about books they'd read, or movies they'd seen. She'd never been to a sophisticated party, one where people dressed up and talked about things that mattered. She pretended to be deep in thought as she stared at the fire. Maybe if she stared at it hard enough, people would just think she was really stoned. If there was more light, she could study the faces of the people around her, and try to figure out how to draw them. Instead, she looked at the shadows playing on people's faces. Everything was more sinister this way.

"Hey," she heard as Jeff sat down beside her. She was surprised to see a beer in his hand.

"I didn't know you drank," she said. She sounded stupid even to herself.

"Sometimes," he said. "My dad likes me to drink Johnnie Walker with him every once in a while."

Allyson twisted the cap off her Fresca and listened to the satisfying fizz of the air escaping the bottle. Tipping her head back, she took a long pull on it, tasting the citrus tang and the burn from the carbonation.

"What have you been up to?" Jeff asked. "You here alone?"

"Not much," she said. "Same old. Reading and drawing. I came with my cousin and her friends, but I don't know where they are."

Even as she said the words, she knew she sounded lame. Even though she talked to Jeff all the time, she felt nervous. Sitting with him in the dark near a campfire was different. Jeff threw his head back and took another gulp from his beer bottle.

"How long have you been here?" she asked. "We came around 9:30."

Why couldn't she think of anything good to talk about?

"We've been here for a while," he said. "Came down with Emily earlier."

"Really?"

"I think there's something going on between her and Tim," Jeff said. "Are you sure you don't want a sip of my beer?"

Allyson hated beer, but she didn't want to tell Jeff. She put her Fresca on the ground and took the bottle from him. When the cold glass of the bottle touched her lips, she thought about how his lips had touched the same bottle. She swallowed, handed the bottle back to him and took a swig of Fresca to chase the taste away.

"Can I tell you a secret?" Jeff asked. He leaned towards her and she smelled beer on his breath. She shivered. The sun was completely gone and the air was a lot colder.

He put his hand on her knee. She thought about moving his hand off her knee just because it felt so strange. It felt sort of nice, though. Should she lean closer towards him? Before she could think about it, his mouth was on hers. He was kissing her. Her first kiss. She wasn't sure what to do, so she stuck her tongue in his mouth. That's what you were supposed to do when you were kissing, right? That's what happened in the movies. He tasted like beer, but she could feel the soft warmth of the inside of his mouth too. His hand tightened on her knee. Did this mean they were boyfriend and girlfriend now? Were they together? Did he like her, like her? Did she like him?

"Woo hoo!" she heard, and Booger, Colton and Lily approached and stood by the fire. Allyson could tell her brother was drunk or high by the way he was standing, and by the way he stared into the flames, transfixed as if he was searching for something.

"I'm going to lay some pole tonight," Booger said.

"What?" she said, mostly to Jeff.

"I don't know," Jeff said to her. "Maybe it means he's going to get laid."

Jeff had taken his hand off his knee and moved away. "What did you want to tell me?" she asked. She leaned towards him, so he could whisper it in her ear if he wanted to.

"I'm kind of drunk," he said. He touched her hair. "You're so pretty," he said. "I just think you're pretty."

"Are you hitting on my sister?" Colton asked. Lily laughed, a loud high-pitched cackle. Her laugh didn't match her looks, Allyson thought. But maybe it suited her personality.

"He's a nice boy," Lily said. "Leave them alone."

"I don't know," Booger said. "You gotta be careful with Chinks these days. They're the ones who carry SARS. Everyone knows they're the ones who brought it to Canada."

Jeff raised his head to look at Booger, whose hulking shape towered over him.

"Shut up, asshole," Jeff said.

Booger laughed. "What did you call me, chink?"

"Shut up, Booger," Lily said, and Allyson was glad she was there. Colton laughed and slumped down on his back to watch the stars. He held out his arms and made grabbing motions with his hands.

"They're so close," he said. "Feels like I could touch them."

Jeff hauled himself to his feet and stood beside Booger, who looked at him and laughed.

"What's up, Chinaman?" he said. "What are you going to do, cough on me?"

Jeff lurched forward, and Allyson could see that he was drunker than she'd originally thought. He bunched his fingers into a fist and aimed for Booger's face. Booger grabbed Jeff's hands with one hand and punched him in the nose with the other. Allyson froze. She couldn't move, couldn't believe this was happening. She leaned over and grabbed at her brother's hands, trying to make him pay attention, make him stop laughing at the sky.

"Do something," she said, yanking at his arm. She kicked him with one foot, but he didn't move. Booger kept on punching Jeff. Jeff tried to punch back, but he wasn't big or fast enough.

"Booger, stop," Lily said. She moved in and tried to grab Booger's arms. "Just stop it. Calm down."

A crowd had gathered, moving from the other fires to watch.

"Fight!" someone said. She couldn't tell who had yelled the word, but she hated that person, hated their voice and all the other people who were gathered around. None of this would have happened if she'd stayed home, safe in bed with a book.

Colton sat up. "Fight!" he said, and laughed a crazy gurgling laugh.

Lily forced her thin, small body between Jeff and Booger. Jeff's arms swung out wildly as he tried to hit Booger. Then someone grabbed Jeff by the shoulder and started to pull him away. Allyson stood up and grabbed Jeff's other hand. "Come with me," she said, even though she wasn't sure where she was taking him. She looked to see who had pulled Jeff away. It was Tim Coates.

"Colton, help me," Lily said. Colton pulled himself to his feet. "Help hold Booger back," she said.

"Break it up, guys," Tim said. "No fighting down here. We don't want the cops to shut us down."

Jeff nodded and took a deep breath through his mouth, inhaling it in a whinny. "My nose hurts," he said to Allyson. His voice was a high-pitched whine.

She had to get Jeff away from all this, as far away from Booger as possible.

"Chloe," she called. "Chloe, where are you?"

She scanned the groups of people, but couldn't see her cousin. She searched for her cousin's familiar strawberry blonde hair, but it was nowhere to be seen.

"You need to get him out of here," Tim said, looking down into her face. "You need to leave."

Allyson grabbed Jeff by the arm and started away from the river, weaving through groups of people. Her breath was rough and shaky in her chest, as she pulled at Jeff, yanking him through the crowds. Away from the bonfire, everyone was just shadows and bodies, and she couldn't find the way back to the house. Branches from a bush scraped against her face. "Ouch, ouch, goddamnit," she said, waving her arm in front of her to push them away.

"Do you know where the path is?" she asked Jeff.

He brought his hand to his nose. "It's bleeding," he said.

"Chloe!" she called again. "Ben!" She wished they would come to help her. She felt as if she was trapped in a funhouse maze. How come the entire school was here, and she didn't recognize anyone? How come no one would help her?

"Emily!" she yelled. Maybe Jeff's sister was there.

"Where is the path?" she asked a girl standing beside her. When she took a good look at the girl's face, she recognized her as one of the girls who went to the Catholic school down the road. The party was so big that even the Catholics were there.

The girl looked from her to Jeff, who was holding his nose with one hand.

"Follow me," she said. "I'll take you."

Allyson followed her back onto the gravel path. She had never been so happy to see dirty old gravel in her entire life.

She started up the path, holding Jeff by one arm. The two of them walked without speaking until they arrived at the house. After they'd climbed the steps, Allyson stood on the porch, wondering what to do. After a few minutes, she walked to the door and knocked. No one came to the door. She tried the handle. It was unlocked, so she opened the door and walked into a back hallway of the house. Jeff followed her inside and as they entered the house, two small Shih Tzus came running towards them, barking.

"Gotta find a bathroom," Jeff said, as he lurched down the hallway. Drips of blood slipped through his fingers and spattered onto the floor.

"You're dripping," she called after him.

She sounded like her mother.

The dogs ignored her and went off after Jeff.

"Hello," she called. Was there anyone else inside the house? It was as fancy as it looked from the outside. She walked a few steps down the hallway, which opened into a large, white kitchen. Pots hung from a copper rack on the ceiling and a stainless steel stove and fridge gleamed against the white walls. Allyson had only seen kitchens like this on television. Jeff leaned over the sink. There was a roll of paper towel next to the sink. Jeff unwrapped a few sheets of it and pressed them to his nose.

This kitchen was nothing like her kitchen at home. Even though her mother kept their kitchen spotless, the kitchen at the Klassen house looked used, like people actually lived there. The Coates' kitchen looked like a showroom. And here was Jeff, wearing dirty running shoes, bleeding on all the whiteness.

Allyson heard a door open and shut and turned to see who was coming through the door. Tracy.

"Tim sent me here," she said. She opened a drawer, pulled out a white tea towel and handed it to Jeff. He pulled the bloody paper towel away from his nose and winced. "I don't think it's broken," he said. "Do you want me to put this nice towel on my nose?"

"It'll be ruined," Allyson said. "Don't you have any rags?"

Tracy shook her head. "Don't worry about it. We've got lots."

"I'm sorry," Jeff said, his voice nasal and scratchy as he pinched his nose with the towel. "I'm sorry about this."

"You should probably just go home when you're done bleeding," Tracy said.

Had Tracy seen what happened? Had Tim told her to tell them to leave? Had Booger been asked to leave? There was nothing Allyson wanted more than to go home. But how would she get there? There was no way she could go back to the river and look for Ben or anyone else who could give them a ride home. If she lived in town, it would be another story. Uncle Craig, Aunty Linda and her parents had always said that any of the kids could call any time they needed a ride and someone would come get them, no questions asked.

"Can I use your phone?" she asked.

Tracy handed her a white cordless phone. Allyson dialled the number. Her mother picked up on the third ring.

"Mom," Allyson said.

"Are you okay?" her mother asked, and there was a wave of panic in her mother's voice. "Is Chloe okay? Is everything all right?"

She heard her dad ask who was on the phone. He must be lying in bed beside her mother.

"Mom, I'm fine," she said. "We're fine."

"You freaked me out," her mother says. "Every time the phone rings at night, I think . . ."

"I need you to come get us," she said. "Me and Jeff. We need a ride home."

"Where's Chloe?" her mother asked.

"I don't know. She's fine. She's down at the river. Just come get us."

"Why isn't Chloe with you?"

Allyson wished she could reach through the phone and slap her mother upside the head.

"She ditched me," she said. And as she spoke the words, she felt like crying. "Now can you come get me? I want to come home."

"I'll go get her," Gord said. "Is she still at the Coates?"

Her mother must have put her on speakerphone. Allyson heard the creak of the bed as her father shifted his weight and sat up.

"Yeah, we're at the Coates," she said.

"He's on his way," Donna said. Allyson pressed the off button, cutting her mother off before she could say anything else. Why had she come to this stupid party anyway?

"Thanks," Allyson said, as she handed the phone back to Tracy.

Tracy put the phone in its cradle. "You can wait in the front room if you like."

"It's probably better if we wait on the porch," Allyson said. "That way he doesn't have to come into the house."

"Suit yourself," Tracy said.

Outside, Jeff and Allyson stood on the porch, looking out towards the yard, which was still full of cars and trucks.

"Your dad doesn't have to give me a ride home," Jeff said. "I'll go back down to the river and find Emily. I think Cody's down there too. Doesn't make sense for your dad to drive all over town."

"What about Booger?" Allyson asked. "If he finds you, he'll beat the shit out of you."

How could Jeff have been so stupid? Why had he hit Booger? Everyone knew you didn't touch Booger. He'd broken someone's arm back in grade school and had been the enforcer when he played hockey.

"I'll take my chances. I'll find a ride before he finds me." He touched her on the shoulder. "Thanks for helping me tonight."

"Whatever," Allyson said. Jeff was just like the rest of them. She'd thought he cared about art, books and movies and all the things that mattered, but he was like everyone else in town. Just another person who wanted to drink, and get into fights and get involved in the town drama. Just another townie.

She started down the steps. It would be a while before her dad got here. Maybe she'd walk to the end of the driveway. There was a large streetlamp at the end of the road. If she stood by the Coates family sign, her dad wouldn't miss her.

Jeff stood at the bottom of the steps. She thought he had already gone back to the river, but he was waiting for her.

"Remember earlier when I wanted to tell you a secret?" he asked. She could smell the scent of beer and the iron tang of the blood that had soaked into his jacket.

"Go away, Jeff," she said. "I don't want to talk to you right now. I just want to be alone."

Jeff opened his mouth, like he wanted to tell her something. Then he leaned in, and hugged her tight. She wanted him to let go at the same time that she wanted him to keep holding on.

She let go of him and walked a few steps away. "You're just like everybody else. I thought you were different. I thought you were like me."

"I'm sorry," he said. "I just got caught up in things. I don't like it when Booger insults me. How can I let him say all that racist shit to me? It's hard."

"Just go," she said.

She stood under the lamp at the end of the driveway, watching the cars on the highway. She wasn't sure how long she waited, but it felt like a long time. When her dad's familiar, tired-looking truck trundled up the driveway, she'd never been happier to see anyone in her whole life.

CHAPTER 12

The next day, Donna caught Chloe in the yard, and chewed her out for abandoning her cousin at the party. Allyson stopped talking to her mother for a few days. Donna felt like shit. She'd just been trying to help, and she'd made things worse.

Right before August ended, Chloe left for school. They had a family burger night to commemorate her leaving. During dinner, Allyson sat at the other end of the table from her cousin, and they didn't talk at all. Donna wondered if she was the only one who noticed the silence between the two girls. The night revolved around Chloe. She told them all about her new apartment with Jamie and the classes she was going to take. She was excited to visit the West Edmonton Mall more often. Gord, Donna, Craig and Linda toasted Chloe and wished her well. The next day, Craig and Linda packed up their truck with Chloe's things. Chloe fired up her Celica, and Donna watched the convoy trundle out of the yard. Everything seemed so quiet after the two vehicles left.

In early fall, representatives from Alberta Agriculture came to town to hold a session on animal nutrition and applying for government assistance. People had talked about aid packages for a while, but nothing had come down the pipe. There were rumours people in government were working round the clock trying to pull something together. The Ministers of Agriculture, both provincial and federal, were lobbying hard, trying to get the border open. Phil Hill said Alberta Beef Producers was trying hard to find a solution and get the ranchers some money. Everyone was working.

"You know this is serious," Phil Hill said, when he told Donna about it. "Those government boys don't work on weekends."

Donna normally wouldn't attend an Alberta beef seminar, but she was still working with Carmen's Catering.

This gig meant Donna had only one full day off and worked double shifts sometimes, but she didn't care. Keeping busy was better than being home, worrying about money, about her family, or about the farm.

Since they found out that the farm was in Abby's name, the two couples still hadn't had a conversation about it. They pretended her outburst last fall had never happened.

Donna walked into the multiplex, carrying a tray of lemon squares, haystacks and butter tarts as Carmen followed behind her with her arms loaded up with trays of sandwiches. They walked past the pool and daycare to the room full of farmers at the back. Baking for Carmen was one of Donna's greatest joys right now. Back in the kitchen at Carmen's shop, she turned up the country music, danced a little, and concentrated on baking, something she could control and was good at. She loved the smells and the satisfaction she got from making everything perfectly, and the praise Carmen gave her when she saw the results of Donna's work.

The meeting was packed. Gord had told her sometimes government sessions weren't well attended, but people had driven in from other counties to make it to this one. Everyone was hurting and needed government money.

Donna and Carmen walked past the rows of men sitting at long tables. As Donna passed by, she heard one man in a black Stetson say to his neighbour, "How long is this going to take? I can't handle this anymore. We're bleeding out."

A man in a burgundy sweater and dress pants stood in front of the room.

"We're trying to get the money out as fast as we can," said a young woman standing next to him. She had long brown hair and freckles and couldn't have been much older than Clay. Was the government so in need of workers that they had started to hire children?

"You just need to fill out these forms and we'll get the show on the road," the woman said. "You'll get the money as soon as possible. No one wants anyone to go under."

Donna helped Carmen refill the coffee pot and replaced the creamers sitting in a bowl of ice. The government officials kept on trying to respond to questions from the men. The men wanted answers, wanted to know what was happening, why the money wasn't going to come sooner. One angry man in a green John Deere cap asked if the money would be enough. When was the border going to open?

"Let's just take a coffee break now," the young woman said. "I can see that the snacks are here, and the coffee's been refilled."

"One thing before we break," the man in the burgundy sweater said. "We've got a grief counsellor travelling with us. She's got cards and pamphlets and she's out there if you want to talk."

He looked down at his shoes. "We'll start up again in twenty minutes."

The men stood up and began talking to each other. There was a lot less laughter than Donna had heard when she'd wandered into farm meetings in the past. The men looked tired and resigned. The yellow paint on the walls and the fluorescent lights didn't make anything better. Some of the men got up and clomped down the hall in their cowboy boots. Some of the men stayed sitting, leaning towards each other as they talked. There were a few women in the room, but not many. A woman wearing a green sweatshirt sat in the back, her fingers flying as she knit.

A group of men came to the back of the room where the food was set up and lined up to go past the plates of sandwiches and snacks. Donna watched Gord as he walked toward her.

"Always nice to see my woman in the middle of the day," he said, touching her on the elbow. She gave him a light kiss on the cheek. Donna patted her husband on the arm, then went to check the coffee pot and chat with the other men as they came to fill their Styrofoam cups with coffee and pile sandwiches and baking onto paper plates.

"I should get the wife to get your recipe," Phil Hill said to Donna, as he bit into one of her lemon tarts. "I wish she could bake like you."

"Might not be a good idea," said Doug Miller, as he walked up to take a cookie. "If my wife could bake like you, I'd be even fatter," he said to Donna, giving her a wink.

She winked back. The butter tarts were running low. She opened the Tupperware container on the counter and loaded up another plate.

"Has anyone heard from Ray?" Doug Miller said, looking at Phil and Gord. "I haven't seen him for a while. Normally we catch up at Joe's. He lets me know if he's going into town or not."

"I haven't heard from him in a while either," Gord said. "Maybe I'll drive out there on my way home."

The man in the burgundy sweater had returned to the front of the room and was looking at the crowd. The young woman standing next to him rang a bell.

"Guess we're starting up again," Gord said. He rested his arm on Donna's shoulder. "See you at home."

He walked back to his seat and Donna studied his ass. Damn, even at forty six and with a couple of extra pounds, her man still looked fine in his jeans.

Carmen came up beside her, standing so close that Donna could feel the warmth of her body. Carmen's fleshy body took up space, but in a cozy way that made you want to hug her. Her cheeks had a flush to them, and she wore pink sweatshirts with cats on them, and hung Anne Geddes prints (which Donna hated), in the back room of her café. Donna would have hated the sweatshirts on anyone else, but on Carmen, they seemed to work.

"Hot in here," Carmen said, fanning her hand in front of her face.

"Mind if I sneak to the washroom and get a bit of air?" Donna said.

Carmen nodded. "I can handle it."

After using the washroom, Donna pushed open the heavy main doors of the multiplex and walked outside into the warm air. Sitting on the bench outside the main doors, she saw a farmer she recognized. He was having a smoke and chatting with a woman. The farmer turned and saw her, and then moved in closer to the woman. They leaned close together, their heads almost touching. Then the man stood up, took a pamphlet from the woman's hands, and walked back into the hall, avoiding Donna's gaze.

The woman turned toward Donna.

"It's nice out, isn't it?"

"Yes," Donna said. She was never much for small talk with people she didn't know.

The woman stood up and shook her hand. "I'm Melody, the counsellor. I'm here if you need to talk. I know a lot of people are having a tough time."

There was something about this woman that made Donna want to tell her everything, but she kept her mouth shut.

"This whole border closure is hard on people's stress levels," Melody said. "I've been travelling around with the government as they do their presentations, just letting people know about their options. There are people available if you need to talk." She shook her head. "You know, I've heard that people are calling the government lines, just asking for help and what they can do. They're not even calling the aid people. They're calling anyone they can get hold of. You got cattle?"

Donna nodded.

"You doing okay?" the counsellor asked.

She wasn't sure what to tell the woman.

"I gotta go," she said. "I need to get back in there."

Melody pushed a pamphlet into her hand. Donna looked down at the paper, saw bright coloured letters advertising therapy, family and marital counselling.

"We have an office in Lloyd," she said. "We find rural people are more comfortable talking to people outside the town. You know, secrets and town gossip. I grew up in a small town, so I know how it goes."

The heavy door of the multiplex closed behind them. Donna turned her head, feeling as though she'd been caught doing something she shouldn't. Craig walked by her. "Just getting something from the truck," he said. "Nice job on the lunch."

Donna didn't acknowledge him. "I need to go and check on the coffee," she said.

Melody caught Donna's eye and her big brown eyes reminded Donna of Maggie.

"Will you be around for my presentation?"

"I'll probably be back at the café, cleaning up," Donna said.

"It was nice to meet you," Melody said, sticking out her hand. Her peach nail polish made Donna feel self-conscious about her own bitten nails and dry hands.

"You can call any time," she said. "My door is open. And costs are low. The government has some programs for farmers right now."

"Thank you," Donna said. She turned and walked towards the door of the multiplex.

"There's help if you need it," Melody called.

Donna shoved the pamphlet into her coat pocket, pretended she hadn't heard, and let the door of the multiplex close behind her.

CHAPTER 13

Gord picked Allyson up from school that afternoon, after the meeting.

"I want to stop by Ray's on the way home," her dad said. "Haven't seen him a couple days and it's always good to check in."

Allyson hadn't seen Ray since before his cattle had been killed. She had heard her parents say that he had gone into the city to visit his kids a few times. Her mother had driven out to his ranch with some pies for him. He loved her pecan pie.

"He's had a long face for a while now," her dad said, as they drove down the highway. "He's not cracking jokes the way he used to. He lost a part of himself when they took those cows away."

And to make it worse, Ray still hadn't heard anything about his cows. They might have BSE after all. Sure, the government was doing their job, but the cows might have been killed for nothing.

"Sometimes you gotta wonder if Ralph Klein is right," Gord said, his eyes on the highway. "Maybe it would be better if everyone just shot, shovelled and shut up. Then we wouldn't all be in this mess."

Allyson looked out the window as they drove. Soon she'd be eligible to get her driver's license and she'd be able to drive anywhere she wanted.

They drove past the Wray farm and Allyson studied their flock of black-faced sheep.

"Did you know sheep and bison can't get past the border either?" her dad said, as he caught her looking at the sheep. "The border is shut to everything that could have the same type of disease. It's like the whole world has gone crazy. Everyone is suffering."

They reached the end of Ray's long driveway. Allyson had been here many times when she was a little girl. When Ray's wife, April, was alive, they'd had a large, scary black dog. April, who smiled just as much as her husband, tried to make Allyson feel better by chaining the dog up to the doghouse whenever Allyson came to visit. She looked for the dog, even though she knew he had been dead for many years. An old tractor rested by the fence, and there was a large planter house in front of the bungalow that read "The Sharps."

Ray's golden lab, Cheese, came over to greet them, running up to the truck when they stopped on a bit of gravel near the barn.

"Hey, girl," Gord said, giving the dog a scratch behind the ears.

Ray's blue truck was parked near the barn. A couple of abandoned, rusty cars were parked next to it. Why did some people have so much junk at their places? They just seemed to collect crap and let years of hobbies and projects pile up around their home. It was like they were afraid to get rid of anything. She would never be like this when she grew up. She would have a room full of books, but she wouldn't keep useless junk around.

Allyson got out of the truck and followed her dad up to the house. The blue paint on the outside of the bungalow was weathered. Allyson looked at the drawn, floral curtains in the window as her dad knocked on the door. April had probably bought the curtains before she died and Ray hadn't bothered to replace them, even though she'd been gone for years.

Gord opened the door and went in, motioning to Allyson to follow. Her mom hated that people just walked into other people's houses without knocking, but her dad had grown up doing it and had no qualms about it.

"Ray," Gord called. "It's Gord. Allyson and I are here."

Inside Ray's kitchen, the tap dripped. There were a few coffee-stained mugs in the sink. The red light of the coffee pot glowed, but the kitchen was quiet.

"Maybe he's watching TV and can't hear us," Gord said, taking his boots off at the door. Allyson took her shoes off, too. In the front room, the coffee table was piled high with magazines and cat-alogues. An old recliner angled itself toward a faded brown love seat while the TV's big grey eye surveyed the empty room. The grandfather clock in the corner ticked. As she and Gord walked through the room, the clock struck, breaking the eerie silence.

"Ray?" Gord called again.

"I don't think he's here," Allyson said.

"His truck is out front."

They went back to the kitchen. "I'm just going to check the rest of the house," Gord said. "You stay here."

Allyson could tell her father was worried, and didn't want to state the obvious. Ray was an old man. He could have fallen or passed out. Maybe he'd had a heart attack.

After a few minutes, her dad came back to the kitchen. It was warm in the house. She could feel her armpits starting to get sweaty.

"I wouldn't think this was so unusual if I hadn't heard from him for a while," Gord said. "Usually someone knows where he is. He's good at letting people know when he goes into the city."

Her dad opened the door and they walked back outside. Cheese came running up to them.

"I'm just going to check the shop and the barn," her dad said. "Why don't you wait in the truck?"

Allyson opened the door and climbed into the truck. From the front seat, she watched her dad walk into the barn. She'd fin-ished her book at lunch and had nothing to read. As she looked out the window, a calico barn cat walked across the yard, mean-dering in front of the truck. Her dad came out of the barn, shaking his head. He walked over to the shop.

The cat sat under a tree in the yard and licked its paws.

The door to the truck opened and her father leaned across the seat. His face was pale.

"I need you to get into the house," he said.

She didn't ask questions, just hopped down from the truck and ran across the yard. The dog loped behind her.

Inside the house, Gord walked across the kitchen floor with his muddy boots and grabbed the phone. Allyson stood in the doorway, watching as her dad jabbed at three numbers. He was shaking.

Maybe there had been some kind of gas leak. At school, they had had to take farm safety and they had learned about a kind of gas that killed people immediately. When you saw someone lying down dead, you shouldn't even bother trying to save them. This gas was so deadly that if you even stopped for a second, the gas would kill you too.

"I need RCMP or ambulance," her dad said. There was a pause. "He's dead," Gord told the other person on the line. "Ray Sharp. I found him in his shop."

Allyson stood still. Ray was dead. Did he have a heart attack? A stroke? She wanted to cry, but her entire body felt brittle and dry. She couldn't move; she was frozen by the news.

Her dad listened for a bit, thanked the person on the other line, and then dialled again. He waited for a bit, swore, and then dialled another number.

"Linda," he said, when she picked up. "I'm at Ray's place and he's dead. I need someone to come here and pick up Allyson. We're inside the house. The RCMP are going to be here right away."

He listened as she talked, but Allyson couldn't hear what her aunt was saying. "I can't answer your questions right now."

"How did he die?" Allyson asked. "How long has he been dead?"

Her dad took off his coat, draped it over a chair, and sat down. "I don't know," he said. He put his head in his hands.

Allyson was clammy and hot. Her dad stood up again and walked over to the coffee pot. "No sense leaving this on," he said. "No one's going to be making coffee around here any time soon."

He turned away from the coffee pot and walked towards her. He leaned over and gave her a big bear hug, and she relaxed into the solidness of him.

After a few minutes, Gord let go and went to sit back down at the table. There was nothing to say. The silence was heavy and awkward, but every time Allyson tried to think of something to talk about, it seemed banal and stupid. One of her grandpa's best friends was dead.

"How did he die?" she asked again.

Gord shook his head. "Not now."

The doorknob jiggled and Linda and Craig came into the house. They'd beaten the RCMP.

"It's so awful," Linda said, walking over the kitchen floor to give Allyson a hug.

Craig gave a curt nod. "I'm going to stay with you, and Linda is going to take Allyson," he said.

"Let's go," Linda said to Allyson.

As Allyson walked to the car, she felt as though she was watching a movie or floating above her own body, watching everything from far, far away.

Linda moved back towards the door and motioned to Craig. "Call me if you need anything. I can come back if you want, right after I get the girl home."

Linda and Allyson walked out into the yard. A bird chirped and the sound was eerie; too cheerful for the experience. As they got into Linda's car, Allyson saw the RCMP car coming up the long driveway. Linda waited until the car reached the yard and parked. Then she drove past the car, waving as they passed.

Growing up on a farm, Allyson had always known about death, but it had never been as present as it was this past year. She'd seen calves die, and sometimes cows dropped dead for no reason. Her family raised cattle and then took them to the slaughterhouse, where they died. But that was different from human death. A few years ago, she hadn't had anyone close to her die. Now she'd lost both Grandpa Al and Ray. Maybe you let go of your childhood when the people around you started to die. The older you got, the more people would die. That was the price you paid for growing up.

As they drove, Allyson looked out the window. Did her dad know how Ray died? Could he tell? Or did it really matter?

It was a short drive from Ray's house to their farm, but tonight the drive felt long, the driveway interminable.

"Your mom is still in town," Linda said, when they pulled into the driveway. "Do you want to come over? I have cookies. Or I can make you some tea."

Allyson hadn't been in her aunt's house for a while. She used to go there all the time, almost every day. But she'd stopped going there when she and Chloe had stopped spending time together. Now Chloe was gone.

"I just want to go home," she said.

Linda gave her a hug. "Do you want me to come in with you?"

"No, it's okay," Allyson said. "I'll just read or something."

"Your mom should be home soon. If you want company, just come over."

Inside the house, Allyson climbed the stairs to her room. She lay down on the bed, grabbed a copy of *Harry Potter and the Prisoner of Azkaban,* and flipped through the pages. But she couldn't concentrate on the words. She put the book down, went back downstairs and out the door. Outside, she walked past her grandparents' house and down to the edge of the pasture. Wind bit at her face, and strands of her long brown hair blew about. She looked at the fields in front of her. Her dad and grandfather had always talked about the beauty of the landscape, how breathtaking everything was and how lucky they all were to live here. But they were wrong. This land was killing them. She could see what was happening to her parents, and what had happened to Ray. How different things could have been if she'd been born somewhere else. What kind of person would she be if she had grown up in Vancouver or even Saskatoon?

She could smell the warm, earthy smell of the cows off in the distance. What was she doing out here? What had just happened? She didn't want to think about any of it. She trudged back across the yard to her house, and went back upstairs to her bedroom. She lay on her bed and turned on the stereo. Maybe music would help. As she lay down, she realized how exhausted she was and felt her body relax. She fell asleep in her clothes, without bothering to eat supper. In the middle of the night, she woke up and put on her pyjamas, and went to the bathroom to wash her face and brush her teeth.

She didn't see her dad in the morning. Her mother said that he had gotten home late, and he was still in bed when Allyson got up for school. At school that day, a few people asked her if she had seen Ray's body. News travelled fast in the town, and by noon, everyone knew Ray was dead and her father was the one who had found him. She'd blown them all off, saying that she didn't want to talk about it, saying she'd seen nothing.

At dinner that night, Colton was chatty, talking about how they'd hired a new guy at the auto shop. The guy was clueless and didn't know what he was doing. But he was the boss' nephew so they had to train him and help him out and pretend he was competent, even though he would have been fired if he were anyone else. Allyson found herself annoyed by her brother and his candour. She missed Clay. Everything was better with Clay around. He just seemed to have an innate ability to calm everyone down, to soothe the prickly spaces between everyone.

She watched her parents as they chewed. She hated the sound of her family as they ate, hated the workman-like crunch of their jaws, the sound of swallowing. The exhalation and gulping sound her dad made when he finished a glass of milk. They were like barbarians.

Colton stopped talking, and the table was quiet.

As she looked around the table, at the faces of her family, the whole thing felt so wrong. How could they all just be sitting here, eating as though nothing had happened?

"How did Ray die?" she asked.

Donna looked at her, and speared a piece of broccoli. "It's not appropriate dinner conversation."

Her father coughed. "I don't really want to talk about it."

Allyson put down her fork. "Why can't we talk about it?" she said. "Why do we keep on keeping secrets? I just want to know how he died. What did the RCMP say?"

She looked from her parents, who both stared down at their plates. Colton chewed his macaroni and cheese, looking from one face to another.

"You need to start telling us things," she said. "I'm not a baby any more. And it's not that hard for us to find things out. You think you can hide things from me, but you're kidding yourselves. You can't pretend everything is fine." She took a deep breath. "I want to know how Ray died."

Her dad put down his fork and looked at her. "Well, I guess you want to be adult enough to hear this," her dad said. "Ray shot himself in the head."

Donna's voice was soft. "You never know what is going through someone's head when they take their own life. It's always so horrible. Just such a terrible loss."

Allyson could see the tears starting in her mother's eyes.

Gord cleared his throat. "The stress of losing his cattle probably did him in." He scraped his fork across his empty plate. "I don't have that much else to say about it. I don't want to talk about it anymore. Didn't sleep much last night," he said. "I'm going to go out in the yard and go check the cows and then turn in early."

He stood up, picked up his dishes, and placed them on the counter with a clunk. Allyson watched as he left the room, still trying to process what her father had said.

CHAPTER 14

After Gord found Ray Sharp's body, everything seemed to stop. He had been looking for a job, asking around, trying to find work and some extra money. But all that ground to a halt after Ray died.

In the nights afterward, Donna listened as Gord tossed and turned beside her. She woke up every time he got out of bed and started pacing through the house. One night, when he had been up more times than a jack in the box, making the bed creak every time, she offered him a sleeping pill.

"You're barely sleeping," she said. "Just take one of these pills and you'll at least get a good night's sleep."

Gord turned over to face her. "Part of me wants to say no, but I'm tired enough to try anything," he said.

"Just lay back down and I'll get it for you," she said.

Until a few weeks ago, Gord never had much trouble sleeping. He was concerned a few years ago when she came home with the sleeping pills.

"It's just for when I feel anxious and can't sleep," she told Gord.

"You need to be careful with those," he said. "I hear it's really easy to get addicted."

"I'll be careful," she said.

They never talked about it again. She kept the small vial of blue pills on her side of the medicine cabinet.

Donna left the room to get a glass of water and a pill. Gord sat up in bed when she returned to the bedroom. Looking at him, she remembered all the nights tending to their children when they were sick. She would bring them cough syrup or flat ginger ale and they would struggle up from their prostrate positions, their bodies sticky with a thin film of sweat, helpless and vulnerable. She flipped the light switch so she could see Gord and he squinted into the light.

"You'll feel better if you sleep," she said, holding her hand out to him.

He took the blue pill from her and swallowed it. She handed him the glass of water and watched his throat as he drank. He placed the tall glass on the bedside table when he finished, and lay back down, pulling the blue quilt up over himself.

"Thanks," he said. "Every time I close my eyes, I see Ray's body."

Donna hadn't asked Gord to tell her about what Ray's body had looked like. She didn't want to know. There hadn't been any funeral. People in town whispered about it at the coffee shop. Doug Miller said he'd seen Ray Sharp's kids driving through town, probably on their way to the farm. Figured they'd probably sell it.

Donna asked Gord if he wanted to talk to someone about finding Ray's body.

"It's a pretty big deal. I think you should maybe talk to someone. See a doctor. You might need some antidepressants. Or you might need a therapist to help you get those images out of your head."

Gord was quiet for a minute. "I'll think about it," he said and rolled over, indicating that the conversation was finished.

Pam was calling Donna more often. It used to be that Donna was the one who called Pam when she had a spare moment, but now Pam called her twice a week, like clockwork.

"Just checking in," Pam said, her voice bright. Pam and Mary Anne must have talked to each other and created a checking-in schedule. Mary Anne had been calling a lot too, asking Donna if she wanted to come into town, offering to bring the Klassens food, asking Donna if she needed anything done. One time, Mary Anne had driven over and brought a bottle of wine and a gift certificate for a massage.

Donna told Pam the news about Ray the day after it happened.

"Why did he do it?" Pam said.

"He just couldn't take any more," Donna said.

Everyone with cattle knew why Ray had done it. Donna had heard that awful little voice in her head. That voice had come to her, whispering that she had nothing worth living for when she had postpartum depression after having Allyson.

"I feel like you guys can't catch a break," Pam said when she called one night.

"I feel like I'm ready to curl up and die," Donna said.

"Don't say that," Pam said. "Things can only go up from here. They can't get worse."

Donna was quiet for a moment. "They can always get worse," she said.

"I'm worried about you guys," Pam said. Her voice sounded far away. Sometimes she put Donna on speakerphone when she was cooking or moving around the kitchen. It just reminded Donna of how small, quiet and contained Pam's life was. She could never put Pam on speakerphone in her own kitchen. "You're always welcome in the city if you need a break from everything."

"We'll survive," Donna said, rubbing her neck. It was always stiff lately. "We always do."

"You need to do better than survive," Pam said. "I hate seeing you guys like this."

After she hung up the phone, Donna lay back down on the bed and thought. She had run out of fingers to count how the number of times she had heard Gord say, "The border will open. Things will get better."

He said it so often that it started to feel like a refrain, the chorus of a popular country song playing on the radio. Almost every week, Gord had a meeting or a rally to go to. A couple weeks ago, the cattle ranchers had rented a big refrigerated truck, filled it with packaged meat and gone to Edmonton to sell it. They drove to the Alberta Legislature to protest on the front lawn and try to tell the city folk how much they were suffering. Some of the men, like Phil Hill, called around to restaurants in the city to see if they'd be willing to buy meat.

One night, when they were watching the news, Gord rocked back and forth in his La-Z-Boy, causing it to creak.

"They are starting to forget about us," he said, staring at the TV. He turned, and started flipping through the pile of clippings sitting next to his chair.

Donna had been paging through *Chatelaine*, looking for new beef recipes.

"What do you mean?" she asked.

"The newspapers are moving on," he said. "When was the last time they reported on the border closure on the news? It's like the world has forgotten about us and we're still out here bleeding."

"You sound like your dad," Donna said. "That's something he would say."

Linda had talked about renting out Al and Abby's house, but no one had done anything about it yet. Donna still hadn't been inside. She knew Linda and Craig had gone in a few times, but she couldn't make herself go in there. Even though she had walked in without knocking when Abby and Al were still living there, she didn't dream of going into the house without them. The thought of strangers, of people they didn't know renting the house and living in the yard and knowing her business, well, it was enough to make her puke.

Donna was tired. She'd been working a lot at both of her jobs. There were signs all over town that things would not be fine. Convinced that the cattle business was never going to come back, some of their neighbours sold their cattle, even though they were worth nothing. They'd quietly gone out of business. There was less joking at the coffee shops. Donna had become obsessed with their bank account. Every time she was in town, she went to the ATM and checked the balances. How could they have so little in savings? Why couldn't they have saved more? She watched as the number went further and further down. Gord kept on talking about an aid package from the government, but no one had seen anything of the sort yet. He'd heard rumours one night that the government was working around the clock, staying at night inside their offices, sleeping on cots so they could figure out a way to get money to people.

Donna heard the thump of footsteps coming into the living room. She turned to see Colton.

"I want to take you guys out tomorrow," he said.

"What?" Donna said.

"Let's go for steak," he said. "My treat."

"That would be nice," Gord said, shifting in his chair.

"Six o'clock," Colton said. "Lily and I will meet you downtown at Dinah's steakhouse."

"What's the occasion?" Donna asked.

"I've got news," Colton said, and left the room before they could ask him anything else.

Donna knew something was up. She looked at Gord, who shrugged.

"That boy wants something," she said.

"Don't know," Gord said and turned back to the TV, dismissing the subject.

The next day, Donna, Gord and Allyson drove into town and parked the truck in front of the restaurant.

Donna tried to quash her thoughts as they walked towards Dinah's. The whole thing was making her anxious. What did Colton have to tell them? Maybe he just wanted to announce that he was finally moving out. It would be nice not to have to feed him. She hoped that was it. He was making decent money at work and he was barely ever at home anyway.

Knowing Colton, he had probably knocked Lily up, and figured the best way to tell them was to invite them all to a celebratory dinner. He would make the announcement, and they would have to lift their wine glasses high and pretend to be happy. Donna and Gord wouldn't be able to say anything, because they'd done the same thing themselves.

Inside the restaurant, Colton waved to them from a booth. Lily sat beside him. He smiled at them, and Donna was taken back to his childhood. He'd been a frequent smiler, always getting into things, trailing along behind Al like a baby duck following its mother. Al had been the one who had first noticed his mechanical ability, encouraging him to work on the farm vehicles, teaching him about cars and tractors.

"I ordered a bottle of wine for the table," Colton said as they clambered into the booth.

They seated themselves, and the waitress, who bore a striking resemblance to Mabel Jacobson, brought them waters and menus.

They studied their menus. Donna was game for anything but beef. The waitress returned with their wine and uncorked it. Colton made a show of taking the first sip. Donna reached for the glass the second it was placed in front of her. She had a feeling she was going to need it. The wine tasted bitter, but she managed to choke it down.

The waitress took their orders. Gord and Colton were the only ones who ordered steaks.

They sat and made small talk for a few minutes, talking about nothing until Donna couldn't stand it anymore.

"What's your news?" she said, interrupting Gord. "You brought us here for something. What do you have to tell us?"

She looked at her son across the table. Lily took a sip from her wine glass. So she wasn't pregnant. Or if she was pregnant, she was irresponsible.

"I've been feeling like I want to do something different with my life," said Colton. "So I'm going to make a big change."

Donna leaned forward in anticipation.

"Spit it out, son," Gord said.

"I've joined the military," Colton said.

Donna let out a breath of air she didn't know she was holding, and raised her glass to take a big gulp of wine.

"The military?" Gord said. "Why? Where did you get that idea from?"

"I knew you would say that," Colton said. Lily put her hand on the table and he reached out to hold it. "I knew you would think I was crazy to join up. But it makes sense. I'll have a job, and I can use my mechanical skills. I've done the research and talked to people about it. It's the right thing to do."

He looked from Gord to Donna. Donna remembered how he had looked when he was a child and had been caught doing something he wasn't supposed to do.

"Why?" Donna asked. "Why do you want to do this?"

"Just watching the war on the news," Colton said. "And then after Grandpa Al died, I felt like I needed to be doing something meaningful."

Allyson, who had been quiet, stirred her Sprite around with her straw and said, "So you're going to kill people?"

"Allyson," Gord said. "Shut up."

"But people die when they go to war," she said. "And they have to kill people."

Colton ignored her. "I just have this feeling that this is what I need to do. The idea got under my skin and it won't go away."

Gord reached for his wine glass and knocked back some of his wine. He wasn't normally a wine drinker.

"There are a lot of things in this world that are worth doing," Gord said. "I could use your help, especially with Dad gone. You should stick around."

"You don't get it," Colton said. He picked up his napkin and twisted it around in his hands. "There's no future here. I can't stay here. I don't want to. I want to do something that matters."

Gord flinched as if he'd been hit. "Farming matters," he said. "We produce food for people. We're keeping your grandfather's dream alive. What could be more important than that?"

Colton shook his head and ripped up a small piece of the napkin. "It's not for me," he said. "I want more out of life."

Donna watched Gord's body tense.

"Come on now," she said. "Don't talk like that to your father."

"I'm not like the other people in this family," Colton said. "I'm never going to be good at school and I'm not someone who can turn everything I touch to gold. I'm just going to go off, and work hard and try this out."

"This isn't the right decision," Donna said. They'd just lost a family member. Why would Colton pick something so drastic, so dangerous?

"You could die," she said, her voice small. "I couldn't take it if you died. I can't take anything more."

He shook his head. "Don't think about it like that. Think about it like I'm doing what I need to do. Like I'm following a calling. Besides, it would be a long time before I could get stationed anywhere."

"Following a calling?" Gord said, his voice low and dark. "Come on, boy. What kind of hippie talk is that? Klassens don't talk like that. You could do some good around here. What's wrong with you?"

The waitress showed up, her arms full of platters of food. A young, skinny guy with acne scars followed behind her, and placed steaming dishes in front of everyone. Colton leaned forward, picked up his wine glass and took a long swig, as if he hadn't had anything to drink in days.

"How are we doing here?" the waitress chirped. She was too cheerful, Donna thought. She must never have suffered or experienced any sadness. Why did everything have to happen to them? If Donna had believed in God, really believed in God, the way Abby and Al believed, she would have thought that God hated them and wanted to get back at them.

"We're fine," Gord said, forcing a smile. "Just fine."

"Need anything else?" the waitress said. She was nosy, just like Mabel Jacobson. Donna couldn't remember the relationship between them. Anita would have known. The waitress reminded Donna of a bird, with her pointy nose and bright eyes. A small annoying bird.

"We're fine," Donna snapped, and then she felt bad. It wasn't the waitress's fault that Colton had some crazy ideas in his head. She felt her mouth contort into a smile. "Thank you," she said, smiling like a beauty pageant queen.

The waitress left. Gord and Allyson started eating. Colton drank a glass of water. He was holding Lily's hand on top of the table. Now Donna wished that they had sprung an engagement or pregnancy announcement. Anything but this.

"You can't stop me from going," Colton said. "I'm an adult."

Gord put down his fork. "You think you're an adult, but you're not. You won't be an adult until you have to deal with adult problems."

Colton leaned forward. "I'm going to do what I have to do," he said. "Whether or not you approve of it. I'm leaving for Shilo in a couple of weeks."

For a minute, Gord looked as though he was going to say something. Then he curved his head towards his plate, picked up his fork again and started eating. He kept his head down, lifting his fork to his mouth again and again. Maybe he believed that if he ignored Colton, the problem would go away. Colton was smart. If they had been at home, someone would have run out of the room or there would have been yelling by now. Donna glanced around the restaurant. A family with three young children sat in a booth. A girl of around six years old leaned against the corner of the table. Braids framed her face as she concentrated on colouring with crayons, pressing down hard on the table. A blonde woman, her face puffy with weight from a recent pregnancy, nursed a baby while a man about her age spooned food into a toddler's mouth. Donna remembered the noise and constant want of young children. How her body ached for sleep. How she loved them and resented them and their loud voices, sticky fingers, constant mood swings, and petty demands. But things were easier back then. Things were simpler when she had Abby and Al and years stretching ahead of her, years that promised a bright future. The future ahead looked dim.

An older farming couple sat a few booths down from the family. The man wore a dusty ball cap and the woman a blue windbreaker. The two of them sat in a companionable silence, raising soup spoons to their mouth almost in unison. The waitress came by to refill their coffee cups and the old woman smiled at her. She put her hand on her husband's for a minute, and the two of them held hands. Donna felt a wave of longing for Abby and Al, followed by sadness. Would she and Gord end up being like those people? It was hard to think about the future, about being that old, when it felt like the world was trying to wipe them out.

She looked around the table. Everyone seemed to be off in their own world, concentrating on their plates. Lily's hand was on Colton's knee.

"What do you think about this?" she asked, addressing Lily.

"It's what he wants to do," Lily said. Donna had never noticed how blue her eyes were. "I don't like it, but I have to let him do what he wants. He says it's important to him."

"We're going to figure it out," Colton said. "She'll join me at some point and we'll get married. Just need to see what happens after basic training. We'll see how it plays out."

Donna hadn't touched her food. She wasn't hungry, even though the food smelled good. She pushed the plate towards the centre of the table and reached for her wine glass. The wine tasted like it had gone off.

"Even though your dad would love to stop you from doing this, we can't," she said. "You're old enough."

Colton nodded.

"I just wish you hadn't settled on this path," she said, taking another sip of wine. It was definitely off.

Colton looked down at the table. "You don't even like me."

"How can you say that?" Donna said. "I'm your mother and I love you."

The words felt hollow in her mouth.

Allyson, who had finished eating, pushed her plate away, pulled out a book and started reading at the table. Donna and Gord had stopped her from reading at the table in the past, but no one said anything about it this time. Donna's stomach churned.

"Are we done here?" Gord asked, as he scraped his plate.

"I'm ready to go home," Donna said.

"But you didn't even eat anything," Gord said.

"My stomach doesn't feel so good," Donna said. "I'll get a doggie bag."

"I'll get the waitress," Colton said, standing up.

After he paid, they all left the restaurant.

"Well," Gord said to Colton, as he walked them to their truck. "Guess we'll see you at home."

Gord, Allyson and Donna got into the truck. As they drove away, Donna looked back at her son and his girlfriend as they stood on the street. She watched as the two figures got smaller and smaller, watched until she couldn't see them anymore.

CHAPTER 15

The morning after Colton left, Donna came down for breakfast. Her face was puffy, and Allyson could tell she'd been crying. Allyson didn't say anything about it; just glanced at her mother, then stuck her spoon back into her cereal.

Alyson spent a lot of time alone that fall. Jeff had contacted her on Messenger and apologized after the party and they'd chatted a bit. But they hadn't done anything together. He'd apologized to her, but she wasn't sure how to act around him anymore. They barely talked. The only person that Allyson really talked to was Amber, but she was busy practicing piano all the time, studying for her Royal Conservatory of Music exams. She wasn't around very much.

Allyson couldn't help but notice how much her mother was checking in on her since Ray Sharp's death. A couple nights after Allyson had found out how he'd died, her mom came into her room and asked her if she wanted to talk about it. Allyson didn't have the words to express how she was feeling inside and how dark and sad she felt because of Ray's death.

Her mom sat down on the bed next to her and sighed.

"This is tough stuff," she said.

"Is Dad going to be okay?" Allyson asked, studying her mother's face. "I mean, he was the one who found him."

Her mother was worried about her dad. Allyson could tell by the way her mom looked at him at the dinner table. She knew her mom talked about her dad to Pam or Clay on the phone. She couldn't always hear what was discussed because Donna typically went into another room to talk, but she could hear the tone of her voice and the rise and fall of her words.

Her mother looked down at her hands. "I don't know," she said. She turned to look at her daughter's face.

"I'm worried about him, Allyson. He's been through so much."

Allyson sat up, crawled across the bed and gave her mother a hug. At least her mother was honest. She wasn't trying to pretend she wasn't worried, that there wasn't something deeply wrong with her father. Allyson didn't know how to talk about how she felt inside, about the big pit of darkness growing inside her all the time.

"Ray's death is sad," she said, and the words sounded stupid and babyish even to her.

"I know," her mom said. "I think so too."

They hugged for a few minutes. Then Allyson told her mother she was tired and wanted to go to sleep. She just wanted to be alone.

In the weeks after he'd left, Colton phoned a few times. Allyson still couldn't believe he had joined the military. The last time he phoned, she heard her mom asking him what he was doing.

"He sounds like he's fine," her mom said to her dad after she hung up the phone.

"Maybe this was what he needed to get his life together," Gord said.

The last time Allyson had been to Joe's with her dad and the other farmers, she saw Lily walking around the restaurant, wiping tables, looking aimless. Allyson had never had much use for Lily, but she waved at her anyway. Allyson left the men at their table and went to sit at the back booth, where she usually met Jeff. There was no sign of him.

"Have you heard from Colton?" Allyson asked, when Lily came over to the table.

"He calls and he sends email when he has access to a computer," Lily said. "We talk a few times a week. Things are going well. I'm going to go visit him soon."

Allyson started to rifle though her backpack, pretending to look for a book, so she didn't have to talk any more.

"Do you need anything?" Lily asked. "Another pop?"

"No, thanks," Allyson said.

★

Clay and Chloe were home for Thanksgiving weekend. The families had planned to go to the lodge to have dinner with Abby. When Clay arrived, Allyson joined him on a trail ride around the back forty. She hadn't been on a trail ride in a long time. She used to ride with Chloe before things changed between them, or with her dad before Grandpa Al died. Her dad was even busier since Colton left. They hadn't bred many cattle this year, but there were still calves to wean. Allyson hated this time, hated the bawling of the animals, the frantic cries of the calves when they were separated from their mothers. The only person who hated it more than she did was Donna. She said the bawling of the calves reminded her of babies crying. During weaning week, her mother spent more time in town. She stayed late at work, or went to visit Mary Anne. She never fessed up to these habits, but everyone in the family knew.

It was good to have Clay back. Hanging out with him and riding over the trails together made Allyson feel more relaxed than she had in weeks. She watched her brother's back. How many times had she looked up at him in front of her and felt safe? He was the one leading the way, the one who could make everything better. The air was cold and crisp as they rode along the path.

"It's so quiet here with Colton gone," she said, as Clay stopped Temple on the top of a hill so he could look at the cows. Temple's brown eyes surveyed the scene as she nickered and then put her head down for a few bites of grass. Gord had owned Temple for years, and loved her. Clay stroked her mane with one hand, and turned back to look at his sister.

"I bet," Clay said. "Less stress for Mom and Dad, but another pair of hands gone."

"I've been trying to help more," Allyson said.

Clay squinted at her. "You should come visit me in the city if you need a break. I'd try to get home more, but I just have so much work to do for school. Makes it hard to get away."

He gave Temple a kick and they started back towards the house.

Back at the barn, Clay hopped off Temple. She dismounted from Crow, and started getting ready to put the horses away.

"Who knows how long this will go on?" Clay said. "And the thing is, it's never going to be the same as before. At least the aid package should be coming soon. That's what Dad said."

They brushed the horses and put their tack away. Allyson and her brother led the horses into their pen and Clay gave them a fresh bale of hay. As they ate, Allyson stroked the sides of Temple's face, admiring the animal's lovely blonde colour and her huge dark eyes. There was something calming about being around the horses, the cats and the dogs. Maybe she'd come out to the barn and draw the horses later.

"How are Mom and Dad doing without Colton?" Clay asked as they started towards the house.

Allyson shrugged. "Fine, I guess. They've talked to him a few times."

"He called me when he was thinking about signing up," Clay said, raising his hand to scratch his nose. "I told him to go for it."

"Why?" Allyson said. Her brother's face was shaded by the brim of his cowboy hat.

"He was lost," Clay said. "If he stayed here, he'd just end up working at the mechanic shop for his whole life. He'd knock Lily up and have to marry her. He wanted something. I could hear it when I talked to him."

"But he could get killed," Allyson said. "Or he could kill somebody."

Clay shook his head. "It'll be a long time before he gets sent anywhere. Besides, what else does he have to do?"

"He could have gone to work in the patch," Allyson said.

"He'd make scads of money, but he'd end up a caveman like Booger. This way is better. He'll get to learn about the world. Get out, like I did."

Maggie ran up, and Clay leaned over and scratched her behind the ears.

"Don't worry," he said to Allyson. "You'll get out of here. I know how badly you want to leave, how being on the farm is sort of killing you. The world will still be there by the time you're done high school. Maybe by that time I'll be thinking about coming back to the farm."

He looked towards Craig and Linda's house.

"What time did they say Chloe was coming? Today or tomorrow?"

"Tomorrow morning," Allyson said. "She wanted to spend Friday night in the city."

Chloe hadn't even called Allyson to talk to her since she'd left. Linda had been over a few times, and Allyson had overheard her aunt and her mother talking about how her cousin was doing. She was loving the city, making lots of friends and taking a great course in animal science. This sounded more interesting than Allyson's life. All she did was go to school, practice her trumpet, watch TV and read. Sometimes she went to Joe's diner or the library. Boring compared to the adventures Chloe was having in the city.

"It's going to be weird to have Thanksgiving at the lodge," Clay said. "But I guess there's a first time for everything."

Allyson wasn't looking forward to eating at the lodge. The lodge creeped her out. Some of the female residents were nice and asked her questions when they saw her, but many of them spent a lot of time staring into space, nodding off in their wheelchairs. People moved and talked slowly, and some of them sat and stared into space, like upright corpses. Whenever Allyson was there, her chest felt tight. The corner of the lodge that housed the dementia patients frightened her the most. She'd ended up in that ward one day by accident and had seen a woman sitting in a chair, rocking back and forth and wailing. Another man had a puzzle in front of him and he jammed the puzzle pieces against one another, unable to make the pieces fit together. She'd turned and fled back to Abby's room, where she had stayed until her dad was ready to leave. Since then, she never left Abby's room whenever she was at the lodge for a visit.

★

It was mid-afternoon on Saturday by the time Chloe's car came barrelling into the yard. Allyson was in the front room reading when the car pulled up and Chloe got out. Allyson could see that she'd cut her hair to her chin and coloured it a dark, reddish purple that made her look like something out of *The Matrix*.

Chloe saw Allyson in the window and waved. Allyson waved back. Chloe gestured to her to come outside. The dogs came up to greet Chloe and she crouched and embraced them as they jumped on her, trying to lick her face. Allyson went to the door, put on her shoes and went outside.

Chloe stood up when she saw her.

"Hey," she said. When she got close enough to her cousin, she could smell a new perfume. Her cousin smelled musky, a sharp scent like an old book that had been left in an attic.

"Did you get a new perfume?" Allyson asked.

"Sandalwood," Chloe said.

"I like your hair."

Chloe touched the ends of her hair, then moved away from Allyson and walked to the trunk of the car. She popped the trunk and pulled out a suitcase and a large duffel bag, and then looked around the farm.

"Everything here looks the same," she said. "It feels like I've been gone forever."

"The only thing that's really changed is that Colton is gone," Allyson said.

"He's called me from the base a few times to talk," Chloe said. "Seems he's doing okay."

Allyson felt a sting in her stomach, like someone had poked her with a sharp finger. She wasn't even talking to her cousin and her brother and cousin were talking? She didn't even know what she would say to Colton if he asked to talk to her, but learning this news still hurt.

"I can take the duffel," Allyson said as she picked it up. The duffel weighed a ton. What had her cousin packed? It wasn't like she was going on a trip to a foreign country. They had everything here.

Allyson followed Chloe as she walked towards Craig and Linda's. The dogs, happy to see Chloe, ran beside them, tails wagging. The group only walked a few steps before the door to Linda and Craig's house was flung open and Linda came hurrying out.

"I thought I heard your car," said Linda, as she grabbed her daughter in a bear hug. "I'm glad you're here."

Chloe hugged back. "Where's Dad?"

"Went to town for something or other," she said. "But he's excited about you coming home."

Linda reached out her hand and grabbed a piece of Chloe's hair. "Honey," she said. "Oh, your beautiful hair."

"I didn't think you would like it," Chloe said. "Jamie did it for me."

"But your natural hair is so pretty," Linda said. "Your dad is not going to like this."

"It's not his hair," Chloe said.

"Let's not start off like this," Linda said, frowning. "We all want to have a nice Thanksgiving."

Chloe turned towards the house. "Are you going to come in?" she asked Allyson.

Allyson hesitated. She didn't want to hear about Chloe's amazing life, while she was stuck on the farm with the adults. She knew how this would go. Chloe would tell her about all the fun things she was doing, and the people she had met and Allyson would have nothing to say.

"Your mom probably wants to talk to you alone," Allyson said. "I'll catch up with you later."

She turned and walked back towards her own house. Her mother was at work, and Clay had gone into town to help her dad with something. She spent the rest of the afternoon in her room re-reading Nancy Drew books. Nancy Drew would have known what to do if she was stuck on some boring farm out in Alberta. There would be a mystery to uncover. Some town intrigue would lead to a wild and wacky adventure. Nancy Drew never spent hours in her room, reading and drawing. Allyson put the book down and picked up her drawing pad. She started to doodle, drawing curlicues around the edge of the page. Soon the curlicues transformed into a dark, menacing tree leaning against her grandparents' house. For the past year, everything she drew turned dark and dangerous. Her pen was possessed and these images needed to get out. Allyson ran her pencil down the sides of the tree and added some shading. Then she lay down on her bed and closed her eyes. The next thing she knew, Clay was in her room, saying her name.

"We need to go soon," he said. "Time to get ready."

Allyson rubbed her bleary eyes. "Do I need to get dressed up?"

"Not really," Clay said. He ruffled her hair. "But you might want to brush your hair. It's tangled."

"Can I get a ride with you?" Allyson asked.

Clay nodded. "Be ready in a few minutes."

★

Clay was waiting in his truck when she came outside, his stereo blaring pop music.

"What is this?" she asked, pointing to the stereo.

"Tatu," he said. "Great dance music."

Allyson turned it down as Clay started the truck and they drove down the driveway and out to the road. The music had moved on to some woman singing about how her milkshake brought all the boys to the yard.

"You've been listening to some weird music lately," Allyson said. Clay just smiled and turned the stereo back up.

"Here goes nothing," Clay said as he pulled into the lodge parking lot. Inside the dining room, Craig, Linda, Chloe, Gord and Donna were seated at a table with Abby, who had a pink, white and lavender knitted afghan draped over her knees. Abby had made it herself a few years ago.

"Nice to see you, Gramma," Clay said, moving forward to kiss Abby on the cheek. Abby smiled a small, wan smile and reached up her good hand to pat Clay on the cheek. Allyson walked over and patted her grandma's frozen hand in greeting, but Abby only had eyes for Clay. Donna gestured to the two empty chairs at the end of the table. The large cafeteria-style kitchen was decorated with pumpkins, paper leaves and paper turkeys that reminded Allyson of preschool. She half expected to see turkeys created out of the residents' handprints. When you became old, you got treated like a preschooler. She took a seat at the end of the table and Clay sat down beside her.

"We're going to go up and get our food in the cafeteria line," Donna said, leaning across the table. "Normally they bring the food to the residents, but with so many people, they want us to go up and serve ourselves."

Allyson looked around at the other tables. There were some large families like hers, but there were smaller tables as well. Some of the tables only held three people. Allyson wondered what it was like to come from a three-person family. At least Abby had lots of people who could visit her. Clay bumped Allyson's knee with his own and smiled at her. A young woman with bleached blonde hair and dark roots came over to their table. Allyson recognized her as a lodge staff member.

"You can go serve yourselves now," she said. "If you're ready to go."

"I'll make up a plate for Abby," Linda said as she got up. The family went to stand in the long line. As Allyson moved down the line, women wearing hairnets served her a big dollop of mashed potatoes, warmed frozen vegetables with peas, corn and perfectly cubed squares of carrots, a bun, coleslaw, gravy and turkey. Her mother's food would taste better, but what could they do? Both of her parents felt guilty about abandoning Abby on so many other holidays over the past year. So here they were, eating mediocre food in a cafeteria with a bunch of sad souls.

Staff members had placed big pitchers of red Kool-Aid and water on the tables. Allyson reached for the Kool-Aid and poured some into a plastic glass.

"I'll have some too," Clay said, pushing a Styrofoam cup toward her.

"Can someone say grace?" Abby asked. Craig started, saying what they all had to be thankful for. As his voice droned on,

Allyson thought about how wrong he was. What did they have to be thankful for? Al was dead. They didn't have any money. Colton was gone, and her family were ghosts of the people they had once been. Maybe she should be thankful that she could read. That was something to be thankful for.

"Amen," Craig said and Allyson bowed her head a little, trying to pretend she had been listening.

"Chloe, honey, didn't you get a drumstick?" her mother asked, looking over at her cousin's plate.

Everyone knew drumsticks were Chloe's favourite. Whenever they had a dinner, one of the drumsticks was saved for Al and the other for Chloe.

Before Chloe could answer, Craig spoke. "Our daughter says she's a vegetarian now."

"For crying out loud," Abby said. "Why would you do a thing like that?"

"I've just been thinking about it," Chloe said as she lifted peas and carrots onto her fork. "Killing animals is wrong."

"Never mind that it's how her family makes a living," Craig said. "All of a sudden it's not good enough for you."

He picked up his knife and started sawing away at a piece of turkey. "Never thought I'd have to say that my daughter has become a hippie vegetarian. Just embarrassing."

Gord giggled a little and everyone looked at him. "She eats like k.d. lang," he said.

"Not quite," Chloe said, as she drew her fork through her mashed potatoes.

Allyson concentrated on her food as her family chattered around her. The potatoes and meat were dry and the vegetables tasted like cardboard. Some celebration, she thought.

"Hey everybody," Craig said. "Abby's got something to say. We need you all to listen."

Gord straightened up and look toward his mother. Donna reached out for Gord's hand. Allyson could tell that they were expecting big news, and it wouldn't necessarily be something good.

"Right now, the farm is in my name," Abby said. "Since Al didn't have a will, everything went to me. But Craig and I have been talking a lot and I've decided that I'm going to transfer everything to him and Linda. They're going to be the owners of the farm," she said. "The only thing that's got to be done is that we've got to sign all of the paperwork."

Craig looked at Gord. Gord's face turned white and then flushed to red. Gord let go of Donna's hand and gripped the table with both hands.

"This won't change anything," Craig said to Gord. "You'll still be farming the land and everything will stay the same. It's just that I'll be the owner."

"What in the hell?" Gord said. "I can't believe you went behind my back to arrange this all with Mom."

Donna put her hand on Gord's shoulder, but he shook it off and stood up.

"Just makes sense," Craig said. "We talked about it and discussed it with the lawyer. It just comes down the fact that Linda and I can be more of a team on the farm. With you and Donna, there's just you. Donna's not involved."

Donna stared down at her lap and hunched down, as if she was shrinking into herself.

"But I'm the one who is more involved in the day-to-day operations," Gord said. The wheedling tone in his voice reminded Allyson of her own voice when she tried to convince her parents they were wrong about something.

"I'm the oldest," Gord said. "It should have been mine."

"This was Mom's decision," Craig said. "We talked about it with her and the lawyers and this is what she decided."

"Are you sure this was her decision?" Gord said. He wasn't yelling, but his voice was loud enough that people at other tables were starting to look at him. "Were you behind her, pulling the strings? Did the two of you bully her into this?"

"Lower your voice," Craig said sternly. "You're making a scene."

Donna reached for Gord's arm, trying to get him to sit down, but he brushed her off.

"I can't believe you did this without us," Gord said. "We're supposed to be a team. If Dad knew about this, he'd lose his mind."

Craig glanced at Clay. "Right now, Linda and I are going to be the actual owners, but nothing else is going to change. You'll still make the same amount of money. You'll still have some control. It's more of a legal thing, really. Just some paperwork."

"It's not like that at all," Gord said. "What I see is you going behind my back. And now you'll be the owner and I'll be the employee."

"Dad was the owner before," Craig said. "You've always been the employee. If Dad hadn't messed up the finances and the cattle crisis hadn't happened, we wouldn't be in such dire straits. But it's Dad's fault. He was stupid."

For a minute, it looked as though Gord was going to walk out of the room, and then he turned towards Craig, walked over to the other side of the table and grabbed Craig by the collar. His movements were so fast that no one in the family had time to react. They could only watch as Gord pulled Craig toward him and punched him in the face.

"Oh my god!" Linda screamed. "Stop it, just stop."

"Don't talk about Dad like that," Gord said, holding Craig by the collar. "Don't blame your greed and your need for control on our father." Craig struggled and he pulled his arms free and punched Gord. The entire dining room stared at the Klassen family. The sounds of chatter and eating had stopped as everyone turned in their direction. Allyson wished she had a portable hole to escape into.

Clay stood up, encircled his father in a bear hug and pinned his arms to his chest.

"Dad, you need to stop," he said. "We can't do this." Linda stood up and tried to position her body in between Craig and Gord. Gord attempted get out of Clay's grasp, but Clay was stronger. One of the hospital staff, a big, burly man, rushed over to help. Gord struggled against the orderly and Clay, breathing hard, snorting like a bull. Craig moved away and stood across the room, glaring at Gord.

Donna finally stood up. She was shaking. "I'm going to make sure your father gets home," she said to Allyson and Clay.

"We'll meet you back at the house. We might stop for a drink if your father needs one. Take as long as you need."

She looked at the orderly. "Just walk us to the front and we'll leave now."

The orderly was still holding Gord's arms behind his back. Allyson heard the heavy, wet sound of her father's breathing.

Donna gave Linda and Craig a dirty look.

"What you did was low," she said. "Just low. That's no way for family to treat each other."

She turned and walked out of the cafeteria, following Gord and the orderly. As they neared the doorway, the orderly released Gord's arms. Donna caught up to them and Allyson watched as her parents disappeared down the hallway. At the end of the table, Abby sobbed, her good hand over her face.

"Look what we've become," she said.

Linda leaned over her wheelchair and said something into her ear.

"Clay, I need to get out of here," Allyson said.

Clay stood up and looked at Craig. "I know I'm not supposed to talk back to you because you're my uncle and I'm supposed to respect you and all that crap, but what you've done is horrible. You just kicked a man when he's down. You didn't even talk to him about joint partnership. It's like you just want to screw up the farm."

Clay touched Allyson on the arm. "Let's go," he said.

He turned and started towards the hallway, not bothering to say goodbye to anyone. Allyson followed him out to the truck. Outside, she gulped the cold air into her lungs. The air had a bite to it, as if it was trying to warn them that snow would be coming soon. Waves of adrenaline coursed through her body.

"Screw Uncle Craig," Clay said as he opened the truck.

Allyson scanned the parking lot, looking for her parents' truck, but it was already gone.

"I just need to sit here for a minute and calm down," Clay said.

He grabbed the steering wheel and stared straight ahead. "I can't believe Uncle Craig did that to Dad. It might just kill him."

Allyson hadn't eaten a lot at dinner, but those words made her stomach hurt, like she might throw up. What would happen to them if her dad died?"

"Want to go get some fries?" Clay said. "I'm kind of hungry. Let's go find a burger or something."

"Sure," Allyson said, and Clay started up the truck.

CHAPTER 16

Outside the lodge, Gord gave Donna the keys and asked her to drive.

"Just take me home," he said.

Donna turned on the country music station and adjusted the volume to high. Shania Twain sang them out of the parking lot. When they got back to their yard, Gord stepped out of the truck and walked over to the corral that held the horses. Donna followed him instead of going back in the house. She didn't want to leave him alone. The fight had riled her up too. Her stomach hurt and her mouth tasted dry and stale, as if she'd been sleeping for weeks and had just woken up.

This latest blow, this indignity to Gord, was all her fault. If only she were a better ranch wife, and learned how to do everything. If only she loved the farm as much as he did. But she didn't, and she couldn't and she hadn't. And now she and Gord were being punished.

Gord stood by the fence and held out his hand. Temple came forward, her big eyes curious. Gord stroked her face. Temple's breath was visible in the air as she snuffed Gord's hand and smelled the top of his head. Gord calmed down as he petted the animal. Animals always had that effect on him. Gord's world would have been better if there had been fewer humans in it.

"Gord, I'm so sorry," she said.

Normally, Gord would have turned his head to look at her, but he kept his attention focussed on the horse.

"I'm sorry," she said again.

"I need you to leave me alone right now," he said without looking at her. "Just go away."

"Are you going to be okay?" she asked. She wanted to touch his arm, snuggle into his body and have him hold her, but she was scared to reach out and touch him. The space around her was too big, the sky overhead too enormous, as if she was a speck floating in infinity.

"The worst thing about what Craig did is that part of me knows they're right," Gord said, turning to look at her. "I can see why Mom wanted to give the farm to them. I'm not mad at her. She isn't all there anymore. She's just an old lady in a wheelchair. Even Dad would have approved this decision."

Donna could feel her breath in her chest, fast and jagged. She counted to ten, forcing herself to concentrate on her breathing. Her feelings didn't matter right now. As she watched, Gord slumped against the wood of the fence. Temple moved away from him as he started to sob. Donna stayed still and continued to focus on her breath. There wasn't enough air. Was she going to choke? She closed her eyes and made herself count and breathe, count and breathe, until she felt a semblance of calm.

"God, I hate him. I hate him," Gord said, his voice terrible through his tears.

Donna walked forward and put a hand on her husband's back. When he didn't shake it off, she rubbed his back through the bulkiness of his coat and concentrated on moving her hand up and down.

"Goddamn," Gord said, covering his face with his hand. "Why did he have to die? Why couldn't he have taken care of things before he died? Why did he have to fuck it all up?"

Donna didn't say anything. If Gord was feeling anything like her, he was tired, simply exhausted from all that had happened. All she wanted to do was sleep. She could sleep for years and still need more. She hugged Gord and let him cry. He leaned into her arms and let her hold him.

"I'm sorry," she said. "I should have been a better wife. A better rancher. Or left you years ago and let you find someone who could ranch. You deserved better than me."

Gord didn't say anything. Donna felt as if she'd been sliced through her belly. She'd wanted him to protest, to tell her that she'd been a good wife and mother, and that he never would have wished for anyone else. She was part of the reason why they were in this mess. They might lose the whole farm if the cattle industry didn't get better. And then what would they do? She looked up at the sky. There was no snow yet, but it would be here soon. When winter came, things would be worse. Gord had talked to her about the feed bills, and how much feed they would need to keep the animals though winter. They would be able to sell some of the cows, but prices were so low it was like they were giving them away. Feeding the cattle over the winter would be hard. Their bank account was bleeding. Who knew how much longer this would go on? Maybe they'd need to move into the city and get jobs. Maybe things would be better if Craig had control of the farm. Would Gord be able to get another job?

Donna pictured leaving the farm, packing up, heading to a city and creating a new life. How many times had she fantasized about that over the years? She would be a completely different person if she lived in the city. Calmer and not as anxious. She'd have a good job. Colton wouldn't have joined the military and Allyson wouldn't be such a bookish loner. They wouldn't be in the cattle business. She wanted to go live in that perfect alternate universe. She loved the world in her head, that whole other world where her life fit together and made sense.

Gord stopped crying and wiped his nose on his sleeve, reminding her of the boys when they were small. How many times had she told them not to do this? And now here was her husband, a cowboy in his late forties, wiping his sleeve on his nose like a baby.

A truck clattered down the driveway and Donna turned to look. Clay parked the truck and killed the engine.

"You guys okay?" he called, as he got out of the truck.

"Checking the horses," Donna said. "You go on inside."

Clay ignored her, and started towards them, Allyson following behind. Allyson looked both old and young at the same time. She was only fifteen, but she'd aged so much in the past few months, the way a person did when grief moved into their home. The events of the past year had aged all of them. Donna had more white hair and lines around her eyes and mouth. Gord's spare tire was bigger, his movements slower and heavier.

"I feel like we lost," Clay said, as he stopped and stood beside his dad. "I didn't even know we were fighting."

Allyson shivered and Donna was aware of how drastically the temperature had dropped.

"Let's go," she said. Gord rubbed his face again, probably trying to hide his red eyes from the kids. The four of them started towards the house.

"I'm going up to bed," Gord said when they got inside. "Just feeling beat."

It was only a little after nine, but Donna didn't say anything. She listened as Gord walked through the hall and trudged up the stairs.

Donna went into the kitchen and turned on the kettle to make tea. She heard the television go on. Once her tea was ready, she took the cup and sat in the family room with Clay and Allyson. The three of them watched a re-run of *Buffy* and an episode of *Saturday Night Live*, but Donna wasn't following any of it. She sat, trying to focus on the television, but she was thinking about what had happened in the lodge. The brothers had never hit each other before. They argued when Al was alive, sure, but it never came to blows. What would happen now? How would they work together? Everyone might go on pretending that everything was the same, that nothing had happened. Could they do that?

Allyson and Clay laughed at something on the television, and Donna realized she should just go to bed. She said goodnight to the kids and went towards the stairs. Inside the bedroom, Gord was already snoring.

She changed into her pyjamas and crawled into bed next to him. The reassuring warmth from his body crept across the sheets. She lay next to Gord and focused on his breathing, making herself breathe along with him. Sometimes this helped her lull herself to sleep. She lay there for a while, her thoughts racing. How much say did Abby have in this decision? Would they really be okay? How much longer would the border be closed? Did they have enough money to survive? Would they have to move off the farm? Could they go bankrupt? Gord had said something the other day about creditors and how Al owed some money to some people and they had to pay the creditors back. Maybe they could turn their land over to crops. Would they be able to send Allyson to university in a couple of years? She might have to get another job now. The extra catering money helped, but maybe there was something else she could do. She could find something else in town. Part of this was her fault. She was the failure. Maybe this attempt at control was Craig's way of dealing with things. It was as if the Klassen family was in a car driving down the freeway in a city they didn't know. Craig and Linda thought they knew the way to go, and they'd turned the car towards an off-ramp. But it was the wrong off-ramp, and the entire family was headed in the wrong direction.

Donna rolled over in bed. Thank God Gord was still snoring. She was hot, so hot. Maybe it was the change. It wouldn't surprise her if that happened now. It would be just her luck.

She sat up, careful to keep her movements slow and even so she wouldn't wake Gord. She walked to the bathroom and thought about taking a sleeping pill. She'd been trying to cut down, because she suspected they made her mood lower the following day. There were some days when she woke up and realized she just didn't want to be alive. She didn't want to kill herself, but she didn't want to exist.

She walked out of the bathroom and stood in the dark hallway, listening to the creaks of the house. She could hear the light sound of Clay's snores as she walked by his room. Perhaps she should go downstairs and read a book or watch some TV. She continued down the hall past Colton's room. The door was shut, and she pushed it open and flicked the light switch, half expecting Colton's normal chaos: his clothes strewn on the floor, the smell of dirty socks and the scent of cigarette smoke and sweat that followed him. But the room was clean and the bed made. Colton had even vacuumed before he left. Some of his things were still there; his stereo and posters of rock bands on the walls, a guitar and a shelf filled with books. A wave of sadness passed over her as she entered the room. One of his dresser drawers was open a crack and she bent over to close it. As she leaned in, she saw the corner of a plastic Ziploc bag. She opened the drawer and pulled out a bag full of green, gnarled buds. She reached into the bag, touched the dry buds and crushed a few of them between her fingers. A small glass pipe and some rolling papers lay in the drawer on top of black t-shirts, an old black hooded sweatshirt, several pairs of white socks that had gone grey and a few navy blue t-shirts from the auto body shop where Colton had worked.

Donna held the baggie in her hands and sat on the bed. Colton's packing had been a whirlwind affair and he'd had so much to do before he left. It happened so fast. He told them he was leaving, and then he was gone. Maybe he'd meant to get rid of this pot, or give it to Lily or Booger. Donna had only smoked pot a couple times when she was in university, before she met Gord. The first time it didn't do anything to her, but the second time, she smoked it with her friend Rebecca in college and they watched cartoons and laughed, and she felt warm, relaxed and full, like a pregnant ant. Rebecca had some cotton candy and when they ate it, higher than kites, Rebecca told her they were eating cartoons.

Maybe pot was what Donna needed tonight. They gave pot to cancer patients and people in pain, didn't they? Some dope might take the edge off. She walked back to the dresser and took the glass pipe out of the drawer. There was a lighter on the top of the dresser. She'd seen people smoke pipes in the movies. She could figure out how to do it. But she couldn't just sit in her son's room and smoke a pipe. Someone might smell it. And she'd feel so bad if Clay, Allyson or Gord saw her, especially after all the times she and Gord had berated Colton for smoking pot. Gord hated it. Said pot made you stupid and started you down the pathway to other, harder drugs. Donna had actually liked it when she'd tried it with Rebecca, but after hearing Gord talk about it, she hadn't bothered to smoke it again.

She took out one of Colton's black hoodies and put it on, stuffing the baggie, pipe and lighter into the hoodie's front pocket. She could sit in the barn with the horses, dogs and cats and freeze her ass off. Or she could walk across the yard and go to

Abby and Al's. She hadn't been inside the house since they died, but somehow it felt right to go there tonight.

Standing near the door, she pulled her winter boots on over her bare feet and put on a warm coat. She was careful not to let the door slam behind her as she ventured out into the cold. Flakes of snow were falling. The snow might here to stay. She felt a pang of sadness. Snow meant another long winter. She wasn't sure if she could handle it. The cold greyness and long stretches of darkness made everything worse.

As she walked across the yard, Maggie and Rascal raced to join her. She was glad for their presence. When the children were younger, she worried about them accidentally stumbling out of the house at night and getting attacked by a coyote, even though Gord told her again and again that the chance of that happening was almost nonexistent. She must have seen it in a movie once and that put the idea in her head, and now she couldn't get rid of it.

She reached Abby and Al's front door and pulled it open. Part of her felt guilty and horrible, as if she was doing something wrong. But Linda had been in the house numerous times since the accident. Why couldn't she go in there too? Just thinking about Linda made her think about Craig, and anger wormed its way through her body.

As she flicked on the light switch, she caught a glimpse of a tiny brown body skittering across the tile floor. She willed herself not to scream. She hated mice and always had. The erratic way they moved scared her. Abby would lose it if she knew there were mice in her house. Donna smiled at the thought. She hadn't yet let herself feel angry at Abby for the decision about the farm. How could Abby do this to them? Granted, she wasn't fully aware of what she was doing. But still. Donna pulled off her boots and held them in her hands. If she put them down, a mouse might run inside. Better to keep them with her.

The house smelled musty, but it also smelled like Abby and Al, even though they hadn't been here for over a year now. It was cold, so Donna kept her coat on. Craig and Linda must left the heat on to keep the pipes from freezing, but not enough to heat the house. She walked towards the stairs and turned that light on, before hurrying back to the front hall to turn off the entranceway light.

She climbed the stairs, looking at the photos that decorated the walls of the staircase. There she was holding Clay. In another picture, the family beamed at the camera, all of them except Colton, who never smiled on cue. He stared straight ahead, stone faced. Donna stopped at a picture of Abby and Al smiling, their entire bodies angled toward each other. She noticed a thin coating of dust on the top of the picture frame and brushed it off with her finger. Upstairs, she turned on the lights and the hallway lit up. Part of her felt she should be going room to room, inspecting the entire house. The house felt lifeless, even though it looked the same. She walked through the other three upstairs bedrooms, visiting the rooms where Craig and Gord had grown up. Abby had redecorated a long time ago. One of the rooms had been her sewing and crafting room. Linda must have taken things out of here, because it didn't look the same as when Abby lived there. The two spare bedrooms, known as the pink room and the blue room, looked the same, except for the thin layer of dust coating the furniture.

She got to Abby and Al's bedroom and turned on the light. The closet was bare and she could see empty hangers and the white wall behind them. The pictures that had been on the top of the dresser were gone. The bed was made, but it was covered with a plaid quilt Donna didn't recognize. Linda must have dusted. Even though the house smelled stale, the room was clean, without the coating of dust Donna expected.

She'd been in this room when Abby and Al were alive, but not for a long time. She'd spent more time in here when the kids were small. She pulled off her coat and got under the plaid quilt. Reaching into her pocket, she pulled out the baggie of pot, the lighter and the pipe. She put a couple of buds into the pipe and lit them, inhaling the warm, skunky smell. She wondered if Linda would recognize it if she came into the room. Maybe she would think a skunk had made its way into the house. The thought made her smile, and she took a quick pull on the pipe, inhaling the smoke in her lungs and holding it there. It burned and she coughed, letting the smoke out. Then she laughed a little to herself, thinking about the strangeness of the situation. Here she was, sitting in her mother-in-law's bed, smoking pot like a petulant teenager.

She felt calmer now. She inhaled again and held the smoke inside her lungs. How much did she need to get high? It had been so long since she had done this. Had Chloe and Clay smoked pot? For a second, she felt guilty about berating Colton for smoking. What a hypocrite. But Colton had probably done stronger drugs. She took a few more pulls off the pipe, careful not to burn her fingers on the lighter as she held it over the buds. She wasn't sure how much to smoke, so she stopped when her lungs felt like they were about to ignite. Then she put the pipe on Abby's nightstand, checking first to see that it wasn't hot enough to leave any sort of mark. She settled down under the covers and stared at the ceiling, transfixed by the stucco patterns. The bed smelled musty, but she could also smell the faint scent of Al. Or maybe she was just imagining things. What would have happened if he had been here? Would he have been able to pull his sons into some sort of united front against the border closure? Abby wouldn't be so crazy and useless, just waiting to die.

She could see faces in the stucco pattern. When Clay had been about four, he ran into the room to jump on the bed. She didn't want him to jump, so she made him lie on his back and look for things in the stucco. He found a shoe, a rocket ship and faces that reminded him of the man in the moon.

As she studied the ceiling, the whole thing struck her as absurd. She had entertained her child by making him look at shapes on a ceiling. She started to giggle. Her warm body relaxed, and her toes tingled. The warmth radiated up her body in lines, shooting up from her toes, travelling all the way to her head. She closed her eyes and relaxed into the glow.

★

It took her several minutes to realize where she was when she woke up the next morning. She was so hot, still wearing Colton's hoodie over her pyjamas, her face smashed into the pillow, drool congealed by the side of her mouth. She rolled over, remembered where she was and what she'd done the night before. There was no clock in the room. Linda must have taken it to the hospital for Abby.

The baggie, lighter and pipe sat on the nightstand, and she put them in the front pocket of the hoodie, got up and made the bed. There was something comforting about being in this room. It felt like a sanctuary. She could pretend she was back in another time, waiting for Abby and Al to come home. Here, she could listen to her thoughts and not have to worry about others. But she had to leave. Gord and the kids might have woken up and they would wonder where she had gone.

Her boots rested by the side of the bed, and she picked them up and started towards the door of the bedroom. Downstairs, she put on her boots and opened the door. She would come back and clean the house later, when she had more time. It was still dark outside as she crept back across the yard.

As she walked to her house, she heard a screech and a scream, coming from the barn. She started to run. Inside the barn, she saw her daughter and Chloe. Her daughter's hands were buried in Chloe's hair and she was yanking hard. Chloe yowled like an angry cat.

"Girls!" Donna said. She pulled on her daughter's arms, trying to force her back. But Allyson was strong, and able to resist her mother's movements. Donna grabbed onto her daughter's arms and tried to pull her back. Her daughter didn't move. The two girls were in a deadlock. Donna pinched her daughter's neck hard and fast, driving her nails into her daughter's skin. Her daughter recoiled in shock, and her hold loosened. Donna was able to pull her off her cousin.

"Stop!" Donna said, even though the two girls were already apart.

Chloe put her hands on the side of her purple haired head, and wept. Allyson was breathing hard, like one of the horses after it had been running.

"What is this about?" Donna said. "Why are you acting like animals?"

Neither girl answered.

"I'm not sure what happened, but you can't act like this," she said. "Enough is enough."

She pulled Allyson by the arm and led her towards the house.

As her mother led her out of the barn, Allyson burst into tears. Donna kept heading back towards the house. She knew she should ask what was wrong, but she didn't want to. She didn't want to deal with the mess, or unravel teenage feelings. No need to get involved in any of that. She didn't want to spend the little bit of energy she had trying to figure out what had happened.

"Go to your room," she said to Allyson once they got to the house. She knew this wasn't a punishment. Allyson would be happy to be alone in her room. She'd just read or draw or listen to music. At least it would keep her away from her cousin.

Inside the house, Donna kicked off her boots and climbed the stairs to her bedroom. If she could get to the shower without having to deal with anyone else, she'd be able to hide in the shower alone for about half an hour, and let the water wash everything away. In the shower, she could stare at the tiles, focus on the feeling of the water massaging her back, and try to forget.

★

It was an early morning in late November when she heard the first shot. Donna was getting ready for work, and Allyson was off at school. Donna had heard shots before on the farm. You couldn't live on a ranch and not expect to hear a gun go off. Sometimes the men needed to shoot sick cattle, and one time, Al had taken their old dog, Bruce, behind the barn to put him out of his misery.

Donna's mind went to the worst possible place. Gord hadn't told her he would be using a gun this morning. She jammed on her boots, pulled on her jacket and ran outside. She stood, listening and waiting for the next shot. Maybe there was a hunter on the property. Maybe Craig or Gord shot a coyote. The door of Craig and Linda's house opened and Craig walked out and stood on the stoop. He put one hand out towards her, telling her to stay put. They'd barely talked at all since Thanksgiving. He went back into the house and returned wearing his jacket and boots. As he started towards the barn and the back of the corral, there was another shot, followed by the bawl of a cow. A third shot pierced the air. Donna remembered the first time she'd heard the loud, angry crack of a bullet. It sounded exactly like the guns she had heard on TV. Every time she heard a shot, her heart beat faster. A shot was never a neutral sound. It always meant something was going to die, or something needed to be scared off.

Her boots crunched through the crust of the snow as she walked towards the corral. When she arrived behind the barn, she saw Gord aiming a rifle at a pen full of cattle. The gun went off again and the cow in front of Gord fell to the ground. Blood gushed from its head onto the snow, the red a startling contrast against the white.

"Stop it," Craig yelled as he approached. "What in the hell are you doing?"

Gord was wild-eyed. His face was puffy like he'd been drinking. A small herd of cattle clustered together at the back of the corral, their eyes wide, breath coming out of their mouths in quick, anxious puffs. As Craig and Donna watched, Gord raised the rifle and fired again. The bullet hit a small red cow right between the ears. Her eyes rolled back in her head as she sank to her knees, falling in a series of spasms and jerks. The other cattle moved to the far corner, breathing hard. The little red cow shook once more, and was still.

"You need to stop," Craig said.

"We can't afford to feed them anymore," Gord said, his voice hoarse. "I'm thinning out the herd. They aren't worth anything anyway."

Donna could smell the iron tang of blood mixed with cow shit, burned hair, animal and the sharp, acrid smell of the animals' fear. Several dead cows lay in the pen, their faces contorted, mouths open, large pink tongues exposed. She gagged. Panicked, a couple animals charged the fence, threatening to go over. Donna stepped back, terrified of being trampled.

Gord raised the rifle again and shot a cow. Donna covered her ears and closed her eyes.

"You've lost it," Craig said. "These animals are perfectly fine. We won't even be able to sell the meat the way you're killing them."

Craig started to move towards his brother. Gord raised the rifle and for a millisecond, it looked like he was going to aim the rifle at Craig. He didn't hold it on him, but Donna could see it happen inside her head. Craig froze. He said something, but Donna couldn't make out the words. He closed his eyes and moved his lips, like he was praying. Gord's face was empty, like a robot out of a late-night science fiction horror movie. In her mind, she saw the bullet fly and hit Craig in the chest, saw his body pitch forward as the blood poured out of him. She was too scared to speak or breathe for fear of startling Gord. Gord exhaled, a long deep sigh, and a puff of his breath hung in the air. Then he turned and shot another cow.

While Gord was busy, Craig backed away and moved towards Donna. She could tell he was scared but his movements were slow and careful, as if he'd wandered into a bear's path and was trying not to spook it. He reached her and leaned down so his mouth was near her ear.

"Call the cops," he said. "Call them right away. I don't know what else to do."

Donna nodded and started walking back towards the house, not wanting to turn away from Gord and his gun. She was having problems breathing again. There wasn't enough air. She couldn't get it into her lungs fast enough. What if something happened while her back was turned? She tried to count, tried to breathe, willed herself not to have a panic attack. That wouldn't do anyone any good. If she lost it now and something happened, she would be partially responsible. She gulped and gasped and tried not to think about what she was seeing, tried to think about getting air into her lungs. She couldn't make it to the house. She closed her eyes and leaned over, trying to stop herself from hyperventilating. If she closed her eyes, she could pretend she was somewhere else. She couldn't call the cops on her own husband, could she? Breathe, breathe, breathe. Count, 1, 2, 3, 4. Inhale, exhale. The oxygen entered her lungs. She bent over, counted and breathed. Then she stood up and started walking back towards the corral.

By the time she got closer, she could see Craig had gotten Gord into an arm hold. As she watched, Craig punched Gord in the face. Gord didn't try to fight back, just let the blow fall. Craig hit him again. She scanned the pen for the rifle. Finally, she saw it leaning up against the fence. Taking a deep breath, she climbed up the side of the fence and hopped over, praying the cows would stay away from her. Her focus was on the rifle and getting it away from the men. She ran a few steps across the snow, picked up the rifle and headed back towards the fence. She pushed the rifle under the fence and then climbed up and over. She couldn't remember the last time she'd climbed the fence. She didn't even know she could still do it.

Her breathing was jagged and she could feel a panic attack coming on. Oh God, don't come now, don't come, no. Just breathe.

On the other side of the fence, she picked up the rifle and held it to her chest. Craig held Gord by the collar and punched him.

She screamed as loud as she could and turned the rifle toward the sky and fired. The kick back reverberated through her body.

The sound of the bullet soared through the air and then everything went quiet. Craig stopped punching his brother and they both looked at her. Gord's nose was bleeding.

"Let him end this," Gord said, breaking the silence.

Craig held his brother by the back of his coat.

"That's what you want, isn't it?" Gord said. "You just want us out of here. Just want to push us off here and take the farm for yourself. I can't do this anymore. Can't live like this. We lost Dad. We're losing Mom. My son is gone. Who knows if my other son will ever come back? Ray's dead. Everything I know and love has gone to shit. And now you want to kick me out of here. Might as well just kill me and be done with it."

Craig loosened his grip on his brother's collar.

"I never meant for it to come to this," Craig said.

Craig let go of his brother, stood up, walked away from him and leaned onto the fence. Gord stood alone in the pen. Craig covered his face and Donna could tell he was crying.

"I never wanted to rip this family apart," Craig said, when he raised his head again.

He stood at the fence and sobbed. Donna stood, rifle heavy in her hands, breathing and watching. Gord's face was dirty and he would probably have a black eye tomorrow. He walked towards his brother. Craig turned, grabbed his brother and pinned his arms to his sides. Gord let his brother hold him.

A small group of cattle huddled in the corner, away from the bodies in the pen. Donna watched as the brothers stood still, frozen in their awkward, uncomfortable embrace.

CHAPTER 17

When Allyson came home from school after band practice, her dad was sitting at the kitchen table, drinking a coffee and reading *The Western Producer*. Linda had picked Allyson up at school, which was unusual. When Allyson walked out into the school yard, carrying her trumpet case, Linda was waiting in the truck.

Gord looked up from his paper, and Allyson started at the sight of his face. His lip was cut and swollen, his eye bruised black.

"Dad, what happened to you?" she asked, her voice loud with alarm.

Her mom came into the room. She had been waiting in the doorway.

"There was a major incident today," she said, her voice so calm that it was scary. She told Allyson about how Gord had shot the cattle.

Allyson looked at her father. "Dad, are you okay?"

Her father shook his heavy head. "I don't want to talk about it."

Allyson turned away from him, and ran back out to the yard, abandoning her backpack and her trumpet case in the kitchen. She heard her mother's footsteps behind her, but she didn't stop. Outside in the yard, she saw Doug Miller, wearing coveralls that were splattered with blood. Phil Hill stood beside him.

"I wouldn't come any closer if I were you," he said, but Allyson didn't listen. She saw the blood on the snow, the bodies of the cattle lying down, their red hides still and lifeless.

Doug Miller was beside her now, his heavy breath making fog in the air. Allyson wasn't wearing a jacket, and the cold was biting.

"It could happen to any of us," Doug said, touching her into the arm. "He just didn't want to feed them any more. We've got to clean up this mess."

As Allyson watched, the men loaded the bodies onto the flat bed of a truck. Craig was helping too. She turned around, shivering and stormed back into the house.

"Dad," she yelled, when she got back inside. "Why did you do it?"

Her mother stood in the doorway of the front room, her face drawn and tired.

"He lost it," her mom said.

"I'll say," said Allyson, and she sank down onto the couch. She couldn't take this anymore. Her dad shooting the animals he loved, her mom, looking so broken and out of it. She thought of Chloe and Clay in the city, away from all this. How she wished she could escape, far away from the farm and this madness. The constant ache, the closed border and all of the pain.

Her mother patted her on the hair, but Allyson jerked away. She stomped back up to the kitchen, where her dad was still sitting with the newspaper.

"What is wrong with you?" she asked him. "Everything is falling apart."

Her dad looked up at her, and suddenly she was afraid. She could see everything that had happened to them in the past year.

"Dad," she said, putting her small hand on his worn, leathery one, his nails tinged with dirt and blood. "Don't be like Ray."

He looked into her eyes. "Allyson, I won't," he said. "I would never do that to you." And without saying anything else, he leaned forward and gave her a hug. He smelled like Old Spice, metal and coffee. She had so many questions, but she felt that if she started asking them, she would never be able to stop.

She heard the door open and Phil and Doug clomped into the house. She heard them kick off their boots and come up the stairs.

"I've got some lasagna in the fridge," Donna said as the men came into the room. "In case you boys are hungry."

"I'd love some," Doug Miller said. "I sure do love your cooking."

"I'm not hungry," Allyson said. She grabbed her trumpet case and backpack and escaped up to her room.

She snuck into Clay's room, and listened to the noises in the kitchen. She could hear the sound of the microwave beeping, and Phil making small talk, asking about Colton and talking about the Oilers. Her dad gave one-word answers, as if talking was too much effort.

She wondered what Craig's version of the events would be, and what he would say. How crazy it would have been to see her dad out in the yard with a rifle, shooting the cattle. How easily something could have gone wrong, and ended badly. The worry in her was like a gnat, buzzing around her skull. It was so deep inside her that she couldn't even figure out how to swat at it. Her mother was talking now, her voice low. But it didn't sound as soothing as Allyson remembered. There was an edge to it, as though she was merely speaking lines.

"Let's watch the game," she heard Phil say. From down in the kitchen, Allyson heard the sounds of the table being cleared, and footsteps as the men retreated to the family room. She could almost smell the lasagna. Maybe she was hungry after all. But if she went downstairs, she'd have to face everyone and she couldn't deal with that. She needed to get out of here, go somewhere else. See the one person she wanted to talk to. Sitting in her bedroom, she knew what she would do.

Allyson stayed in her room, drawing and reading. She was glad that she had learned Clay's address, and that she knew where he lived in the city. When it got dark and she couldn't hear any movement and she felt like everyone had gone to bed, she snuck down to the front door. She had already packed a bag. The door creaked when she opened it, so she had to be fast. But a minute later she was outside, standing in the snow. The key was still in her father's truck. She started it up, half expecting her mother and father to turn on the lights, and come out after her.

"Please," she said quietly to herself. "Please." Adrenaline surged through her body. Finally, she could get away, and have a talk with her brother. Get off this farm, where her dad was doing crazy things like shooting perfectly good cattle. Get away from the grey ghost of her parents, the spectre of her grandparents. She fumbled around for the lights on the vehicle. The headlights lit up the yard. She held her breath as she started the truck.

She thought about stopping and looking at the pen again. But there was no time for that now. She pulled the truck out of the yard, and headed down the highway.

As she drove down the road, Allyson tried not to think about how she'd just basically stolen her father's truck. Colton had done this a number of times when he was younger. Both she and Clay knew about it. She drove toward town, feeling strangely victorious. She was free.

She loved listening to music in the truck, but she was afraid to turn on the radio. Thank God it was a clear night. Her grandfather had warned her about all the dangers of driving in storms, and she'd been in a few bad storms herself. She was a country girl after all.

Ahead of her, she could see the lights of the town looming in the distance. All she had to do was come over the hill, and the lights would light up the horizon, like miniature lights on a Christmas tree. She had loved that view when she was a child, soaring through the darkness in the truck, warm and safe next to her grandparents. How she longed for that now. And then she was over the hill, and in town. She drove past the 7-Eleven, hoping no one would see her. What if she got reported? That was one of the things about living in such a tiny place. You were bound to see someone you knew. She thought about abandoning the truck and taking the bus, but there was a bigger chance that someone would see. News travelled fast, and someone would ask her where she was going. If anyone asked, she wouldn't be able to lie or tell them with a straight face. So she drove on. She had gone this way so many times. The highway signs were easy to read and the markers were clear. She merged onto the main road

to the city. There wasn't a lot of traffic tonight. Why would anyone be driving to town on a school night? The highway stretched
ahead of her, open and clear. She could go anywhere she wanted.
Why hadn't she done this before?

A pair of eyes flickered on the side of the road in the ditch.
It was a deer. She'd been in the truck once when Clay had hit
one. She concentrated, pushing down the thoughts of her parents back at home. The faces that popped into her mind were
Chloe's and Jeff's. Would she and Jeff ever talk again? She
missed his friendship. What would be different between them if
she hadn't seen him drunk that night? Sometimes she thought
about kissing him, about running her hands through his hair.
She squelched the thought from her mind and concentrated on
driving. Soon enough, she would be in the city. She'd travelled
this route so many times in her life as a passenger. One day, she
would move to a city and not have to leave. There would be
no reason to go back to the farm, with its depressing history and
her parents, stone-faced and serious. She'd have her own place
in the city. She wouldn't have to live with the scent of cattle in
the air. The face of one of the dead cows came to her, and she
saw it again, its tongue lolling out of its mouth, its eyes open.
Its body crippled and broken and surrounded by the heavy
whiteness of the snow.

The lights of the city approached and she panicked. She was-
n't legal to drive. The traffic was getting heavier, and suddenly it
was all around her. A car filled with a bunch of boys leered at her.
Maybe they could tell she was underage. Perhaps she shouldn't
be driving in the city by herself. What if she got the truck into
an accident? What if she died? Would that be what her parents
needed, after they'd been through so much shit? She pictured her
funeral. Would Chloe even bother to come? It would probably
kill Gramma Abby. Who knew what would happen? Maybe she
should pull over and call Clay.

She pressed the turn signal and shoulder checked, the way
she'd seen her mother do. A large hauler was behind her. She
could see that it was full of cattle. Well, as least someone was
moving them.

A cab almost hit her, and she shook and held up her hand as if she was protecting her head. There was a 7-Eleven on the side of the road and she almost cried as she pulled into the lot. She drove the truck up to a parking space and stopped. For a second, she couldn't believe what she had done. Her parents, if they were awake, would be worried. What would happen to them? Did they know that she had taken the truck?

What time was it? Her mom must have awakened in the middle of the night. She didn't really sleep well, although she'd been taking more sleeping pills. Would they have gone to her room and seen that she wasn't there? Maybe her dad would have noticed. Or the dogs. But there was only one person she wanted to call now, and that was Clay. She wrapped her parka tighter around herself and got out of the car. An old homeless man immediately approached her.

"Got any change?" he said.

She looked down, feeling embarrassed. The man followed her for a while, but she looked away, intent on finding a pay phone. Finally, she found one around the corner of the store, and made her way over to it. With shaking hands, she fumbled through her wallet. A woman walked around the corner and Allyson jumped. She hadn't expected to see anyone else. The woman gave her a dirty look and continued on. Allyson shoved the quarter in the slot of the phone and dialed her brother's number. Thank God, she knew it by heart.

The phone rang once, twice, and she prayed that he was there. What if he wasn't? What would she do then? She looked out onto the street. A woman driving by looked suspiciously like Mabel Jacobson, and Allyson pulled up her hood, covering her face. If Mabel saw her, everyone back in town would know she was gone in two seconds.

"Hello," she heard on the phone. She didn't recognize the voice.

"Can I speak to Clay?"

"Who is this?" the voice said, and she hoped she hadn't misdialed.

The man from the front of the store walked by again.

"It's Clay's sister, Allyson," she said. "Can I talk to him?"

The man looked at her and smiled. She waved at him, and then turned her back. She said the only thing that came to her mind. "It's an emergency," she said, and then it sounded like the phone hit the ground. After what seemed like an eternity, she could hear her brother's voice on the line.

"Hello," he said, and she felt bad for waking him.

"Clay," she said. "I'm in town. I drove here."

"You aren't legal yet."

"I know," she said. "I had to escape. Did you hear what happened at the farm today?"

There was a long silence.

"So you left Mom and Dad and drove here?"

The man approached her and tapped her on the shoulder.

"Got any change?" he said.

She shook her head. "No."

Clay sounded exasperated. "What's happening?"

"I wasn't talking to you. There's a guy bothering me for money."

Clay sighed.

She whispered into the phone. "Come get me, and quick."

"Where are you?"

"At 7-Eleven."

She realized then that she didn't know the address, so she asked the man. He gave her an address, which she repeated to Clay. He told her he would be able to find it, and she should expect him in about half an hour. She hung up, rifled through her wallet and gave the man a couple dollars. She went back to the truck and waited for what seemed like a long time. Eventually, she could see Clay in his truck. As the truck approached, she could make out the shape of a person wearing a turban beside him. Arjun.

She got out of the truck and stood in front of it. As Clay drove up, she waved at him. He parked in the spot beside her and got out.

"I've called Mom and Dad," he said. "They know you're here."

He gave her a hug, but she could tell he was angry at her. "They know you took the truck," he said. "They're just glad you got here in one piece. What the hell were you thinking?"

She felt small before him. One harsh word and she was a toddler all over again. The wind was starting to pick up and it was cold against her face.

"I needed to get away," she said. "Did you hear about Dad and the cattle? I feel like they've all gone crazy."

"Yeah, and you taking off didn't help them any," Clay sighed. "Get back in the truck. I'm going to drive it, and Arjun is going to take mine back home."

Allyson looked over at Arjun and he gave her a little salute, a tip of his hand to his turban.

Her backpack was starting to get heavy.

Without speaking, she went to the truck and got back into the passenger seat.

"I don't like to think about what could have happened to you," Clay said. "What if someone had caught you driving? Like the police? That might do Grandma Abby in."

Allyson was silent. This was not how she had pictured her reunion with her brother. He started the truck, waved across at Arjun and pulled out of the parking lot.

She looked out the window at the city as they drove. How wonderful it would be to live here, where you could go out and see so many different things every day. Nothing like the boring old countryside, with just farms full of cattle and endless space. They drove by a strip club and she looked away. She was more interested in the Chapters, the Lebanese restaurant and the comic book store. It seemed like they were driving forever before she recognized where she was.

They went across a bridge which she recognized as the High Level. She'd been over it a million times before, when she visited Clay with her parents. She was glad that she had called him to come get her. The intersections going across the bridge were confusing. There was no way she could have made this trip by herself.

"I understand why you wanted to get away," Clay said, finally as he pulled in front of a small house in the university area.

"I mean, the whole thing with the cattle, it sounds crazy. Mom told me all about it."

Gord had woken up in the night, and had gone out in the yard, he said. But he hadn't even known that Allyson had taken off or taken the truck until Clay phoned to tell them.

"Mom was pretty angry," Clay said. "She started crying. She was worried about you driving in the dark by yourself. I can't believe you would do that to her. She's got enough on her plate to worry about without worrying about you too."

Allyson opened her mouth to protest, but one look at her brother's face told her it was the wrong thing to do. She looked behind her, and watched as Arjun parked behind them.

"I'm sorry," she said.

"It's okay," Clay said, putting his hand on her shoulder and giving her a squeeze. "I probably would have done the same thing."

She leaned into him and gave him a hug. He still smelled the same, like that Calvin Klein scent he was so proud of. He hugged her back and then ruffled her hair.

"I told Mom and Dad you can stay for a few days," he said. "I'll take care of you here. You can hide out."

"Thank you," she said, and buried her nose in the side of his parka. She felt relieved, and alive, like she'd finally moved from a world that was grey into a world full of colour. She would be able to relax in the city, a place where no one would notice her and she would blend in. She felt a twinge of guilt because she'd left her family behind, but she pushed it down. Chloe wouldn't have felt a thing if she was in her position.

"Let's get inside," Clay said. "I'll make some tea and then we'll go to bed. It's late."

She undid her seatbelt, jumped out of the truck and followed him into the house. Arjun was waiting inside when she entered.

"I'm going to leave the two of you alone," he said. "I have a feeling that you might have a few family things to discuss and I don't want to get in the way."

Clay nodded at him.

"You can put your stuff in my room," he said to Allyson. "You know where that is right?"

She nodded. His words were curt and she was afraid to say anything else to him. She wouldn't be able to handle it if he started yelling at her.

"I'm sorry," she said. "I shouldn't have come."

"Well, you're here now. I told Mom and Dad that you could stay for a few days. I understand the need to get away. I can barely handle it out there. Why do you think I've been spending so much time in the city?"

She could feel the shadow of a smile creeping onto her lips, but she bit it back. At that moment, she was glad she had driven to the city. Time with her brother would make her feel better.

"I know you probably want to talk about some things," Clay said, as he hung up his coat and took off his boots. "But I don't want to do that right now. I just want a cup of tea and to go to bed."

She nodded, scared to say anything else. She followed Clay into the kitchen and watched as he made her a cup of peppermint tea. He handed the Co-op mug to her, and she smiled. He must have nicked it from home. She looked at the clock. It was about midnight. She listened. She could hear some music, it sounded like Moby, coming from Arjun's room down the hall.

Clay sighed. "It's been a long day," he said.

Allyson had one question. "How long can I stay?"

Clay ran his hand through his hair and leaned against the kitchen counter. "I told Mom that you could stay here three days. You can't miss too much school."

Allyson opened her mouth to complain, but then shut it. Instead, she sipped her tea. It was comforting.

"You know where the bathroom is and everything," Clay said. "I'll get you some clean towels."

She sat in the kitchen as her brother left and returned with a set of blue towels.

"Thanks," she said.

"I'm going to hit the hay," Clay said. "I've got a long day coming up tomorrow. Classes and work. But we'll go out for dinner, and talk or something. Whyte's right there. You can do whatever you want."

"Okay," Allyson said. She listened as her brother went into the bathroom. She could hear the sound of the water running, and his toothbrush swishing back and forth. After a few minutes, she finished her tea and wandered down the hall to Clay's bedroom.

This wasn't quite what she had pictured. She had hoped that Clay would be glad to see her. She thought about Chloe. Maybe she should meet up with her tomorrow. But what would she say? The last time she'd seen Chloe, she'd attacked her. Did she know about the cattle?

Standing in Clay's room, Allyson couldn't stop thinking about her dad and the dead cattle. How scared her mom must have been when the gun went off. For some reason, she thought of the grain elevator coming down. How it had looked over the town, and been standing there for years. And then all it took was a couple good swings from a bulldozer, and it was toppled and destroyed forever. Like Jeff had gone down after Booger's fist met his face.

She put on her jams and got into her brother's bed. It was covered in a warm green and red plaid quilt. She turned out the bedside lamp, and tried to get to sleep. But her thoughts were like gnats, buzzing around her head and sleep would not come.

She listened, trying to hear what she could from the other rooms. But all she could hear was quiet, and the creak of the house. There were footsteps and the sound of Clay and Arjun talking to each other. She couldn't make out what they were saying, and then things got quiet again. She was alone, and she couldn't quite remember why she had left the sanctuary of her room to spend a night alone at her brother's.

She turned on the light so she could look through her brother's bookshelf. He had turned her on to so many books. She stood up and padded across the floor. Looked at the pictures on the top of his bookshelf. There was a school picture of her from a few years ago. She looked like a dork. She looked at the picture of Colton and wondered how he was doing. She let her eyes rest on the picture of Grandpa Al and Abby for a second, before she looked away. What would they say about this whole mess?

She scanned through her brother's bookshelf. There were a few of his old favourites here. A Louis L'Amour? What was he doing with that? *The Lord of the Flies*. Her eyes settled on a copy of Neil Gaiman's *American Gods*. Jackpot! She remembered Clay telling her about it at Christmas. It must have slipped her mind, because she hadn't gotten around to requesting it from the library. She pulled the book out of the bookcase and tiptoed back to bed, opening the book after she slid under the covers. But as she tilted the book up to read it, photographs tucked inside fell out onto the bedspread.

There was her brother with his arm around Arjun. A second picture showed the two of them with their faces close together, smiling at one another. And in a third one, they were kissing. This was the one that confused her the most. She knew that guys got drunk and sometimes kissed each other. But these pictures, this was something different.

Allyson flipped through the pictures. Were Arjun and her brother lovers? Something about the pictures and the expressions on their faces, the way they were staring into each other's eyes, told her this was not made up. They were together. Boyfriends, she guessed.

Maybe she should shove the pictures inside the book and pretend she had never seen them. She studied the pictures again and again, memorizing the details, looking for clues. Did anyone else know? Part of her was tempted to walk into the living room right now, even though it was the middle of the night, and wake Clay up so she could get some answers. It didn't matter to her that he was gay. Sure, she had to think about some things and it made her want to look for clues throughout the years, but she loved him just the same. But he hadn't told her. He had a secret.

The blanket was too hot and she kicked it off. She stuck the photos back into the book and put the book onto the bedside table. The light from Clay's bedroom illuminated the hall as she crept down the hallway to the bathroom, where she peed, brushed her teeth and splashed water on her face. After she was done, she walked towards the kitchen. The living room was blue from the flickering light of the television, which was on without any sound. Clay snored on the couch, his face turned away from the screen. She stared at his back, wondering how long he'd had this secret. She stood, silent, willing him to wake up, but he didn't move. After what seemed like a long time, she went back to bed. She couldn't wake him up in the middle of the night. As she crawled back into bed, she thought she would never fall asleep. She would just lay there, awake all night. But in the morning, she heard the sound of footsteps and voices. She had fallen asleep after all. She lay there, wondering if she should get up. Eventually, Allyson heard the front door open and shut and she took this as a cue to get out of bed. The copy of *American Gods* was heavy in her hands as she started towards the kitchen. Clay sat at the kitchen table, his hand around the Co-op mug. He was flipping through a newspaper, but raised his head when he heard her come in.

"You'd like some coffee now, right?" he asked.

She nodded. How was she going to tell him what she'd found? Should she just pretend she didn't know, that this had never happened, that she had never seen the pictures? But she was sick of this tactic. Look at what it had done to her family. Why didn't people just talk about things and address them? The thought that her brother was gay was strange and weird. But if it was the truth, she wanted to learn everything she could. Would Clay be open to talking about it? Or was he still mad at her for stealing the truck and coming to see him?

Clay handed her a mug of coffee. She wrapped her hands around it, grateful for its warmth, and set the book down on the table next to her.

"When did you know?" she asked. "Have you known for a long time?"

"Known what?" Clay asked. He flipped the newspaper to the sports section.

She opened *American Gods*, took out the photos and pushed them across the table towards him.

"I found these," she said.

Her brother put the paper down and looked at the photos, flipping through them.

"They were in the book?"

She nodded.

A look of panic came across his face. She couldn't look away. His expressions changed from bewilderment, to fear, to understanding.

"It doesn't matter to me if you're gay," she said. "I just want to know the truth. Does anyone else know?"

He stood up, knocking his knee against the table and spilling his cup of coffee. Clay paced around the world, as if his chair was too hot for him to sit in.

"No one back home knows," he said. "Don't tell them."

"I won't," she said, feeling sort of special that she knew something that other people didn't. "Have you known for a long time?"

"I think Chloe may have figured it out, but she's not saying anything," Clay said.

"I won't tell," she said.

Clay stared down at the floor, avoiding her eyes.

"Just tell me," she said. "I'm tired of secrets."

"I've known for years," he said. "Since I was about your age. When I went overseas, that's when I was finally able to get out there. Arjun is my first real boyfriend. That only happened a few months after Grandpa died."

He still wasn't looking at her. "I spent years hating myself, wishing I could be different. Just throwing myself into activities and into the ranch. Left as soon as I could."

He finally met her eyes. "You get that, don't you? You know you're different and you don't belong. You don't fit in. Only you can't hide it like I could. People back home only know a small part of who I am."

He walked back to the table, sat down and took a sip of coffee. "Part of me actually feels relieved that you know. I've been hiding this from everyone for so damn long."

"Maybe Mom and Dad will be okay with it," Allyson said. But even if they were okay with it, people in the town wouldn't be. She'd heard people at the coffee shop talk about fags. And there was a jeweller in town that everyone said was light in the loafers. He had a male roommate and everyone talked about how they were actually more than just roommates.

"I don't want to tell them yet," Clay said. "They don't need to deal with anyone else right now."

He took a sip of his coffee. "You know, I admire you."

"Me?"

Clay nodded. "You don't pretend to be someone you're not. I don't even think you know how to do that. You're just who you are. And even though that makes things hard for you, you don't try to be anyone else. Someone like Chloe is never going to be like you."

He started towards his bedroom. "I've got to get ready for work. I'll leave you the key. And I've already written down Chloe's address and directions on how to get there if you want to do that. You know how to get to Whyte Avenue from here?"

She nodded.

"I've got to shower and run," he said, walking toward the bathroom. Allyson couldn't help but think he was trying to escape from the conversation.

She remained at the table, trying to piece everything together. It all made sense. He'd never had long-term girl-friends, even though there were lots of girls who liked him. Every time someone asked him why he didn't have a girlfriend, he blushed and changed the subject. This was one of the reasons why he couldn't seem to commit to coming back to the farm. It might have to do with this mad cow thing, but that wasn't the whole picture. This might be why he never seemed certain about what he wanted to do. What kind of life would he have if he came back to town? Would Arjun come with him? Could he have a life with a boyfriend at the farm? At this point, she didn't see that happening.

For a second, it made her feel special to be the only one in the family who knew Clay's secret. Now she and her brother had something shared between them, someone that no one else in the family had.

After he showered, Clay said goodbye to her and left. Alone in the house, she walked to the coffee pot and filled her mug again. She should probably call her parents, but she didn't want to. Right now, she could pretend the farm and her parents didn't exist. She showered, dressed and blow-dried her hair, and read *American Gods* for a bit. After noon, she put on her tuque, jacket and boots and ventured out of the house onto the city streets.

That afternoon, she soaked in the atmosphere of the city, watching people bustling up and down the sidewalks. She walked into Chapters on Whyte and marvelled at the rows and rows of books, walked down the street to a comic store, looked at manga and flipped through posters. She walked past the Princess movie theatre, and stared at its large marquee. Maybe she and Clay could go see a movie tonight, in a real movie theatre—not the tin can they had in town. Here in the city, she was surrounded by the sound of traffic, people walking and talking around her. There was so much to look at. She sat in the window of Starbucks and stared out at the street, her hands clasped around a paper cup of warm, syrupy hot chocolate. This was home. Eventually, around four, when the sky started to turn dark, she made her way back to Clay's. He'd left Chloe's address for her. It was on the way. She turned and went down the street. She saw the building where she thought Chloe was living, and glimpsed her cousin's face in the window. She thought about ringing the buzzer and surprising her cousin. Maybe they could talk. But what would she say to her? What would happen between their families now that the cattle had been killed? Did Chloe even know? She didn't want to start into all that now. Maybe things would get better between them eventually, but now was not the time. She turned her back on Chloe, and walked towards Clay's place.

When she got to Clay's, the house was dark and quiet. She scrounged around in the fridge and cupboards and found crackers, cheese and apples and ate them sitting at the kitchen table.

What if she stayed with Clay in the city? Her parents would never go for that. What was going to happen next? She had too many questions. She opened her book and read until she heard the familiar sound of the key in the lock. Should she call her parents and talk with them? Part of her felt guilty that she hadn't yet.

"Hey," she heard Clay say, and she looked up from her book to see him standing in the kitchen.

"How was your shift?" she asked. Clay was working at Earls as a waiter right now.

"I was run off my feet," he said, sinking into the chair across from her. "Always busy this time of year. I'm beat. I'd rather do chores than wait tables, any day. At least with farming you don't have to deal with so many miserable, rude people. You get out of the house today?"

She told him what she had done.

"There's decent Chinese food a few blocks away," he said. "I thought we could go there for eats. Just let me rest a bit and then we'll go. And then we can head to the Metro downtown. They're showing *The Wizard of Oz*. I thought you might like to see that on the big screen."

The phone rang and Clay went to answer it. Allyson didn't even pretend she wasn't trying to listen. She could tell her mother was on the other end. The sound of Donna's voice came through, but the words were muffled, lost to her.

"Have you talked to Dad?" Clay nodded. "You've left."

Where had her mother gone?

She'd heard Mary Anne talk about her ex-husband a few times and how she couldn't stand him and how they fought for months before he finally came clean about his affair. Once she finally kicked him out, she was so happy and relieved. But Allyson's parents didn't fight like that.

"Is that Aunty Pam's suggestion?" Clay asked. "Are you making a plan?"

She wished she could hear more, or that Clay would give her an indication as to what they were talking about.

"I have a few ideas," he said, pacing around the kitchen. "I'll try to help. I'm glad you're doing this. Do you want to talk to Allyson?"

The phone was in her hand before she had time to say anything.

"Hi honey," her mother said. "Are you having a good time in Edmonton? I'm in Saskatoon. The weather's nice here."

"Like for a vacation?" Allyson asked. She couldn't believe that her mother had just abandoned her dad right now. Even though she wasn't on a farm, her mother couldn't avoid talking about the weather.

"I just needed to get away," her mom said. "It was too much. Sort of like you, if you hadn't stolen the car. I'd ground you, but I don't have the heart to do it. Plus, it seems dumb to ground you when you're in Edmonton."

"Clay is going to take me to see *The Wizard of Oz,*" Allyson said, pretending everything was normal and that they hadn't just abandoned her father, who seemed to be having a nervous breakdown.

"Won't that be fun," her mother said, and her tone reminded Allyson of Abby. "On the big screen? I'm glad you're with your brother."

"When are you coming home?" she asked.

Clay tapped her on the shoulder. "Let me talk to her again."

Allyson handed the phone to her brother. "Keep me posted," he said into the phone.

They murmured a few more things at each other before Clay hung up.

"Things are going to get better," Clay said.

"How do you know?" Allyson said. "Did she say when she's coming home? Is she coming home at all?"

He started towards the hallway. "Things will be okay," he said. "Now forget about all that. We're off to see the Wizard."

★

The next morning, Allyson woke up in Clay's bed filled with sadness and dread because she didn't want to go home. Clay was going to drive her, so he could see Dad, and take the truck back. Then he would take the bus back to the city, in time to work his shift and study for finals. When she dragged herself into the kitchen, Clay was making pancakes and frying bacon.

"Mom raised me to make a visitor at least one good meal," he said, sliding a plate in front of her. He pushed a bottle of maple syrup towards her as she took a seat at the table, and she opened it and doused her pancakes.

"Where's Arjun?" she asked as she chewed. She hadn't seen him since that first day.

"He decided to visit his parents," Clay said.

She normally liked bacon, but the piece she had just eaten tasted burned. She chewed it and swallowed.

"He could have stayed," she said.

"Arjun's not out to his family yet," Clay said. "Same as me. It's just a few of our friends that know."

What did he and Arjun do in bed? She didn't want to think about that, any more than she wanted to think about Colton and Lily. Or her parents. Just thinking about her family members with anyone made her feel uncomfortable.

"It's just hard to know how to talk about it," said Clay. "How much to tell you. Now finish up and get dressed, because we've got to leave."

A few minutes before they had to go, Clay went outside to start his truck so it could warm up. It was snowing out.

"So many idiots don't know how to drive here," he said, as they got into the truck. "Dad is right when he talks about how people in the city lack common sense."

As they drove, Allyson shivered and buried her nose and mouth down into the collar of her coat as she watched the streets pass outside the truck window. Fewer pedestrians and cars were out because of the snow. She willed the truck to break down, to get stuck so she didn't have to head back to the farm. Maybe she could just stay here. She could transfer her credits and finish the year in the city. It wouldn't be impossible.

She sat still as Clay drove across the city, and then out to the highway.

"You know what," he said, eyes on the road. "I'm glad you came and I'll glad you know."

She looked down at her lap. "I don't want to go back," she said. "Can I just stay with you? Things are so much better in the city."

"I wish you could," he said, leaning over and patting her on the shoulder. "But you and I both know you can't. Mom and Dad need you."

She looked down at her hands. "Being there is breaking me into little pieces."

"It's broken all of us. We want to go back to being the people we were before Grandpa died, before the border closed, but we can't. We aren't those people any more. But think of it this way, you don't even have two full years of high school left. Just a year and change. Then you can take off and be whoever you want. I know it seems long now, but it'll go by fast," he said. "You need to just stick it out. Maybe you can come visit more often. You can do this. Think of everything you've already been through. Not even two years."

She leaned in and hugged in and rested her head on his shoulder as he drove.

"Just think of this time like a test, in one of your fantasy books. Do your time and then you can get out. It'll happen."

He turned on the radio and they sat in silence for a few minutes.

"You need to go back or Dad'll lose it," Clay said. "You're his special girl."

"I'm his only girl."

"He never picked me up from school," Clay said. "I had to take the bus."

On the way home, she thought about the couple days that she'd been in Edmonton, and Clay's secret and what she was going back to. The farm houses along the highway passed by, small blips of colour in the endless white. Hoar frost coated barren trees. When the truck entered the town, the streets were empty and quiet. She realized that she really wanted to see Jeff, right away.

"Can we go to Joe's?" she asked Clay. "I've got something I got to do."

He gave her a bit of a sly smile, and said, "You like Jeff, right?"

And she nodded, because she wanted to be honest with him.

"No problem," Clay said, and he parked right in front of the building. "I'll head on home and check on Dad and you can call for a ride whenever you need one. Do you want me to take your stuff too?"

"Sure," she said, wondering how this was going to go.

Clay leaned across the seat and hugged her and then she stepped out of the truck. As she walked towards Joe's, Clay rolled down the window and leaned towards her.

"Call me when you need to," he said. "And I'm glad you know. Just don't tell anyone else."

"I won't," she said. It felt good to know his secret.

She looked down the street, as Clay backed the truck up. The town buildings loomed large and still, muted after the noise and activity of the city. She felt a wave of sadness and despair at the thought of being back in town. But Clay was right. She could get through this. She could hate every minute, or she could grit her teeth, steel herself and git 'er done, like Grandpa Al. She thought of all she'd been through in the past couple of years. All that, and she was still here, still going. She had her whole life in front of her. Clay was right. She could handle a tiny bit more.

She pushed open the front door of Joe's, putting all her weight against it to open it. The smell of French fries, cigarette smoke and fried meat assaulted her nostrils. The restaurant was empty except for two tables. Lily came to greet her as she sat down in a booth.

"How's it going?" Lily asked, sliding a menu in front of her.

"Just got back from the city," Allyson said. "I was at Clay's."

"Talked to Colton yesterday," Lily said. "He's doing all right. He might come home for Christmas. He says to see if they're going to let him take time off."

Allyson pushed the menu back towards Lily. "Just a hot chocolate with whipped cream."

Lily nodded and went back to the kitchen. Allyson looked around the restaurant. Was Jeff around? Maybe he was in the kitchen.

Lily came back with the hot chocolate. Allyson thanked her and wrapped her fingers around the mug. Chocolate shavings dotted the surface of the whipped cream swirl. Allyson took a sip and studied the horoscopes on the paper placemat before her. She flipped the placemat over and took a pencil out of her backpack. She made a quick sketch of Jeff, taking time to shade his hair, and his dark eyes. In her drawing, he was looking down, sketching in a notebook, a contemplative expression on his face. Underneath the drawing, she signed her name.

Once she finished the drawing, she pushed it to the middle of the table, and finished her hot chocolate.

Lily walked by, carrying plates of fries to two old-timers who had come in while Allyson drew. Allyson caught her eye and gestured to her to come over. After she'd served her customers, Lily came back. Allyson had never noticed the graceful way that Lily walked, moving across the floor like a dancer.

"Is Jeff here?" she asked.

Lily nodded. "I'll go get him," she said.

For a second, Allyson felt her heart in her chest, and a feeling of nervousness, like a small bird was flying around her ribcage. But then she took a deep breath, steeled herself, and waited for him to come out.

She turned when she heard footsteps. And there he was, standing beside her.

"I made this for you," she said, pushing the drawing into his hand.

He looked down at it. "Thanks," he said. "It really does look like me."

"Can you come outside with me for a second?" Allyson said. She'd never felt so nervous or so bold in her life, but she wanted to do this, even though she was terrified.

"Just let me get my coat," he said.

She put hers back on, and fingered the cuffs, nervous. A few minutes later he was back, in his coat and boots.

As he came by the booth, she stood up and they walked outside together, wordless for several minutes.

"What do you want?" he asked once they were outside. She moved away from the window so the people in Joe's couldn't see them.

She leaned forward, placing her warm lips on Jeff's mouth. "I miss you," she said. "I've liked you a long time. I just need to admit it to myself. Can you forgive me?"

"I like you too," he said, smiling at her.

She leaned into him and rested her head on his shoulder. The snow had started to fall, and he brushed his hand over her hair. She wasn't sure how long they stood together. The wind was cold.

"I've got to get back to work right away," Jeff said. "Lily is going home."

"I have to go home too," Allyson said.

They went back inside the restaurant. "We'll figure this out, right?" Jeff said as he led Allyson to the front counter and pointed to the black office phone sitting next to the cash register. Allyson nodded, and then picked up the receiver. She punched in the familiar numbers, and listened as the phone rang. Her dad was probably sitting in the family room, watching TV.

"It's me," she said when he answered. "I'm at Joe's. Can you come get me?"

"I just need to warm up the truck for a bit," he said. "Sit by the window. I'll be there soon."

"Bye," said Allyson and she hung up.

She put some money down on the table, and moved to a table near the window. Maybe when she moved away, she would miss Joe's, the way she missed the way things had been a few years ago.

She felt calmer than she had in months. Jeff walked through the restaurant carrying plates and smiling at her. She smiled back. She would see what happened. Outside the window, she saw her father's truck and his familiar shape in the truck's cab. She stood up, picked up her backpack and walked out the door.

CHAPTER 18

Donna drove down the highway. Part of her felt terrible for what she was doing, but she knew she was doing the right thing. After the cattle had been shot, she'd stood in the snow watching Craig and Gord hug and cry for a few minutes.

Then Craig pulled away from his brother.

"We better get this cleaned up," he said.

The rifle was heavy in Donna's hands. She had clicked the safety on a while ago. She hadn't used guns very much, but she knew to do that. In the early days of her marriage, Al had taken her out to the back forty for target practice. He lined up some cans and taught her how to use a gun. She was a poor shot and had begged to stop, telling him she didn't need to learn how to use a gun, that there would be people around who would be able to help her. Craig, Gord or Al would be able to shoot anything that needed to be shot, she argued.

"No," Al said, squinting down at her. "You need to learn to do this yourself."

He'd said that to her so many times, and now she realized just how right he had been. She should have taken the time to learn from him. Things were so much more complicated now that he was gone. Good old Al. He'd tried so hard to turn her into a farm wife, to try and make her into someone who could do her part on the ranch. It wasn't his fault. The failure was hers alone.

What would he say if he could see the mess they were in now?

As she stood there, a wave of panic overtook her and she struggled to breathe. She'd held it together for so long, stayed calm during the situation with Gord and Craig, but now she was breaking down. There wasn't enough air in the world for her.

She tried to count her breaths, watching them as they hung in the air. She wanted to drop the gun, run to the house, get in her car and drive far away.

She studied the brothers and looked at the pen. The live ones huddled in the corner, far away from the dead.

She turned and started crunching through the snow, rifle in her hands. She'd crossed this yard thousands of times in her life, but this time the trek felt immense. Abby and Al's house loomed, the blinds half shuttered, as if the house had narrowed its eyes and was staring at her with disapproval. She looked away from it.

Inside the house, she kicked off her boots and took off her coat, leaving the gun by the door. Thank God all of this had happened while Allyson was at school.

Gord opened and shut the door. She turned on the coffee pot. His feet were heavy on the steps as he climbed the stairs to the kitchen.

"Why did you do it?" she asked, as he sat down at the table.

"I just couldn't handle it anymore," he said. He rested his chin on his hands and stared at nothing. "I just kept on thinking about feeding those animals, and how little we would get for them. It's so humiliating. All that money just draining out. I didn't want us to lose any more."

The coffee trickled into the pot, and the brown drops fell into the carafe.

"I can't think straight," he said. "I'm trying to think and my head is stuffed with cotton and nothing makes sense. And I'm tired, just so tired."

"Gord," she said. "You need to do something about that. Go to the doctor. Go to a therapist, get some help. We should all do that. We all need to do things to get better."

She knew she was going to leave, but she was scared to leave her daughter alone with Gord. Thank god Allyson was still at school. She'd be home soon, and then they'd have to explain the whole thing to her. Craig called Phil, and Doug, and they came over and helped clean up the dead, and salvaged the meat that could be sold. They barely talked, and that night, Donna went to bed early, after she heard Allyson in her room. She fell into a deep sleep.

When the phone rang, she thought she was watching the tv.

"You serious?" she heard him say, his voice groggy.

He turned and nudged her with his elbow, hard, as if he needed to make sure that she was awake.

"You're not going to believe this," he said. "Allyson's in Edmonton."

"What?" Donna said. "How?"

"She stole the truck," Gord said. "Then she got lost in the city. Clay is going to get her."

"He wants to talk to you," Gord said, passing the phone to her.

"She's okay?" Donna asked Clay.

"As far as I can tell," Clay said. He sounded tired. "Did something crazy happen there today?"

Donna threw off the covers, walked out of the room down the hall. She walked into Allyson's room, turned on the lights and saw her daughter's empty bed. She told Clay what had happened—the story of how she'd found Gord, Craig and the cattle out in the yard.

"Christ," Clay said when she finished. "I kind of get why she left."

"Yeah, well. She stole a car and drove illegally."

"Do you want me to send her back home? Are you going to come and get her?"

Donna thought about it for a minute, and that was the last thing she wanted to do. She felt as though she had cinder blocks attached to her feet and a gollum on her shoulders.

"She can stay here for a few days," Clay said. "Just until things simmer down. Kid probably needs a break."

"I'm not happy with her," Donna said, and sighed. "But it would probably do her good to stay in the city for a few days. Keep us updated. As long as she's safe."

She and Clay talked for a few minutes and then she hung up. She walked back to the bed. Gord was still lying there, his back facing her.

"Our crazy kid," Donna said. "We're going to have to figure out a way to punish her."

But Gord was already asleep.

In the morning, she awoke to an empty bed. Gord was already up. She walked down to the kitchen, where he was sitting at the table, flipping through a newspaper.

She took a deep breath and looked him in the eye. "I've got to get away. I can't take it here right now. I need to leave."

Gord kept sitting at the table. The coffee dripped into the pot and sizzled. She leaned into the counter. The weight of her own body was too much for her.

He took his head off his chin and turned to face her. "You're leaving me?" he said.

She blinked hard, and turned towards the coffee pot, trying to hold back tears. She was so sick of crying, of feeling like shit, of living like this. If only there was something she could do. If only she was able to take over the farm, do the books, be the farm wife he needed.

"I can't take any more. I feel like I can't breathe. I think about that dark place I went after Allyson was born, and it's creeping towards me. I can't go there. I can't get any more broken. I can't deal with this. I'm leaving."

"What about Allyson?" Gord said. "What about me?"

"Allyson will be okay. The kid isn't even here for a few days, and I'll have things figured out by then. You'll both get through."

"Are you thinking of this like a vacation? Or are you leaving me?" Gord asked. "Where are you going?"

"I just need to leave," she said.

★

An hour later, she was in the car. She called Pam at work, and told her she was on her way. She called Anita and Carmen and told them she needed to take time off for health-related reasons. Part of her was worried she'd be fired, but Anita seemed to understand.

"You've been a great employee and you've been under so much stress the past year," Anita said. "We'll be fine for a little bit. Kelly can probably come in and help out in the store."

Carmen was equally supportive.

She'd put her suitcase and the rifle in the trunk of her car. They had other guns, and she could have put this one in the cabinet, but for some reason, it seemed to make sense to keep it with her, to keep it away from them. She locked the trunk and walked across the yard to Craig and Linda's.

Instead of just walking into the house, she knocked. It seemed like the right thing to do right now.

"Oh, it's you," Craig said, when he opened the door. "Whenever you knock, I think it's somebody coming to sell me something."

"Just wanted to tell you I'm heading to Saskatoon for a bit," she said.

"You two having problems?"

"Don't try and make me feel guilty about this. And I don't know what's going on between you two, but it needs to stop. You need to start working together. Be a family again. Do you want to run off in different directions or do you want to act like brothers? If you want to stay brothers, you've got to get your head out of your ass and realize that you need to work together. You can't just go charging around, making decisions and tearing things apart."

Before Craig could say anything, she turned away from him and started toward her car. She got inside and steered the car towards the highway. As she drove, she felt herself relax. The roads were calm and clear. But she concentrated, knowing there was a possibility of black ice on the highway. Focussing on the road helped her forgot about the events of the past two days, and how she'd just taken off. Maybe this was another way she had failed. Maybe she should be going to Edmonton to get her daughter instead of escaping. The only thing she could think about now was getting to her sister's house. She'd get to Saskatoon by early evening, when it was dark.

For a minute, she worried about Gord and Allyson. Would they be okay without her? Linda would be able to help them out.

She'd be the capable one, as always. Craig and Linda would probably talk about her behind her back, say she was the type to run away when things got tough.

About an hour out of town, she passed the intersection where Al and Abby had been hit. She pulled off to a small side road on the edge of the highway and put on her hazard lights. Somehow it felt wrong to speed past this terrible place and not acknowledge it in some way. She turned off the radio and its crooning country songs. The road was still and silent, the sky grey. The only sounds were the low buzz of the car heater, the engine and her own shuddering breath. Abby and Al weren't the only ones who had been hurt at this intersection. All of the Klassen family's lives changed that day. How different they all were now. If the farm was a ship, it was a sinking one. A boat full of holes, some of which they'd created themselves. Everything had started here. She wanted to cry, but she was too tired.

Donna took a minute to think about Al and how much she missed him, and how she wished he were still alive, because he would have known what to do and say. If she closed her eyes, she could hear his booming laugh, see the red of his beard, the way his eyes crinkled at the corners. Even when he was angry or disappointed with her, there had been love. Love and pride, at all she and Gord had created, their children, their home. Al had loved them all. She had seen it, and she had known it, without ever having to ask.

She closed her eyes, remembering Al and his strength. What would he want her to do? When she opened her eyes again, she stared at the intersection, willing the former, whole selves of Abby and Al to appear. Then she turned off her hazards, flipped on the radio and drove down the road.

Hours later, she drove over the hill and the lights of Saskatoon welcomed her to the city. Her car travelled the familiar streets until she reached her sister's house. The light from Pam's front room shone out onto the street. The porch lights were a beacon, illuminating the snow around Pam's house. Donna parked the car in her sister's driveway, and went to grab her suitcase from the trunk, ignoring the rifle beside it.

Pam opened the door before she could ring the doorbell.

"I was watching for you," she said. She let Donna take her coat off before she leaned in for a hug.

"You must be exhausted," she said. "I've made the spare bedroom up for you. And there's some leftover chicken soup. I made it on the weekend. Would you like a hot toddy?"

Donna kicked off her boots and lined them up in the corner. Pam's house was tidy, but quiet and bare. That's what happened when you lived alone and could control where everything went. When you only had the detritus of one person to deal with, and not a collection of coats, boots, papers and books and all the other things people carted through their lives. One person's stuff could never fill up a house the way that five people's stuff could. Pam didn't have all the farm junk or the constant chaos of people walking in and out, bringing in dirt. She'd been to her sister's house countless times, but this time the quiet struck her as eerie.

"Do you need to use the phone?" Pam asked.

"I should let Gord know that I got here okay," Donna said, feeling a pang of guilt. How could she just pick up and leave? Was Gord okay? She pushed the guilt out of her mind. She'd done the right thing, for her own sanity.

"Don't feel bad," Pam said. "It's okay for you to be here right now. You can tell me everything."

"Let me make that phone call first," Donna said. "Right after I wash up."

She went to the washroom and ran her hands under the warm water. She used one of Pam's peach washcloths and wiped her face, feeling calmer. In the mirror, her eyes were black and sunken. New lines had formed around her mouth. When did she start looking old? Seeing the exhaustion on her face made her feel worse. She would call, eat some soup and go to bed.

In the kitchen, Pam gave her the phone and retreated to the front room. Donna dialed her home number.

"You okay?" she said, when he picked up the phone.

"I'm surviving," he said. "I'm not going to do anything stupid, if you know what I mean."

He cleared his throat.

"Will you be back soon?"

"I'll let you know," she said.

"Please," he said, his voice small like a child's. "Don't leave me. I can't take any more."

"Gord," she said. "We can't go on like this. Things need to change. This is bad for everyone."

His silence on the other end of the phone was an abyss.

"I love you," he said. "I don't want to lose you. I'll do whatever it takes." And his voice sounded as though he was far away, calling from another planet.

"I love you too," she said, and hung up. She sat in silence until Pam came into the room.

"Clay called," Pam said. "He and Allyson are having a nice time."

She walked to the fridge, took out an orange Tupperware container and dumped the contents of the container into a pot on the stove. "Do you want to talk?" she asked. "I'll just heat up this soup for you."

Donna started to cry. "I'm a bad wife and a bad mother. But I just had to get out of there. I couldn't do it right now."

"Shh," Pam said, stroking her hair. "You've been under incredible stress. You did the right thing. You need to take care of yourself right now. It's okay."

She held Donna, stroking her hair as if Donna were a child.

"I just needed to leave," Donna said, putting her head on her arms. "But I'm so tired that I can't even talk right now. I just need to eat and go to bed."

When the soup was ready, Pam put a steaming bowl in front of her. Donna ate the entire bowl, warmed and comforted by the soup's meaty, savoury broth. When she finished, she put the bowl in the dishwasher and climbed the stairs to Pam's spare bedroom. After washing her face, brushing her teeth and getting into her pyjamas, she got under the covers. But when she closed her eyes, she saw the dead cows and Gord and Craig at the corral. She shuddered. All she wanted to do right now was sleep, sleep and forget. She got out of bed and rummaged around in her suitcase, looking for her makeup bag. Her fingers found the zipper of the bag, and she unzipped it and felt the familiar shape of her bottle of sleeping pills. Normally she took one, but two seemed appropriate for today. She popped them in her mouth, swallowed them without a glass of water, and lay back down. After a few minutes, the drugs kicked in and her thoughts were woozy and blurry. She let the sweet, pharmaceutically induced sleep take her away.

Hours later, she woke up, realized where she was, and went back to sleep. It was all she wanted to do. Even though she'd been sleeping for hours, she still wanted more. She lay back in bed, letting time slip away, letting sleep overtake her, rising once or twice to tiptoe to the toilet. She had no idea how much time had passed. Then there was a weight on the bed, as Pam sat down. "You need to get up," she said.

"I'm so tired," Donna said.

"You've been in bed for over a day," Pam said. "At least get up and eat something."

Donna sat up, her limbs heavy. The sour scent of her own skin filled her nose.

"Just let me take a shower first," she said, standing up, unsteady on her feet. Getting up after that much sleeping was exhausting. A shower warmed her skin and helped clear some her bleariness. She washed herself with Pam's rose-scented soap, helping herself to shampoo from the row of bottles lining the back wall of her sister's shower. A person could spend a lot of money on expensive bath products if they had a good job and no other mouths to feed. She dried herself off, dressed and went downstairs. Pam stood at the stove. She was heating up a pot of spaghetti and meatballs.

"Gord's been calling," she said.

"I'm going to eat first," Donna said. Her head was fuzzy. "Do you have any coffee?"

She looked at the clock. "Don't you have to be at work?"

Pam shook her head, her back still to her sister. "I took a couple personal days," she said. "Figured I might as well, since you're here."

Donna sat at the table, and Pam slid a plate of spaghetti in front of her. She ate as Pam made coffee. The pasta tasted good.

She hadn't even realized how hungry she was until she started eating.

"Do you want to talk about things?" Pam asked, and Donna told her everything that happened. Pam just listened.

"You guys need help," she said when Donna finished. Pam walked over to the counter, poured a cup of coffee and passed it across the table to her sister. She touched Donna's hair. "You've all been suffering for months. It's been hard for me to watch, and I'm sitting five hours away."

"I just worry about all the money. Fixing this isn't cheap," Donna said, looking down at her empty plate.

"We'll figure something out," Pam said. "If you want, I'll lend you the money. I'll do whatever I can. I've been saying that to you for months. I'll help you guys get out of this."

Donna didn't say anything. She stared at her empty plate as if it was the most fascinating thing to ever come in front of her face.

"Are you leaving Gord?" Pam asked. "Is that why you came here? Is the farm too much for you?"

"I just needed to get away," Donna said.

She looked around the kitchen for the phone. "I should call Gord." Pam brought her the phone and left the kitchen.

"How are you doing?" she asked, when she heard Gord's voice on the phone.

"I'm okay," he said. His voice sounded a little stronger than it had when she last saw him. "I finally did what you said I should do a long time ago. I went to see a doctor in Lloyd. He said I was depressed. Gave me some sort of prescription. Gave me the number of a therapist to talk to that's cheap. Phil and Doug keep stopping in. We did some work out in the yard."

"Well," she said. "That's good. That's something. Have you and Craig been working together?"

"No," Gord said. "But Linda has been by. She's been checking up on me. I suppose I could go over there, but I don't know what to say. I caused some scene a couple days ago."

"I was so tired I just slept for over a day," she said.

"When are you coming home?"

She shook her head, forgetting that he couldn't see her. "Not yet," she said. "You heard from the kids?"

"Colton called. Said he misses everything, even though he loves the training. He said the discipline is good for him. Allyson's in the city. Clay's fine. He keeps on calling to check up on me." Gord cleared his throat. "You know, I never would have believed it, but going to the doctor made me feel better," he said. "Should have done it sooner. Made me think I'm not going crazy."

He was probably sitting at the kitchen table, with a beer or cup of coffee in front of him. How could she have left him and Allyson alone? How could she have been so selfish?

"I love you," she said to Gord. "I'll talk to you soon."

He said he loved her too. She said goodbye and hung up.

Pam had left some newspapers on the table. Donna reached for a section and started reading articles to give herself something else to think about. There was so much happening in the city. She shuffled through the sections of the paper. Since she'd left over twenty years ago, entire new neighbourhoods had sprung up. The Saskatoon of today was so different from back then. She didn't know the first thing about living in the city any more. She'd never lived here as a mother or a wife. She'd have to create a whole new life. What would she do with Allyson? She couldn't leave Gord, could she? Even now, she missed him and wanted to see him. Part of her wished he were with her now. But he would hate living in the city. Could she go to Edmonton? That was closer, but she'd still be away from him. Could she live alone? And even if she wanted to, did she really have to do it now?

She flipped to the back of the paper to look at the want ads, apartment listings and house prices. If she rented an apartment, she'd be living like a student. She had no education, and no skills that she could market, other than retail skills and her ability to cook and bake. But there must be jobs for people like her in the city. Maybe she could take a course and get more skills. But she'd need money for that.

The letters in the paper started to blur. She rested her head on the scratchiness of the newsprint. Pam walked into the room, stomping her feet a little as she came closer. Her sister had never been subtle.

"How is he doing?" Pam asked.

"He saw a doctor today." She raised her head to look at her sister. "I didn't think I would miss him so much."

Pam pointed to the classifieds. "Find anything interesting?"

"Just looking," Donna said, closing the paper.

The two of them went to the front room and watched television for a while. Donna was comforted by her sister's presence and the distraction. The phone rang and Pam went to answer it. She came back into the room after a few minutes.

After a few hours of mindless television, Donna went back to bed.

In the morning, she felt strangely refreshed, as if something had shifted in the night. Pam greeted her in the kitchen. "Do you want to do something today?" she asked.

"I think I'll walk down to the mall," Donna said. "But you don't have to come with me. I need some time to wander around by myself."

Pam nodded. "I can give you a ride if you want," she said. "I've got a few errands that I can run."

"No, it's okay," Donna said. "I can walk."

After breakfast and a shower, she put on her parka and boots and started the trudge towards the mall. There were a lot of cars on the road. Probably people getting their Christmas shopping done early. How different her life would be if she had stayed in the city. She still couldn't imagine Gord here. He moved and talked in a way that was wrong, out of place. The kids would be different people if they'd grown up here. The air nipped at her face as she walked. The smell of car exhaust hung in the air. There had more trees along these streets when she lived here. Had the city cut them all down?

She arrived on 2nd Ave and wandered through the shops. The Saskatoon Bookstore looked a little worse for wear. Its shelves used to be full but now there were empty pockets where books were once crammed. She walked out of the store without buying anything and continued down the street, noticing the changes around her. Every time she walked down this street, there were new shops. The city changed so fast. Or maybe she just noticed the changes more. She walked along a side street, past the bank, up to the Midtown Plaza. The air outside was colder than she'd anticipated, and she shivered as she pulled open the doors and stepped inside the mall. Tinny Christmas music played over the loudspeakers. A Starbucks had replaced the A&W in the corner. Maybe she should have a coffee to warm up. She walked towards the counter and stood in line to order.

"I'll have a small coffee," she said.

"Do you want the Pike Place roast?" asked the server. She was a dark-haired girl with a nose ring that was too big for her face.

"Just regular," Donna said.

"You want the tall?" the server said.

"Just small," Donna said. "A small regular."

"So tall Pike," the server said.

"Sure," Donna said. What was wrong with small, medium and large? She looked at the menu board. What was wrong with a medium coffee? When did ordering a coffee become so complicated? The server came back with a steaming cup of coffee and Donna paid. She sat down at a table with her coffee, and watched as the servers made elaborate, foofy drinks, calling out names as they finished each creation.

Three girls around Allyson's age picked up their drinks and sat at a table near Donna. As they arranged themselves around the table, Donna felt a pang of guilt.

Allyson might be like those girls, with their lipsticked mouths and kohl black eyes, if she'd grown up in the city. Maybe she'd be happier. One of the girls moved her hands as she talked. Her bright red nail polish caught Donna's eye. She looked down at her own nails, which were jagged, unpolished and short. She should get a pedicure and manicure. Take care of the things she'd been neglecting. Pay more attention to these types of things.

She took a sip of coffee as she watched the teens. She missed Gord. She'd been away from him for short periods, had even come to Saskatoon to visit without him for a couple of weeks. She'd taken the kids to Vancouver Island when they were small, when she and her parents were still trying to act like a family. As she sat alone, drinking coffee so hot it threatened to burn her mouth, she missed him. She'd actually been missing him for months. She'd been missing the man he was, the one she had fallen in love with, the man she'd been married to for over twenty years. Without him, she'd be like those teenagers at the next table, working a low paying job, living in an apartment.

Her head hurt and she rubbed her temples. She was still wearing her coat, and starting to overheat. She took a sip of coffee. Gord had been to Starbucks a couple of times in Edmonton. He hadn't liked it. He said the coffee was overpriced and tasted burnt.

"Why would someone pay so much for a simple cup of coffee? Why not go to Timmy Ho's or a gas station? People just think it tastes better because they paid more and it's a fancy chain." She could hear his voice in her head.

She'd been fooling herself by even thinking she could leave Gord or the farm. If she left, she wouldn't be helping anything. She'd be even more of a failure. Their problems wouldn't go away; they'd just get bigger. She would be carrying the burden of knowing that she was the type of woman who couldn't stand by her man, who left him when things got rough. She couldn't be that person.

She needed a therapist. Something. Anything. Someone to help her through this mess. Her family was a tangled ball of yarn, with threads snarled around each other. They all had to help untangle it.

She took another sip of coffee. The teens at the next table talked about some party they went to the night before and how Jordan was going to come meet one of them later. Watching them made her miss her girl. She drained the dredges of her cup and stood up. Out in the main hallway of the mall, she surveyed silver and gold Christmas balls and bells hanging from the ceiling, and looked down at the row of stores. She didn't want to be here. It was time to go home and talk to Pam. Figure out what she needed to do to go back home. She needed to go back, but she couldn't go back to the same place. Something had to give.

She trudged through the cold and snow back to Pam's. When she opened the door to the house, she was greeted by the warm, homey smell of chocolate chip cookies. She took off her boots and parka and went into the kitchen, where Pam stood at the sink, washing dishes.

"Cookies will be ready in a bit," Pam said.

Donna slumped down at the table.

"You weren't gone for very long," Pam said. "You okay?"

Donna looked at her sister. "I can't leave the farm," she said.

Pam took her hands out of the dishwater. "I know."

"We need to make things better out there," Donna said. "And I need to be the one who starts it."

Pam left the sink and sat down at the table. "We'll make a plan," she said. "It's been hell for me to watch you suffer like this. It's going to take help to make things better. And time. And the whole family on board."

For the rest of the day and part of the next, Donna and Pam talked and discussed plans for what Donna could do. She used Pam's computer to look things up on the Internet. When Donna got home, she would look for the name of the therapist she'd met at the multiplex, and make an appointment with her. She called Gord to check how he was doing.

"When are you coming home?" he asked.

"As soon as I can," she said. "But I need you to do something for me. I need you to call a family meeting. We need to talk about things. If we're going to keep running the farm together, we need to start talking and come up with a plan, even if Craig and Linda have already signed that paperwork to take the title. We need to sit down and discuss everything. Really start talking."

"You want to get everyone together?"

"Everybody," Donna said. "Even the kids. We all need to be there."

"I'm glad you're doing this," Clay said, when she called him to check in. "I'm glad you're finally going to try to take charge."

She consulted with him and Pam. The Klassens might need a mediator. Counselling. Any services that Alberta

Agriculture could offer to help them. They'd been trying to do it alone for so long, and if they kept trying, it was going to be the death of them. They'd been through too many deaths. She'd learn how to keep the books. Quit letting the world happen around her. They'd have family meetings. She wasn't sure if this plan would work, but it was worth a try. There were people to talk to. Banks and lawyers. She might not be able to handle the cows, but she could learn how to run the business. It was time for her to step up. Pam, Clay and Gord would help.

Later that night, she sat down at Pam's kitchen table and called Linda. Craig answered the phone.

"Hey," she said. "It's me."

"You coming home soon?"

"Yeah," she said. "How are things?"

"It's okay," he said. "We've started getting some things done around the farm. Some cows got out and we had to chase them down together. Gord seems calmer."

"Can I talk to Linda?"

"I'll put her on," he said and the line went quiet for a few minutes.

"Glad to hear from you," Linda said, when she came to the phone. "Craig says you're coming back."

"Tomorrow," she said. "Linda, I need to talk to you. We haven't been doing a good job of things since Al's accident and everything that's happened lately has been proof. We need to start talking and change things and we're all going to have to help. We're probably going to have to get help from the outside. All of us are going to have to work together, or it'll end up just the two of you out there. Do you really want that? Do you think Al would want that?"

She was nervous saying these words, but she felt safer somehow, standing in the warmth of her sister's kitchen, far away from the farm. This was the first of many steps that she would have to take. And part of her was doing it for Al. And for Abby. And for what they would have wanted and dreamed of. The dreams they had of keeping their farm alive.

"I've been waiting for you to call," Linda said. "We've just had our heads down for so long, making decisions that were best for us, not talking about them with you. I wanted to tell you I'm sorry. When I heard about what happened with Gord, and Craig and the gun, well, it nearly did me in."

"I have some ideas about what we can do," Donna said. "But I want everybody to hear them."

"Gord told me about the meeting. We'll figure it out," Linda said. "I'm as tired of this as you are."

The next day, Donna drove back to the farm. The whole way home, she went over the plan and thought about seeing everyone. Darkness had settled by the time she pulled into the yard. It was cold outside, but the lights were on in the house. She would be able to sleep in her own bed, take a bath in her own tub, and cuddle up with Gord while they watched television. As she got out of the car, Maggie and Rascal came to greet her and she bent down to pet them. Donna went to the trunk of her car to get her suitcase. The rifle was still there, and she decided to leave it. The air was calm and still, with a bite of coldness to it. She heard a car behind her, and turned to watch as her daughter and Jeff drove into the yard. Jeff stopped the car and Allyson got out.

Donna looked towards her house. She could see Linda, Craig, Chloe, Gord and Clay in the window of the front room. She saw Gord disappear. A minute later the front door opened, and he came out and stood on the porch. As he stood there, waiting, Allyson caught up to her mother and together they walked toward home.

ACKNOWLEDGEMENTS

People often say it takes a village to build something. In this case, it took the equivalent of a town. Thank you to Now Or Never Publishing for taking a chance on a strange little story. Special thanks to the reporters at *The Western Producer*, who wrote numerous stories that I used for reference when creating this book. Karen Emilson's book "Just a Matter of Time", also helped me understand what happened during BSE.

The idea for this book came to me while I was working my day job. I work as an agricultural reporter, and I learned a lot about the effects of bovine spongiform encephalopathy on Alberta's agricultural community. I want to thank my co-workers Glenn Cheater and Jennifer Blair for a great work environment that enabled me to delve into my own creative work as well.

Many people served as early informal consultants and cheer-leaders for this book. Among them were Laura Thygesen, Laura Bodell, and Chelsea Geiger. An extra special thank you to Wendy and Howie Schneider for their honesty and open hearts.

This book needed the encouragement, faith, and wise words of Larry Hill, who served as my mentor at Sage Hill in 2014. Thank you, Larry.

Twitter and Facebook proved to be wonderful resources for a city person writing about rural life. I'd like to thank all the ranchers whose ranches I visited over the years. I have also had good conversations with many ranchers in person and online, but there are a lot of you, and I'm scared that I will forget someone! Thank you all for helping me get things straight, and for sharing your passion for ranching with me, and helping me develop a stronger love for the land and the work you do.

Early readers who offered advice included Tara Gereaux (who inspired several changes), Andrew Wilmot (who inspired more changes), Lisa Guenther (who gave wonderful technical advice), and Mari Sasano, who listened to me talk about this damned book for far too long.

A special thank you to Danica Longair for always believing in my work, and for sticking with me during tough times. I appreciate it more than you know.

For Nathan Smith, for being my partner, asking questions, having adventures, making food and having way too many conversations. Thank you for everything you do and the life we have built together.

For my parents, Cliff and Doreen—love you forever and for always. I don't even have the words to express how much you mean to me.